INSPECTOR WITHERSPOON ALWAYS TRIUMPHS . . .
HOW DOES HE DO IT?

Even the inspector himself doesn't know—because his secret weapon is as ladylike as she is clever. She's Mrs. Jeffries—the determined, delightful detective who stars in this unique Victorian mystery series! Be sure to read them all . . .

The Inspector and Mrs. Jeffries
A doctor is found dead in his own office—and Mrs. Jeffries must scour the premises to find the prescription for murder!

Mrs. Jeffries Dusts for Clues
One case is closed and another is opened when the inspector finds a missing brooch—pinned to a dead woman's gown. But Mrs. Jeffries never cleans a room without dusting under the bed—and never gives up on a case before every loose end is tightly tied . . .

The Ghost and Mrs. Jeffries
Death is unpredictable . . . but the murder of Mrs. Hodges was foreseen at a spooky séance. The practical-minded house-keeper may not be able to see the future—but she can look into the past and put things in order to solve this haunting crime!

Mrs. Jeffries Takes Stock
A businessman has been murdered—and it could be because he cheated his stockholders. The housekeeper's interest is piqued . . . and when it comes to catching killers, the smart money's on Mrs. Jeffries!

Mrs. Jeffries on the Ball
A festive jubilee ball turns into a fatal affair—and Mrs. Jeffries must find the guilty party . . .

Mrs. Jeffries on the Trail
Why was Annie Shields out selling flowers so late on a foggy night? And more importantly, who killed her while she was doing it? It's up to Mrs. Jeffries to sniff out the clues . . .

MORE MYSTERIES FROM THE
BERKLEY PUBLISHING GROUP...

MELISSA CRAIG MYSTERIES: She writes mystery novels—and investigates crimes when life mirrors art. "Splendidly lively."—*Publishing News*

by Betty Rowlands

A LITTLE GENTLE SLEUTHING	FINISHING TOUCH
OVER THE EDGE	EXHAUSTIVE ENQUIRIES

TREWLEY AND STONE MYSTERIES: Even the coziest English villages have criminal secrets . . . but fortunately, they also have Detectives Trewley and Stone to dig them up!

by Sarah J. Mason

MURDER IN THE MAZE	CORPSE IN THE KITCHEN
FROZEN STIFF	DYING BREATH

INSPECTOR KENWORTHY MYSTERIES: Scotland Yard's consummate master of investigation lets no one get away with murder. "In the best tradition of British detective fiction!"—*Boston Globe*

by John Buxton Hilton

HANGMAN'S TIDE	TWICE DEAD
FATAL CURTAIN	RANSOM GAME
PLAYGROUND OF DEATH	FOCUS ON CRIME
CRADLE OF CRIME	CORRIDORS OF GUILT
HOLIDAY FOR MURDER	DEAD MAN'S PATH
LESSON IN MURDER	DEATH IN MIDWINTER
TARGET OF SUSPICION	

THE INSPECTOR AND MRS. JEFFRIES: He's with Scotland Yard. She's his housekeeper. Sometimes, her job can be murder . . .

by Emily Brightwell

THE INSPECTOR AND MRS. JEFFRIES	THE GHOST AND MRS. JEFFRIES
MRS. JEFFRIES DUSTS FOR CLUES	MRS. JEFFRIES TAKES STOCK
MRS. JEFFRIES ON THE BALL	MRS. JEFFRIES ON THE TRAIL
MRS. JEFFRIES PLAYS THE COOK	

MRS. JEFFRIES
PLAYS THE COOK

EMILY BRIGHTWELL

BERKLEY PRIME CRIME, NEW YORK

MRS. JEFFRIES PLAYS THE COOK

A Berkley Prime Crime Book / published by arrangement with the author

PRINTING HISTORY
Berkley Prime Crime edition / November 1995

ISBN: 0-425-15053-4

Berkley Prime Crime Books are published
by The Berkley Publishing Group,
200 Madison Avenue, New York, NY 10016.
The name BERKLEY PRIME CRIME and the BERKLEY PRIME CRIME
design are trademarks belonging to Berkley Publishing Corporation.

PRINTED IN THE UNITED STATES OF AMERICA

10 9 8 7 6 5 4 3 2 1

With love and gratitude to
Beryl and Gladys Lanham—two very special people
who truly make the world a better place

MRS. JEFFRIES
PLAYS THE COOK

CHAPTER 1

"Before I say another word," Lady Cannonberry said earnestly, "I do have one request. You must keep everything I tell you very, very confidential. You can't breathe a word to anyone, especially the inspector."

Everyone at the kitchen table stared at her. The household of Upper Edmonton Gardens, home of Inspector Gerald Witherspoon, was used to unusual requests. But this was startling, even by their rather relaxed standards of behaviour.

Lady Cannonberry, their neighbour on the Gardens, had popped in only a few moments ago while the household and their trusted friends, Luty Belle Crookshank and her butler Hatchet, were celebrating the successful conclusion of one of the inspector's more baffling murder cases.

Betsy, the lovely, blond-haired maid, looked inquiringly at the housekeeper, Mrs. Jeffries. The eyes of the cook, Mrs. Goodge, bulged behind her spectacles. Smythe, the coachman, raised one dark eyebrow, and Luty Belle Crookshank, an elderly American with a love of six-shooters and a mind sharp as a barber's razor, looked

1

positively enthralled. Hatchet, as usual, was unperturbed.
But the footman Wiggins's mouth gaped so wide that if
it had been June and not November, he would have been
in danger of catching flies.

"Lady Cannonberry," Mrs. Jeffries said hesitantly.

"Ruth, please," their guest said quickly, flashing a
charming smile that took years off her middle-aged face.
"I think we all know each other well enough to dispense
with the formalities."

Mrs. Goodge gasped in shock. Calling the widow of a
peer of the realm by her first name was as unthinkable as
shopping on the high street with her petticoat showing.

But Lady Cannonberry appeared not to notice the
cook's reaction. "It doesn't seem fair that because one is
a servant one is forced to use these ridiculous modes of
address," she continued blithely. "I always thought Lady
Cannonberry was such a ridiculous way to address
someone. Ruth sounds ever so much nicer. Friendlier too,
and as I've come to you as a friend and not a Lady, then
I do think we ought to dispense with the title."

"Er, Ruth, of course, we'll use any mode of address
you prefer." Mrs. Jeffries didn't quite know what to say.
Naturally, she wanted to help her. But on the other hand,
she didn't want any more people than absolutely necessary knowing their secret. The fact that Ruth had come to
them seemed to indicate that she knew they were more
than a housekeeper and servants to a Scotland Yard police
inspector. "But I've no idea what we could possibly do
for you."

"You can hear me out!" she cried. "You can help
someone who's in a great deal of trouble."

Mrs. Jeffries frowned slightly as her conscience did battle with their need for caution. Her conscience won. "Of
course we'll hear what you've got to say. Actually, we're

quite flattered you've come to us. But honestly, I've no idea why you think—''

"I promise I'll not say anything to Gerald," Ruth interrupted, shaking her head earnestly. A lock of blond hair slipped down from her topknot and dangled over her ear. "I know you've been helping him solve his cases. . . . ''

Smythe, who'd just taken a swig of tea, choked.

Betsy dropped a spoon.

Wiggins gasped.

Mrs. Goodge's eyes bulged again, and Luty Belle started to snicker.

Hatchet, as always, remained perfectly calm.

"Where on earth would you get an idea like that?" Mrs. Jeffries said faintly. But the game was up and she knew it.

A half-wit could see by the guilty way they'd all reacted that Ruth was right on the mark. They did help the inspector with his cases, and of course, he didn't know it. That would never do.

"Oh, give it up, Hepzibah," Luty said, slapping her knee and cackling. "Ruth found out the same way I did, by watchin' and listenin'." She grinned at their guest. "I figured out what they was doin' back when that neighbour of mine got himself poisoned."

"Really? Which case was that?"

"Quack by the name of Slocum got poisoned a couple of years back. I spotted Hepzibah and the others snoopin' around and askin' questions. Mind ya, they was right good at what they was doin'. But I figured it out. How'd you?"

"I've suspected for quite some time now," she said with an apologetic smile. "But I didn't know for certain until I overheard Mrs. Jeffries talking to that nice young doctor at the tea shop."

Mrs. Jeffries sighed inwardly and wished she'd been a

bit more discreet in her inquiries on their last case. No doubt Lady Cannonberry had got an earful when she overheard her conversation with Dr. Bosworth that day. But they'd solved the case successfully and that was what counted. Now, though, she had to think of a way to deal with this. "How very resourceful of you," she murmured.

Ruth blushed slightly. "I'm sorry, I'm not usually so bold. But I do have a friend and she's in a great deal of trouble. I didn't know where else to turn. But I promise, my lips are sealed. I'll not breathe a word to anyone about your activities."

Mrs. Jeffries hesitated before answering. She'd no idea what to do or whether or not they could trust their neighbour.

Luty apparently had no such reservations. "If'n she says she'll not say anything to the inspector," she said slowly, "I reckon we can trust her."

"Well, really, madam," Hatchet said pompously. "I hardly think it's our place to speak for everyone."

"It's quite all right, Hatchet," the housekeeper replied, smiling at Lady Cannonberry. She trusted Luty's judgement. "Luty's right. I'm sure we can trust Lady Cannonberry to keep her word."

"Indeed you can," Ruth said quickly. "I've never betrayed a confidence in my life."

Wiggins cleared his throat. "We 'elps the inspector some," he said, an earnest expression on his innocent boyish face, "but 'e does most of it 'imself. 'E's a smart man, our inspector."

"We only does a little bit of snoopin'," Betsy put in. "The inspector does all the rest."

Mrs. Jeffries was touched by their efforts to bolster their employer's status. They were all intensely loyal. Of course they had good reason to be devoted to Gerald Witherspoon, she thought.

Betsy, now a healthy young woman of twenty with rosy cheeks and clear blue eyes, had been a half-starved waif when he'd taken her in and given her employment. Smythe and Wiggins had both worked for the inspector's late Aunt Euphemia. Upon her death, he'd kept them employed even though he rarely used the carriage and he needed an untrained footman about as much as he needed a hole in his head. But jobs were hard to come by, and when the inspector had inherited a modest fortune and this big, beautiful home, he'd decided to keep the two men employed rather than toss them out onto the streets. Mrs. Goodge, having lost her last position because of her age, had also been in need of a place to call home. Gerald Witherspoon had given her one.

Naturally, Mrs. Jeffries was loyal as well. She genuinely admired her employer. Inspector Witherspoon was one of nature's real gentlemen, and of course, being in his employ meant she could use her own rather unique detective skills. All in all, it was a most satisfactory arrangement for all concerned. But she was becoming alarmed by the number of people who'd figured out what she and the staff were up to. They really must be more careful in the future. Perhaps after Lady Cannonberry told them her troubles, she'd call a meeting and they could discuss the problem.

"Betsy is absolutely correct," she said with a calm smile. "Inspector Witherspoon is a wonderful detective. Positively brilliant."

"But of course he is," Ruth agreed.

Mrs. Jeffries thought it best to determine exactly how Lady Cannonberry had caught on to what they were doing. One overheard conversation at a tea shop wasn't quite enough evidence. "I know you overheard me talking with Dr. Bosworth that day," she began. "But is that all? I mean, was there anything else you saw or heard us do that gave us away?"

"Oh, it's been obvious ever since that nasty murder of that woman in my literary circle," Ruth replied honestly. "If you'll remember I was somewhat involved in that myself, only as a witness of course. But I couldn't help but notice that you in particular, Mrs. Jeffries, were always asking questions. Why, every time I took Bodaceia for a walk, there you were."

Mrs. Jeffries wished a hole would open up in the floor. *She* was the one who gave them away. Gracious, how could she have been so careless!

"I've so admired all of you," Ruth continued. "I think what you're doing is ever so interesting. Far more exciting than boring old tea parties and shopping on Regent Street. I've so longed to participate."

"Was that all that gave us away?" Wiggins asked.

"Well," Ruth said thoughtfully. "I did notice that all of you were out and about so much. You never were here doing the normal things that servants do. Frankly, you all do far more dashing about than any household I've ever seen. But only when the inspector is on a case. The rest of the time, you behave just as every other household. But once I realized that you help him, I thought perhaps you could help me with my friend's problem."

"A problem you don't want us sharin' with the police?" Smythe reminded her softly. He was a big, muscular man with harsh features, black hair, heavy eyebrows and the kindest brown eyes on the face of the earth.

"That's right." Ruth nodded. "I really must have your promise you won't say a word to anyone outside this room."

Everyone at the table looked at the housekeeper. Mrs. Jeffries was in a quandary. She didn't wish to turn Lady Cannonberry away, but on the other hand, if the woman confessed to a heinous crime, they could hardly keep silent. "You've placed us in a rather awkward position."

"Don't worry, I haven't done anything criminal," Ruth said earnestly. "As I said, it's my friend who's in trouble. And, well, what she's done is wrong, but it's not criminal. . . . Well, not *too* criminal, that is. You see, poor Minerva can't help herself. Besides, she always puts everything back, so it isn't really stealing. But you really mustn't say anything to the inspector. He is, after all, a policeman. I don't think he'd view Minerva's problem quite the way I do."

"All right," Mrs. Jeffries said cautiously, "we'll not say anything to Inspector Witherspoon." However, if what she heard was too dastardly, she wouldn't hesitate to say something to Constable Barnes, the inspector's right-hand man. "Please, do tell us what's on your mind. If we can help, we certainly will."

Ruth took a deep breath. "I have a very dear friend, Minerva Kenny. She's a very nice woman, a spinster about my age. She lives over on Markham Place. Minerva's a very gentle person, really, rather unworldy, if you know what I mean."

"Keeps herself to herself, does she?" Mrs. Goodge asked.

"Not at all. Minerva's a very social person. She delights in the company of her friends," she explained. "By unworldly I meant that she's not really aware of how cruel and hard the world can be sometimes."

"Bit of an innocent, then?" Smythe commented.

Ruth nodded. "That's it exactly. She's very innocent."

"If she's so innocent," he continued, "then why is she in trouble?"

"Unfortunately"—Ruth paused and cleared her throat—"Minerva has a rather strange affliction. It's not really her fault, though. She can't help herself."

"Can't help what?" Mrs. Goodge prompted. The cook wasn't the most patient of women.

"Stealing," Ruth replied. "But it's not *really* stealing, because she always puts them back."

"She's got sticky fingers, then?" Wiggins said.

"No, she just sees things, usually just pretty knick-knacks and shiny objects in other peoples homes," Ruth explained hurriedly, "and she can't help herself. She puts them in her pocket, takes them home for a day or two to, well . . . play with them, and then manages to put them back. Most of the time people aren't even aware the object is gone. Certainly the Astleys' have no idea their little painted bluebird is gone. Goodness, their drawing room is so full of things, I don't think they'd notice if half of it disappeared."

"So what's the problem this time?" Smythe asked, leaning forward. "Someone catch her filchin' the bird?"

"Oh, no, that dreadful man didn't catch her taking it; he caught her when she tried to put it back."

"Matilda," Adrian Spears said to the parlour maid, "have you seen King?" The middle-aged man frowned slightly as he bent down and peered behind the settee. Sometimes King wedged himself behind the settee when he wanted a good, solid sleep. But there was no bundle of black-and-white fur curled up there. "I've not seen him since lunch."

"I've not seen him, sir," the parlour maid answered. She glanced at the rug by the big walnut desk. Usually the dog lay next to Mr. Spears as he worked in his study. His fat body would be rolled tight in front of the fire and he'd be snoring. But the rug was bare.

Matilda sat the silver tea tray down on a rosewood table next to the settee. On the tray was a pot of tea, milk, sugar, a cup and spoon and a plate with four biscuits. Two for Mr. Spears and two for King. The King Charles spaniel loved his afternoon treat. "That's odd, sir, I've not seen him all afternoon."

"Perhaps Cook let him out in the gardens for some fresh air," Spears suggested. "I'd best go see. I don't want that awful man harassing my poor dog."

"Cook wouldn't do that, sir," Matilda said quickly. "Not after what happened yesterday. Pembroke said we're only to let King out with one of us. One of the footmen took him out at lunchtime, but I saw him bring the dog back inside."

"Has anyone gone in or out?" Spears asked. "Could King have gotten out on his own?"

Matilda swallowed. She didn't want to tell her employer that Janie, the tweeny, had left the back door open. Janie was her friend, and if something had happened to King, Janie'd be out on her ear.

"No, sir," she lied. Someone else might tell, but Mr. Spears wasn't going to hear nothing from her. He was a good employer, God knows she'd worked in worse houses, but he was daft about that dog. "I don't think so. We've all been careful after what happened yesterday. We make sure the doors are closed."

Spears's lips pursed in disgust. "I should hope so. With neighbors like Barrett, we ought to make sure the doors are locked as well. Odious creature. Imagine, throwing stones at an innocent animal."

"He's not a nice man, sir," Matilda said. She began

edging toward the door of the study. She wanted to warn Janie that she'd best get out in the gardens and look for that ruddy dog.

"He's a callous brute," Spears said harshly. He was frightened for his pet but loathe to let it show. "But brute or not, I'll not have him bullying my dog." He walked briskly toward the hall. "I won't have him harassing anyone from my household, including King. We've as much right to use these gardens as Barrett, and if he's thrown any more stones at King, he'll answer to me."

But King didn't come when Adrian Spears called for him.

Alarmed, he called the servants, and together, they searched the huge communal gardens.

Spears peered down the side of Barrett's house, straining his eyes to see in the failing light. He thought he'd heard sounds coming from the passageway. "King," he called. "King, where are you, boy?"

Suddenly a footman shouted, "Over here, sir!"

Spears swiveled on his heel and saw the footman standing in the heavy foliage in the small plot behind Barrett's terrace.

"What is it?" he cried. "Is it King? Is he hurt?" He ran toward the footman, ducking branches and charging through the high bushes. He skidded to a stop at the footman's pale face and then looked down. At the sight of the twisted black-and-white body, his heart broke. King was curled in a semicircle, one paw resting on his snout. There was blood everywhere.

"Oh, my God," Spears moaned. Dropping to his knees, he tenderly lifted King's head. But the dog's big brown eyes were closed forever. Tears of grief—and rage— swam in Spears's eyes. King was dead. His head had been smashed in.

"Look at this." The footman pointed to a spot a few feet away. A bloodstained hammer lay atop a mound of leaves.

The other servants had gathered around. Matilda shot a warning glance at Janie, who was biting her lip and twisting her hands together. God, if Spears found out Janie had left that door open and that she, Matilda had covered for her, they'd both be sacked.

Spears climbed to his feet, turned toward the Barrett house, and bellowed his rage at the open back door. "Barrett, you bastard, come out and face me like a man."

"Sir," Pembroke, Spears's butler, said hesitantly. But Adrian Spears paid him no mind.

"You brute!" he bellowed again. "I demand that you come out here and face me."

By this time servants were coming to the window and the open back door. Spears continued to shout at the top of his lungs. More and more people came out of the house. Even the painters and carpenters who'd been working on the third floor were now out and standing on the small terrace facing the garden.

"What's going on here?" William Barrett demanded. He pushed past a maid. "What are you people doing? That plot you're standing on is private. Get off—get off at once! You'll ruin those plants."

Spears, his voice shaking with rage, pointed to the brush where his pet lay dead. "To hell with your plants, you disgusting brute. You've killed my dog!"

"I'll thank you not to talk to me like that," Barrett replied. He started toward Spears. "And I've no idea what you're talking about. Get all these people out of here."

"I'm not letting you get away with murdering my dog."

"I've nothing to do with your wretched dog," Barrett

sneered. "But whatever's happened, make sure you keep the stupid animal out of my plot."

With a scream of rage, Spears leapt for the man's throat.

Across the gardens from the distraught Mr. Spears, Mr. Thornton Astley paced his study. He kicked a footstool out of the way and glared at the young man sitting at the small desk by the door. "Why on earth should I drop the suit against the devil?" he snapped. "He's guilty of theft!"

"But you may find that difficult to prove," Neville Sharpe, Astley's private secretary, said reasonably. "He covered his tracks quite well. You've no real evidence against the man."

"How much more evidence do I need?" Astley yelled. He picked up a handful of papers from his desk and shook them in the air. "These prove nothing. For all we know, every one of them could have been forged by Barrett himself."

"But they could be genuine too," Sharpe pointed out. "And according to those notices, the overpayments were clerical errors and the overpaid invoices were the result of a mistake. Elliot says the clerk responsible has been sacked."

"But I know Barrett put him up to saying that!" Astley cried. "I know the man's a thief. I've asked a number of questions about Mr. William Barrett, and this isn't the first time he's done this. I'm disgusted that I was ever stupid enough to go into business with him. I must have been blind not to see the kind of man he is."

Sharpe glanced at his watch. "Mr. Astley, I really must get going. This tooth is causing me great pain." He held his hand up to his cheek. "If I don't get there before five, the dentist mightn't be able to see me until tomorrow.''

"Go on and go," Astley said. "There's no need for you to suffer. What time is it exactly?''

"Four-thirty, sir.''

"Maud's late," he muttered irritably. "All right, then," he said as his secretary put his papers away. "Perhaps I'll think about dropping the lawsuit.''

"I think that's wise, sir.'' Sharpe put the pen back in the drawer and snapped the ledger shut.

"But by God, I'm angry.'' Astley began pacing again. "Angrier than I've been in years. I'll see to it that that man can't show his face in any respectable house in London. Just see if I don't. No one robs me and gets away with it. One way or the other, William Barrett is going to pay.''

"He'll claim that it was Elliott who inflated the invoices," Sharpe pointed out. "And then it would be Mr. Elliott's word against Barrett's if we took him to court.''

"I've said I'll think about dropping the damned lawsuit. You needn't keep harping about it, Neville. But I'm not letting that man get away with it. He almost forced me into bankruptcy when he was my partner, and now I've evidence he's been stealing me blind now. I'll not have it, do you hear, I'll not have it.''

The woman pulled her coat tighter against the wind. She wondered if anyone had seen her leave and then decided it didn't matter. If she'd been seen, she'd claim she only went for a walk. There was no harm in that.

She smiled mirthlessly as she went toward the big red-brick house. It was time to take matters into her own hands.

Barrett was a savage.

There was only one way to deal with savages.

And she meant to deal with him before tonight. Before the dinner party. She couldn't stand the thought of sitting across from him, watching the ugly, knowing smirk on his face as he worked his way through soup and fish and meat. No, it was too much. No woman could be expected to endure such torment.

And she didn't intend to endure it a moment more. He'd sit there as if he were the Prince of Wales when he was the one who should be ashamed.

He was a brute. A cold unfeeling cad. But she was the one who would have to endure the pain, the humiliation, the awful agony of wondering when and if he would speak up.

For speak he surely would.

She knew that as well as she knew her own name. Men like William Barrett couldn't be trusted with anyone's secret.

She clenched her hands into fists and drug a deep, heavy breath into her lungs. Her teeth chattered lightly, but it had nothing to do with the cold, damp November air. Nerves, she told herself as she clamped her mouth tightly shut. It's just nerves. But it will be over soon.

It was almost dark now, even if it was only a half past four.

She heard the *clip-clop* of a hansom coming from down the street, so she ducked behind a hedge until it went past.

It wouldn't do to be seen here. She didn't want to have to explain her presence to anyone. Not until after she'd seen Barrett.

She kept her hands balled into fists to keep them from shaking. Fear turned her knees to jelly and made her insides shake. But she had no choice. She stepped out from behind the hedge and started up the walkway.

The front door was wide open. It was almost as if he were expecting her.

" 'E caught her puttin' it back?'' Wiggins muttered. "That's a bita' bad luck.''

"Indeed it was,'' Ruth agreed. "And even worse, the awful man snatched the bird right out of Minerva's hand and put it in his pocket.''

"You mean he's a thief, too?'' Mrs. Goodge queried.

"No, no. I mean he took it to torment poor Minerva. He grabbed it and told her he'd hang on to it until he can decide what to do about the situation.'' She shook her head sadly. "Poor Minerva is in a state. If that awful man says anything to the Astleys, she'll be ruined. Absolutely ruined.''

Mrs. Jeffries realized they'd better learn a few more facts. "First of all, why don't you tell us who this man is and when all of this took place.''

"Oh, I'm sorry. I suppose that might be useful. The man's name is William Barrett. He's some sort of business associate of Thornton Astley's. Everything happened yesterday afternoon at the Astley house. That's over on Kildare Gardens.''

"I take it that Miss Kenny had . . . uh . . . appropriated this bird from the Astleys' drawing room sometime prior to her attempt to return it?'' Mrs. Jeffries was always of the opinion that one couldn't have too much information.

"Oh, yes.'' Ruth smiled sadly. "Minerva and Maud Astley are great friends, despite the fact that Minerva's years older than Maud. She goes there frequently for tea and dinner parties, that sort of thing. She'd seen this ridiculous china bird and she took a fancy to it. Unfortunately, Mr. Barrett was sitting in the drawing room when Miss Kenny was trying to get in and put the bird back

where it belonged. The Astleys kept it up on a high shelf.
Minerva was dragging a chair over to put it back when
Barrett suddenly popped up. She didn't see him right
away; she claimed she was too busy watching the door
for servants. Barrett came sneaking up behind her and
snatched it right out of her hand.''

"Were the Astleys at home?" Smythe asked.

Ruth shook her head. "Oh, no, that's why Minerva
tried to put it back. She was certain she'd be able to do
it without getting caught. She knew Maud and Thornton
were out.''

"Why did the servants let her in?" Betsy asked curiously. "I mean, when the Inspector's not at home, we
don't let people in to go wanderin' about the drawin'
room.''

"She had a story ready," Ruth replied. "She told the
parlour maid she thought a pearl button had fallen off her
sleeve the day before—that's when she took the bird in
the first place. The girl was busy, so she let Minerva go
into the room to search for her button.''

"Sounds like it'd work," Smythe said thoughtfully.
"But why was Barrett there?"

"He'd come to see Astley's secretary." Ruth shrugged.
"At least that's what he told poor Minerva. She was so
shaken by being discovered, she didn't think to question
Barrett further.''

"Perhaps the Astleys were due back soon," Mrs. Jeffries mused. The man being in the house was unusual but
perhaps explainable.

"Oh, no," Ruth said quickly. "Minerva wouldn't have
dared go near the place if any of the family were there.
They'd told her they were going to be out for the day.''

"I see.''

Ruth glanced uneasily around the table. "I know this

is a very peculiar story, but Minerva Kenny is one of the nicest people in the world. Please, you must help her. She's nowhere else to turn and time is running out for her.''

Mrs. Jeffries smiled weakly at Lady Cannonberry. Gracious, this was a problem. She didn't approve of stealing—if what Miss Minerva Kenny did could be called stealing. But on the other hand, she did think that Mr. Barrett's behaviour was rather odious. Imagine torturing a poor woman that way. Surely if this Mr. Barrett were dreadfully opposed to theft, he'd have informed the Astleys immediately about Miss Kenny's behaviour. No, it sounded to Mrs. Jeffries as if this man had something else in mind. Blackmail, perhaps?

''Well, I'm not really sure what to say,'' she began weakly.

''Oh, please, you must help my friend,'' Ruth pleaded. ''You don't understand. She's at her wit's end. If Barrett tells what she's done, she'll be ruined. For a woman like Minerva, death would be preferable.''

''But she's a thief,'' Mrs. Goodge said quietly.

''But that's just it, she's not. She always puts what she takes back.''

''That doesn't make takin' it in the first place right,'' the cook said stoutly.

''But she can't help herself,'' Ruth persisted. ''Please, listen to me. Do any of you think a man ought to be hanged for stealing a loaf of bread because he's hungry?''

There was a general murmur of ''no'' and ''course not'' around the table.

''So in some cases, you'd say that stealing was right,'' Ruth said doggedly.

''Now, we never said that,'' Luty Belle corrected.

''But that's really the point, isn't it? Sometimes the law

is wrong. I know what Minerva does isn't right, but I honestly believe she can't help herself. She's not a criminal, she's ill. Only instead of the infection being in her arm or her chest, it's in her head!'' Ruth cried passionately. ''Minerva Kenny is a wonderful woman. If you knew her, you'd understand.''

''Are you saying, Lady Cannonberry,'' said Hatchet, who wouldn't call a titled lady by her christian name if someone put a knife to his throat, ''that you think we ought to help this person because she's ill?''

''Yes, that's exactly what I'm saying.'' Ruth slowly gazed around the table, taking a moment to meet the eyes of each and every one of them. ''This is a matter of justice. It isn't right that a woman like her could be utterly ruined by a horrible man like Barrett. He isn't concerned in the least about the morality of what she did, but only in keeping her within his power. William Barrett couldn't care less about whether she's a thief, but only in how he can use this information to make her life miserable. That's absolutely wrong. No human being should ever have that kind of power over another.''

Mrs. Jeffries rather agreed. ''What does everyone think?'' she asked, gazing around the table. ''Should we help?''

Betsy spoke first. ''I'm for helpin' the woman. Lord knows, I've been in a tight spot a time or two in my life.''

''Me too,'' Wiggins agreed. ''This Mr. Barrett sounds like a right old prig.''

''Count me in!'' Luty exclaimed. ''Can't stand people who bully others.''

''As Madam has agreed,'' Hatchet said slowly, ''I suppose I've no recourse but to agree as well.''

''Fiddlesticks!'' Luty glared accusingly at her butler.

"You're just as eager to have something else to stick yer nose in as the rest of us."

"I do not, as you so quaintly put it, 'stick my nose' in matters that do not concern me," Hatchet responded. "Unless, of course, a greater purpose—such as justice—is being served. In this case, it certainly sounds as if the poor woman is being treated most unjustly. Lady Cannonberry"—he bowed regally—"I am at your disposal."

Luty snorted.

"Smythe?" Mrs. Jeffries queried.

The coachman nodded slowly. "I'll have a go. Men like this Barrett fellow stick in my craw."

"Mrs. Goodge?"

"Well," the cook said doubtfully, "I'm not sure about this. Where I come from, stealin' is stealin'. But I don't rightly think that's what Miss Kenny's doin'. Oh, bother, of course I'll help."

"Good." Mrs. Jeffries smiled brightly at Lady Cannonberry. "We're all agreed."

"What did ya mean when you said time was runnin' out for Miss Kenny?" Smythe asked.

"Minerva's been invited to dinner at the Astley house tonight. Barrett's going to be there too. She's terrified he'll bring the bird with him and tell them what she's done. A number of other people have been invited as well. Her greatest fear is that he'll wait till everyone's seated at the dinner table and then accuse her of being a thief."

They all looked at one another. "She's left gettin' 'elp a bit late, 'asn't she?" Wiggins said what they all were thinking. "Cor, there inn't much we can do in the next few hours."

"Oh, dear," Mrs. Jeffries murmured.

"I'm sorry." Ruth looked down at the table. "I don't know what I expected you to do on such short notice, but you see, I only got the whole story out of Minerva today at lunch. It's hopeless, isn't it?''

"I don't know," Mrs. Jeffries replied honestly. "Why don't you give us more information." She cast a quick glance at the clock. "We may be able to do something. First of all, where does this Barrett live? Do you know?''

"Kildare Gardens." Ruth replied.

"Is Barrett married?" Smythe asked. "I mean, does 'e live alone or with family?''

"He's unwed," she answered. "And I've taken the liberty of making a few inquiries of my own. He lives alone except for his servants. But the staffing in his house is sparse. I believe he has a difficult time keeping servants.''

"Where does 'e work?" Wiggins asked. "Is 'e gone durin' the day?''

They all began asking questions at once. Lady Cannonberry tried her best to answer them. But it was clear that she hadn't much more information to share.

"All right, so now we knows where 'e lives and that 'e spends part of the time at 'is office," Wiggins complained. "I don't see 'ow that's gonna do us much good. 'E's still got Miss Kenny's bird.''

"You mean he's got the Astley bird," Betsy corrected. She thought Wiggins was right. She didn't see that they were going to be of much use to Minerva Kenny. Not if William Barrett talked tonight at that dinner party. By tomorrow morning Miss Kenny might be the most-gossiped-about woman in London.

"This is a most difficult problem," Mrs. Jeffries murmured.

"No, it's not," Smythe announced. Everyone looked at him. He gave them a wide cocky smile.

Betsy's eyes narrowed dangerously. "You've got a solution, then?''

"Course I have," he replied. "Barrett's got the bird, right? And that's all the evidence he's got against Miss Kenny. Without the bird he's got nothin'. It'd be 'is word against 'ers if he goes to the Astley family tellin' tales tonight. The solution's as plain as the 'eadlines in the mornin' papers." He leaned back in his chair, crossed his arms over his chest, and said, "We'll steal the bird right out from under his bloomin' nose."

CHAPTER 2

"I don't think this is goin' to work," Betsy said. She held up the heavy black wool coat and squinted at the seam she'd just mended. "The plan's daft. It'll be too easy to get caught."

"Don't worry so, lass," Smythe said easily. He frowned at the garment Betsy held up. He'd not put on that old coat for years. He hoped it still fit. But whether it was tight across the shoulders or not, he needed it. "I know what I'm doin'."

"It's not like we've got any other ideas," Wiggins pointed out.

"I'm afraid I agree with Betsy," Mrs. Jeffries said. Her normally placid face was creased with worry. She stared at the coachman. "Are you absolutely certain your information is correct?"

After Lady Cannonberry had left, Smythe and Wiggins had made a fast trip out to learn more about Barrett.

"Sure as I can be," he replied. "Barrett's had workmen in his house today, and he's supposed to be goin' to a fancy dinner party at Thornton Astley's tonight. It'll be no trouble to get in an' out. All I have to do is convince one of the maids that I'm gettin' some tools that one of me mates left upstairs.''

"Servants aren't stupid, you know. They'll know good and well you're not one of the labourers that's been workin' there," Mrs. Goodge snapped. "And even if you manage to sweet-talk your way past some maid, someone's bound to want to go upstairs with you to keep an eye on you."

"Let me worry about that part," he said.

"But I still don't see how you're goin' to do it. Barrett's goin' to that dinner party tonight. What if he's already left and taken the bird with him?" Betsy said worriedly.

Smythe was touched by her concern. "Stop frettin' so. The man only has to walk to the other end of the Gardens, 'e'll not be gettin' there early. Even if 'e is plannin' on takin' the bird, I should be able to nip in and pinch it before 'e leaves for the Astley 'ouse.''

Mrs. Jeffries had a very bad feeling about all this. She wished they hadn't gotten involved. "How do you plan on getting it out of the house while Barrett's still there?" she asked.

Smythe grinned confidently. "Barrett won't be gettin' dressed for a fancy evenin' out in 'is study, now, will 'e? I'll wait till 'e's changin'." The plan was bold as brass and he wasn't sure it would work. But it was worth a try.

"I still don't like it," Betsy mumbled.

"I'll be dressed like a workman," Smythe replied. "In that old coat no one will think I'm anything but one of the bloomin' painters' mates, come back to pick up a tool. This time of night the servant's'll be tired. None of 'em will be wantin' to climb up to the third floor and keep their eye on me."

"But what if someone does come with you?" Betsy persisted. "And how do you know where to look for the wretched bird once you're in there?"

"Betsy's got a point," Mrs. Jeffries said hastily. "Barrett could have put the figurine anywhere. You won't have time to search the whole house."

"I won't have to," Smythe said. "Lay you odds that he's got that bird tucked away in his desk. Isn't that where the Inspector puts important things he don't want to lose?"

"Well, yes," the housekeeper said doubtfully. "But that doesn't mean that that's what Barrett did. For all we know, he could have put it under his mattress or in a drawer in his dining room."

Smythe shook his head. "Nah, he put it in his desk. Now stop yer worryin'. I'll nip up the back stairs, find the man's study, snatch the figurine and be out before you can snap yer fingers. I'll be in and out so fast the only thing anyone'll remember is the back of me coat."

"I still don't like it," Betsy said. "If you get caught, they'll call the police."

Smythe hated to see the fear in Betsy's pretty blue eyes. He wouldn't have her frettin' over him and wringin' her hands if he could help it. But he didn't see they had much choice. If they was goin' to help Minerva Kenny, they had to take a few chances. Far better to try and talk his way past a maid on the excuse that he needed some tools than waitin' about and tryin' to sneak in in the dead of night. "I'll be fine, Betsy."

"I think I ought to go with you," Wiggins said. "I can wait outside with the carriage. Keep everything ready in case we have to make a fast getaway."

"Now Wiggins—" Mrs. Goodge began.

"That's a splendid idea," Mrs. Jeffries interrupted.

"I'd rather there were two of you there than just Smythe on his own."

"Humph," the cook snorted delicately. "I don't know why we're mixed up in this. We don't even know this woman. And I'm not sure that she isn't deserving of getting caught."

"No one deserves being tortured," Betsy said. "And we're mixed up in this because we're all scared that if we don't help Lady Cannonberry's friend, she'll 'accidentally' let it slip to the inspector that we've been helpin' on his cases."

"Why, Lady Cannonberry would never do that," Wiggins said indignantly. "She give us her word."

"Of course she wouldn't," the cook put in.

Mrs. Jeffries wanted to believe that Ruth would hold her tongue. But she wasn't willing to bet her next quarter's wages on it. She didn't like to think that their motives for helping someone in trouble were so self-serving, but she had considered the fact that refusing to help could influence how Lady Cannonberry felt about them.

Barrett's house in Kildare Gardens was built much like the Inspector's home at Upper Edmonton Gardens, so Smythe had little trouble determining the layout of the rooms. He drove past the tall redbrick structure, circled the houses and drove out again through Kildare Terrace. He pulled the carriage up in front of St. Stephen's Church.

Tossing the reins to Wiggins, Smythe jumped down. "It's just gone on six-fifteen. Barrett should be gettin' ready about now. Let's 'ope the old boy is as vain as 'e is mean and needs plenty of time to tart 'imself up."

"Blimey, I hope so." Wiggins nervously clutched the reins. Bow and Arrow, the inspector's carriage horses, snorted softly and tossed their heads.

"If I'm not back in half an hour," Smythe said as he stroked Bow's nose, "you take the carriage and get out of 'ere."

"Drive the carriage! Me?" Wiggins screeched. "But I've only driven it once before. We're a long ways from 'ome. I don't think I can do it."

"Don't be daft, boy," Smythe hissed. "If I'm not back, then you've got no choice. We're less than fifteen minutes away. If you have any trouble, just head for the Uxbridge Road. Bow and Arrow knows their way back from there and the road's wide enough, even for yer drivin'."

"Cor, please come back," Wiggins pleaded. The thought of driving the inspector's great carriage through the London streets filled him with dread.

"I intend to," Smythe snapped, worried now at the thought of Bow and Arrow, his personal pride and joy, being in the hands of a nervous Nellie like Wiggins. He gave the horses one last pat and turned toward Kildare Terrace. Moving quietly, he kept to the shadows as he made his way to the Gardens.

The street in front of the house was as silent as a church. The lamplights were lit but their glow was dimmed by a heavy mist drifing in from the river.

Smythe headed for the side of the house. He paused in the silent passage, his gaze fixed on a brilliant shaft of light coming from a window. Moving stealthily, he crept down the passage and peeked through the glass.

Several scullery maids, a serving maid and a uniformed footman bustled back and forth in the brightly lighted kitchen. On the opposite side of the long trestle table he could see the remains of the evening meal. One of the maids slowly stacked plates while another one emptied scraps into a bucket on the floor.

Smythe tiptoed toward the passage, around the corner and to the back door.

He reached for the handle, praying it wasn't locked. The door opened quietly. He peeked inside and realized this door opened into a long, dark hallway. Holding his breath, he eased inside and shut the door behind him. From the kitchen at the front of the house, he could hear voices.

"What time was he supposed to go out, then?" a woman's voice asked.

"What's it to do with you?" another voice replied. "What he does is 'is business."

Smythe tiptoed past a half-closed door, the cooling pantry probably, he thought. He hoped no one would take it into their heads to go for a walk just now. He reached the end of the hall and wanted to laugh in triumph. Instead of having to cross into the kitchen and try talking his way upstairs, he found another doorway right in front of him. It led directly to the back stairs.

"Watch what yer doin' there!" a maid yelled. There was the sound of laughter and a clatter as something metal hit the floor. Smythe waited a moment, listening for footsteps and then he stepped onto the first stair.

Squeak. It creaked louder than an old granny's bones. He took another step. Squeak. He paused, waiting to see if someone from the kitchen would come and check. Nothing. Holding his breath, he hurried up the stairs. As he neared the top, he heard footsteps coming down the hall.

Smythe took the last two stairs in one leap, glanced to his left, saw that the coast was clear and then dashed forwards towards the second set of stairs leading to the upper floors. He made it into the darkened corridor just as the footsteps rounded the corner and the butler appeared. Smythe waited until the man had disappeared down the stairs before continuing. He made it to the next floor without incident. It took only a moment to locate Barrett's study.

Smythe edged the door open and saw a fire burning in the grate. There was a balloon-backed chair set at an angle in front of the fireplace and beside that was a desk. Bookcases and tables edged the walls. He squinted, trying to adjust to the sudden dimness. From the corner of his eye, he caught a glint of silver. He glanced to the side and saw a sword and scabbard hanging on the wall above a long, low table.

But the room was empty. Breathing a heartfelt sigh of relief, Smythe gently closed the door and walked softly toward the desk. Keeping one eye on the door, he rounded the desk and pulled open the top drawer. Nothing but papers. He tried the second drawer. More papers. He stuck his hand inside and felt around at the back. Nothing.

He tried the next drawer, wincing as it creaked in protest when he yanked it open. More papers, but he'd heard something rattle at the back. As he reached inside, his fingers brushed against china. Smiling in triumph, he pulled the object out.

In the dim light he couldn't quite see what it was, so he leaned forward, closer to the fire. It was the bluebird. He grinned at the china beastie.

As he straightened, he caught sight of another glint of silver. He cocked his head so that he could see the back of the huge, overstuffed chair near the fireplace. Something was sticking out of the upholstery. Curious, he moved closer.

Startled, he blinked to make sure the dim light wasn't playing tricks on his eyes. Cor blimey, he thought as his gaze focused on the curved handle, that looks like the hilt to one of them fancy swords. He glanced at the wall by the door and realized the sword hanging above the desk was only an empty scabbard.

Smythe swallowed, inched closer and peeked over the top of the huge chair. At the sight that met his eyes, he thought he'd lose his dinner.

A man was sitting there, pinned like a bug on a board. His eyes were open, staring straight ahead. The sharp edge of a sword stuck out of the center of his chest.

Smythe knew the man was dead. His chest weren't movin' and with them eyes popped wider than fried eggs, he couldn't be still breathin'. Just to make sure, he reached for the man's wrist and felt for a pulse. Nothing. "Blimey," he muttered, "this is a fine fix I've got into."

He was pretty sure he knew who the feller was too. William Barrett. Someone had skewered the ruddy bastard.

For a moment he didn't know what to do. Then he caught himself, tucked the china bird in the pocket of his jacket and tiptoed toward the door. Easing it open, he checked to see that no one was coming. He had to get out of there. Fast.

Smythe retraced his steps. When he got to the bottom of the steps going into the kitchen, he stopped and listened.

"The master said he wasn't to be disturbed," the butler was saying to someone. "So we'll not. It's hardly our place to remind him that he has a dinner engagement. But as he'll probably be hungry, I'd suggest you get some of that joint out of the cooling pantry and do up a plate. Just in case he decides not to go out. *Some* people consider it the height of rudeness to be late to dinner engagements."

Suddenly a heavy set of footsteps sounded in the downstairs hallway, blocking his escape through the back door.

Damn. He couldn't get out that way. Sounded like there was a bleedin' army in that kitchen now, not to mention the cook rootin' around in the pantry.

Smythe tiptoed back down the hallway. There was a door at the far end. He opened the door, saw a small sitting room and went inside. He hurried toward the window. The ground was a goodly drop, but he'd take his chances. Opening the window, he took a deep breath, swung his legs out and jumped. It was only as he hit the ground that he realized what he'd done. With the window left open, the police would assume that the killer had gotten in or out that way.

Smythe ran to where he'd left Wiggins and the carriage, taking care not to be seen.

"Everythin' go all right, then?" Wiggins asked, clearly relieved to see the coachman.

"I got the bird," Smythe said, climbing up and grabbing the reins. "But we've got us another problem."

"Someone saw you?"

"No one saw me." He made a clicking sound through his teeth and the horses took off with a great lurch. Smythe never used a whip. "But there's a dead body in William Barrett's study."

"Are you sure he was dead?" Mrs. Jeffries asked.

" 'E was dead, all right," Smythe replied. "He 'ad the sword coming out of his 'eart, no pulse and his eyes open wide like 'e was starin' into the bowels of 'ell. I hope I did right, comin' back 'ere. But considerin' the circumstances, I didn't think it'd look good me bein' found there."

"You did the right thing, Smythe." Mrs. Jeffries pursed her lips.

"We goin' to tell the inspector?" Wiggins asked.

She shook her head. "Not directly. No."

"We can't just let a dead man sit there all night." Mrs. Goodge looked utterly scandalized by that thought.

"Why not?" Wiggins muttered. "It's not like it makes any difference to 'im."

"Of course we're going to tell the police," Mrs. Jeffries said quickly. "We're just going to have to think of a way to do it without bringing our involvement into it."

"Oh, dear," Lady Cannonberry said. "This is all my fault. . . ."

"Nonsense," the cook said briskly. "You was just tryin' to help your friend."

"Thank God Smythe wasn't caught!" Betsy exclaimed. She was sitting at the kitchen table, her face pale and her hands clenched together in her lap.

Suddenly Mrs. Jeffries looked at Lady Cannonberry and asked, "Does the inspector know what your handwriting looks like?"

"Why, no."

"Good. Wait here, all of you. I'll be right back."

She came back a few minutes later carrying a plain white paper, a pen and an envelope. Handing them to Lady Cannonberry, she said, "Would you please write what I dictate? We must let the police know about the murder, but we don't want to implicate ourselves."

She told Lady Cannonberry exactly what to write. Then she turned to Wiggins and said, "Go round to the front door and bang on it hard, hard enough for the inspector to hear. Leave the envelope on the doormat. When you hear my footsteps, make sure you're gone by the time I get to the door."

Wiggins grabbed the envelope and dashed for the back door. Everyone else stood around Mrs. Jeffries looking anxious and worried. "Let's hope this little trick works," she murmured. "Now, everyone go sit down and pretend to be going about your business."

Along with everyone else, Lady Cannonberry started toward the table.

"No, no, Ruth," Mrs. Jeffries said. "Please don't think me rude, but I do believe our plan has more of a chance of succeeding if you're not here."

"Oh, yes." She blushed slightly. "Of course. I'll be off, then. Do keep me informed and I'm so very grateful for your help." She smiled quickly at the other servants and held up the china bird. "Whether you know it or not, you've probably saved Minerva's life. I do believe that if that dreadful man had accused poor Minerva of being a thief, she'd have jumped off a bridge."

No one mentioned that the "dreadful man" was now dead and that Minerva would have to be considered a suspect. Lady Cannonberry waved a goodbye and left. A few moments later there was a loud banging on the front door.

Mrs. Jeffries waited for a moment before heading for the stairs. She paused on the step, waited till the banging came again and then started up. She stomped her feet as loudly as she dared. As she reached the end of the hallway, Inspector Witherspoon was coming down the front staircase.

"Gracious, who on earth could be making such a racket?" he murmured. Behind the rim of his spectacles, his blue-grey eyes were narrowed and his long, bony face creased in worry. His thinning dark hair stood straight up in spots, as though he'd been lying down, and he'd taken off his vest. Though it was only eight, the inspector had obviously been planning on having an early night.

"I've no idea, sir," she replied, stomping across the entryway. She reached for the door handle.

"Mrs. Jeffries, don't answer that," he ordered. "Let me get it. Please. I'm always a bit suspicious of people banging on my door this time of night. Especially when they're pounding loud enough to wake the dead."

"Of course, sir," she replied, stepping back.

Witherspoon pulled open the door, and a blast of chilly damp air blew inside. "Drat. There's no one here." He started to close the door.

Mrs. Jeffries dashed forward. "Look, sir, there's an envelope." She pointed to the stoop.

Witherspoon bent down and scooped it up. "It's addressed to me."

She quickly shut the door, keeping her eye on the inspector as he tore open the envelope. His expression turned puzzled as he read the paper. "Goodness," he murmured. "This is most odd." He reached for the handle, jerked the door open and dashed out onto the stairs. Turning left and right, he squinted into the dark night. "No one there. I wonder who brought this?"

"May I ask what it is, sir?" Mrs. Jeffries queried softly.

"Oh, yes, of course. It's quite strange really." He cleared his throat and started to read. " 'Inspector Witherspoon. There is a dead man in the study of Number fifteen Kildare Gardens off the Talbot Road. He has a sword through his heart. Come at once.' It's signed, 'A Concerned Citizen.' "

Perplexed, he stared at the note for a moment longer, then looked at Mrs. Jeffries. "Do you think this is someone's idea of a joke?"

"Well"—she had to be very careful here—"it could be, sir. A note is rather an unusual way to summon the police to a murder. But honestly, you don't have any friends or acquaintances who would do such a thing. Perhaps you'd better go."

"But it's so odd," he protested. He'd just solved one murder, and he really wasn't all that keen to have a go at another. "I mean, if someone's been murdered, why not call a constable? Why bring a note all the way round here?"

Mrs. Jeffries decided to fire every bit of ammunition at her disposal. "Now don't be so modest, sir. It's quite obvious why someone brought the note here instead of taking it to a police station or calling a police constable."

He stared at her blankly.

"Your reputation, sir. You must admit, you've become rather well known for solving the most heinous and complex of crimes."

He smiled and his narrow chest swelled slightly. Dear Mrs. Jeffries, she always knew just the right thing to say. "You're right of course." He sighed theatrically. "I suppose I'd better nip along and see if there's anything to this." He started for the stairs, stopped and turned back. "Send Wiggins over to fetch Constable Barnes, Mrs. Jeffries. Have him ask the constable to meet me at Kildare Gardens. If this isn't someone's idea of a silly prank, I may need Barnes's assistance."

"Should we go right to the front door?" Constable Barnes asked. He was a tall man with a head full of thick, iron-grey hair beneath his police helmet, a lined craggy face and a pragmatic, kind disposition.

"Yes, we've no other choice," Witherspoon replied as he started up the short flight of steps. Dash it all, he thought, this is most awkward. If there wasn't a body in here, he would have a lot of explaining to do. He banged the brass doorknocker. "Skulking about trying to determine whether or not this is a hoax wouldn't be right."

The door opened and a tall, bald man in a butler's uniform stuck his head out. "Good evening," he said slowly, his eyes widening slightly at the sight of Barnes.

"Good evening," the inspector began. "Could you please tell us who owns this house?" He thought it best to learn who the owner might be. That way, if he had to apologize, he could at least use the correct name.

"This is Mr. Barrett's residence, sir," the butler replied, looking even more puzzled.

"Is Mr. Barrett at home?"

"Yes. Who may I say is asking for him?"

Witherspoon identified himself and Barnes. "This is rather awkward, I'm afraid," he explained, "but we really must speak to Mr. Barrett. We've had a communication that claims there is a dead man in the study of this house."

"That is absurd. You're making a dreadful mistake. Mr. Barrett's in the study." The butler sniffed. "And I'm quite sure he'd have noticed if there was a corpse there as well." He started to close the door.

Barnes flattened his palm against the panel and pushed hard. "Then would you mind showin' us in so we can see for ourselves?"

The butler's stiff face looked as if it were going to crack, but he jerked his chin, inviting them inside. Turning on his heel, he called, "It's this way. But Mr. Barrett's going to be very angry about this. He doesn't like to be disturbed when he's working."

The door opened into a wide entryway paved with black-and-white tiles. There was a huge ornate mirror with a gold gilt frame on one side of the hall and an elegant gaslamp, it's flame flaring brightly, on the other side. The walls were papered in white-and-gold empire stripes and decorated with pictures of hunting scenes with red-coated aristocrats riding to the hounds. A mahogany table with a large potted plant stood beside the staircase. Beyond the staircase was a long hallway with doors on each side.

The butler, muttering about chief inspectors just loudly enough for Witherspoon to hear, tromped up the stairs. He led them down a long thickly carpeted hallway to a closed door. Knocking once, he called out, "Mr. Barrett, sorry for disturbing you, sir. But the police are here." He shot them a sour look. "They insist on seeing you."

There was no answer.

The butler frowned. He knocked again. "Mr. Barrett, sir."

Still no answer.

Witherspoon and Barnes exchanged a glance and stepped closer to the door.

"Mr. Barrett," the butler tried again, and this time his voice was high-pitched and frightened. "Please, sir. Is everything all right?"

"Go in," Witherspoon instructed.

The butler nodded, grabbed the brass knob and opened the door. The three men stepped inside.

The room was dim, the dying fire in the hearth being the only source of illumination. The butler stared at the empty desk and moved closer into the room. "Mr. Barrett," he said softly.

"I say," Witherspoon called out. "So sorry to disturb you, but we've had a most unusual note."

"Who're you talkin' to?" Barnes asked. He glanced around the darkened room wondering if the inspector could see someone he couldn't. "I don't see anyone here."

"Perhaps he's in the chair," Witherspoon replied.

The servant hurried forward, angled his head to see into the chair and made a funny, strangling noise. Barnes and

Witherspoon sprang across the room.

Barnes was the first to speak. "Looks like that note wasn't a joke," he said softly. "Poor fellow's been poked clean through."

He grabbed the man's wrist and felt for a pulse. Then he looked into the man's open, glassy-eyed gaze. "He's dead, sir. And as the blood's starting to clump around the wound, I'd reckon it was at least an hour or two ago that he got done in."

Witherspoon forced himself to look. He hated looking at bodies. But weak stomach or not, he knew his duty. Drat. Why did these things always happen to him? And so soon after supper, too. "Er, yes," he gulped and wiped his face as his gaze fastened on the end of the sword sticking out of the man's chest. "He does look . . . well . . . dead. Obviously not self-inflicted."

"It's Mr. Barrett!" the butler cried. "Good God, and skewered clean through like one of the cook's roast chickens."

Witherspoon looked at Barnes. "You'd best get some help."

Barnes nodded. "I'll go up to the end of the Gardens and blow the whistle. There's constables walkin' the beat near the train station."

Barnes left and Witherspoon turned to the wide-eyed servant. Even in the dim light, he could see the man had gone as white as chalk. "Perhaps we'd best step outside into the hall," the inspector suggested.

"We can't just leave him alone," the man mumbled.

"Well, he isn't going anywhere. I'd rather no one touch anything until after the police surgeon arrives."

The butler nodded and shuffled toward the door. As soon as they were in the hallway, Witherspoon asked, "Is there somewhere up here where we can sit down?"

"There's a small sitting room on the next floor." The butler nodded, turned and went down the stairs. He carried himself rigidly, as though he were bracing for a heavy blow.

Feeling sorry for the poor man, Witherspoon silently followed him. But the servant had recovered somewhat by the time they reached the sitting room. He ushered the inspector inside and then started to shut the door. Witherspoon stopped him. "Leave it open. We don't want any of the other staff going upstairs."

"Yes, sir."

"Why don't you sit down." Witherspoon gestured toward a settee. He also noticed how cold the room was.

The man sat. Some of his color was returning. "This is the worst thing that's ever happened here," he murmured. "Never worked in a house where someone's been murdered before."

"What's your name?" The inspector thought the butler must have gone into another state of nerves. He was starting to mumble to himself now. Naturally, it must be quite a shock to find one's employer with a sword sticking out of his chest, so he could understand how the servant felt. But the best thing for shock was to direct the poor fellow's attention elsewhere. Questions, that's right. Lots of questions.

"Hadley, sir." He shivered. "Reginald Hadley."

"Right. Hadley. Tell me, how many servants are there in the house?"

"Not a full staff, sir." Hadley swallowed heavily. "Myself, of course, two scullery maids, a serving maid, a parlour maid, a footman and a cook."

"No housekeeper?"

"No, sir. Not since Mrs. Pretman passed away. Mr. Barrett was trying to find one, sir, but he never found one he liked. Particular he was. Real particular.''

"Is there anyone else in the house? Any guests or relatives?''

Hadley shook his head. "Mr. Barrett doesn't have any relatives and he rarely invited houseguests to stay. The only people here tonight are the staff.''

"Was the entire staff here all evening?''

"Yes, sir. But this time of the night, most of them have finished their duties and gone to their rooms." He wiped a trembling hand across his face. "But none of us would have done a thing like this.''

"I'm not accusing anyone," the inspector assured him. "I'm merely asking a few, very ordinary questions. When was the last time you saw Mr. Barrett?''

"About five o'clock, sir. He told me he was going to be working in his study. He didn't wish to be disturbed. That was the last time any of us saw him.''

"He had no plans to eat supper?''

"Oh, yes, sir. He was going out this evening.''

"I see," Witherspoon replied. "What time was he supposed to go out?''

"He was due at the Astley residence at seven for a dinner party, sir.''

"Didn't anyone go and knock on his door when it got late and he still hadn't come down?" Witherspoon asked. "It's past eight. Surely you realized he'd be late for his appointment.''

"We realized it, sir. But it wasn't worth my position to be telling him what to do. When he went into that office and said he didn't want to be disturbed, then he didn't want to be disturbed. If you understand my meaning, sir.''

Witherspoon did. The late Mr. Barrett did not sound like the kindest of employers. "Was Mr. Barrett expecting any visitors tonight?''

"No, sir."

"Has anyone unexpected been to the house tonight? Have you seen any strangers lurking about?"

"Strangers, sir? No, not really. We had workmen in and out all day. Mr. Barrett's having the third floor redone."

"Were the doors unlocked?"

"Yes, sir, and open most of the day too. Mr. Barrett wanted the air to circulate. As you can feel, sir." The butler shivered slightly. "It's made the house cold. November isn't really the best time for painting, but once Mr. Barrett made up his mind, that was that."

"Did any of the staff have reason to go into Mr. Barrett's study?"

"No, sir. The staff had their supper at six, finished their chores and then went off to their rooms. As Mr. Barrett was going out, there was no reason for anyone to stay on duty except for myself."

"I'll need to question the other servants," Witherspoon said. "Could you please gather them together?"

"In here, sir?"

Witherspoon started to say yes, caught himself and realized he'd probably get a lot more out of them if they were warm and comfortable. This room was wretchedly miserable. His feet were freezing.

"How about the kitchen," he suggested. "Perhaps, if you wouldn't mind, we can have the cook brew up a pot of tea. This has been a terrible shock. I'm sure the rest of the household will need some sustenance."

"It certainly has, sir," Hadley said with feeling as he got to his feet. Suddenly the curtains on the other side of the room billowed as a gust of air blew in.

Hadley stared at them for a moment, a frown on his face. "That's not right," he mumbled. He crossed the room and drew the curtains back. "Look here, sir. This window shouldn't be open."

"Are you sure? You said you'd left doors open for the air to circulate. Perhaps someone opened this window as well."

"It was open, sir, but I remember closing it myself. Right after the painters left at six o'clock."

CHAPTER 3

———✦———

"How long do you think the inspector'll be?" Wiggins asked.

"Several hours, I expect," Mrs. Jeffries replied. She saw that everyone at the table already had a cup of tea in front of him before pouring her own. "He'll have to take statements from the servants and then wait for the police surgeon to arrive."

"Let's hope it's old Dr. Potter, then," Smythe added. "He takes hours before he'll even decide if someone's dead or not."

Everyone laughed. Dr. Potter had been involved in several of their other cases, and he was not held in high esteem by either the household or Inspector Witherspoon.

"Mrs. Jeffries," Betsy said, "they'll let the inspector have this one, won't they?"

"Why wouldn't they give it to the inspector?" Mrs. Goodge interjected impatiently. "He's the best man they've got."

"Yes, but what about that Inspector Nivens?" Betsy explained. "Remember how he carried on the last time?

He's been itching to get himself a murder. You don't think the chief inspector will let *him* have it?''

Mrs. Jeffries shuddered delicately. Inspector Nigel Nivens was a thorn in her side. Not only did he bitterly resent Inspector Witherspoon's startling success, he'd let it be known on more than one occasion that he was certain their dear inspector had help. But she didn't want to dampen anyone's enthusiasm. Not that she approved of murder. Certainly not. However, some degree of anticipation when starting out on a new case was definitely called for.

"Let's hope not," she said cheerfully. "After all, our inspector will be the one who discovers the body. He'll be right there 'on the scene,' so to speak. It wouldn't make sense to bring another inspector in after the trail had gone cold." She hoped the Chief Inspector felt that way.

"Well," Betsy said bluntly. "I don't care which Inspector gets this one, we're going to have to investigate it as well. If anyone saw Smythe goin' in or out of that house, he could be done for. We've got to make sure we find out who the killer is. It wouldn't be fair for Smythe to be gettin' blamed for something he didn't do.''

Smythe stared at her incredulously. Betsy sounded as fierce as a lioness defending her cubs. He wasn't sure if he should be insulted or flattered, but he knew it gave him a nice warm glow inside to see how much she cared.

"I told you, lass," he said gently. "No one saw me. The servants was all in the kitchen.''

"What about when you jumped out the window?" Betsy argued. "Someone might have seen you then.''

"Of course we'll investigate this one," Mrs. Goodge said briskly. "After all, it's our murder. And if Smythe said no one saw him, I expect that he got clean away. Stop all the worrying, Betsy. It'll not do a bit of good.''

Betsy opened her mouth to argue, noticed the strange

expression in the coachman's gaze and then clamped her mouth shut. "All right," she muttered, looking down at her lap. "I guess Smythe knows what he's about."

Wiggins yawned loudly. "What do you want us to do first?" he asked, turning sleepy eyes to the housekeeper.

"What we always do first," Mrs. Jeffries replied. "We learn everything we can about the victim. Smythe, can you recall anything about him or about the study? Anything which might be important?"

Smythe's face grew thoughtful. "Don't think so. I was in and out pretty quickly. Once I'd seen Barrett with that sword pokin' out of 'is 'eart, I didn't notice much of anythin' else."

"Tell us what you can recall about the dead man," Mrs. Jeffries said softly. She wasn't positive the victim was William Barrett—though it didn't seem likely it could be anyone else.

"He looked to be middle-aged," Smythe said, "and 'is 'air was dark but it was thinnin' on the top. When I looked over that chair, I could see a bald spot as big as one of Mrs. Goodge's scones on 'is head."

"How was he dressed?"

"Like a city gent. Dark suit and vest, a white shirt."

"And the murder weapon?" Mrs. Jeffries pressed. "Are you sure it was a sword and not just some sort of long knife?"

"It were a sword, all right. It had one of them fancy hilts to it," Smythe continued. "Besides, there was an empty scabbard 'angin' on the wall."

"A what?" Wiggins asked.

"A scabbard," Smythe explained. "That's the thing the sword fits into when it's not being used." As the footman continued to stare at him blankly, he sighed. "You know, it's what they hung on to their belts to put the ruddy things in when they was goin' off to war or gettin' their pictures painted.''

Wiggins nodded sleepily.

Mrs. Jeffries ran her finger around the rim of her teacup. There was so much more they needed to know. "Anything else?"

"Not really. The room was so dark it was 'ard to see and once I discovered what was sittin' in that chair, all I could think of was gettin' out of there.''

Mrs. Jeffries understood. Smythe might appear to be a big, rugged bull of a man; indeed, he'd proved he was perfectly capable of taking care of himself on more than one occasion. But underneath it all, he was really quite sensitive. And finding a dead body would be a shock for anyone. They could wait until later to get more information. She'd stay up and see what the inspector had to tell her. No need to press Smythe further tonight.

"You want me to start with the pubs in the area?" Smythe asked.

"Oh, yes," she answered. He started to get up, but she waved him back into his chair. "But not tonight. It's too dangerous."

Smythe raised an eyebrow and sat back down. "Dangerous? Mrs. Jeffries, I've gone out hundreds of nights to the pub.''

Betsy snorted derisively.

"If you go out asking questions tonight, the very evening Barrett was murdered, you could be asking for trouble," she explained. "Betsy's concern is valid. Someone may have seen you climbing out Barrett's window. If you were seen, and then a few hours later, you're identified as someone who went round to local pubs asking all sorts of questions about the dead man, well . . .''

"I get yer meanin'," he said quickly. He glanced at

Betsy. She'd gone pale again. "But I don't think anyone saw me. Do you mean you don't want me askin' questions at all about this case?"

"Of course not," she replied calmly. "But do give me a day or two to determine if the police have a witness to your leaving the Barrett house."

"It won't hurt you to wait till tomorrow," Betsy chimed in.

"All right," he agreed. "If it'll keep you ladies 'appy, I won't set foot out of this 'ouse until I'm told to."

"Good," Betsy gave him a quick smile and turned to the housekeeper. "What do you want me to do?" she asked.

"Talk to the shopkeepers in the area. Find out what you can about Barrett and his household." Mrs. Jeffries turned to Wiggins. His elbows were on the table, his chin propped in his hand. His eyes were closed.

"Has he gone to sleep?" Mrs. Goodge asked. "Hey, boy! Wake up. We've not got all night."

"I'm not asleep," Wiggins mumbled around another yawn. "I'm just restin' me eyes. Besides, I already know what I've got to do. Mrs. Jeffries wants me to make contact with one of the servants in the Barrett house, right?"

"Right," Mrs. Jeffries agreed.

"And I suppose you want me to get me sources talking," Mrs. Goodge said. "Course I'll have to get up extra early and do some baking. People talk so much better when you're filling their bellies."

Mrs. Goodge had a whole network of people from delivery boys to chimney sweeps tramping through her kitchen. She plied them ruthlessly with hot tea, fresh buns and savory rolls. She managed to wring every morsel of gossip there was about anyone in London out of them. Add to that her many years in service and the attendant number of housekeepers, footmen, butlers and maids she knew, and she had a veritable army of informants.

"You're correct as always, Mrs. Goodge," Mrs. Jeffries said.

"What about Luty and Hatchet?" Smythe asked. "Luty'll have a fit if we don't give her something to do. You know 'ow she 'ates bein' kept out of things."

"Luty?" Betsy protested. "What about Hatchet? He's just as bad."

"Never said 'e wasn't," the coachman replied.

"We'll have them both around tomorrow," Mrs. Jeffries said quickly. She didn't want another problem on her hands. On their last murder, the women had been utterly furious at the men. Not that they didn't have good reason, she thought. The men had been unbelievably arrogant, convinced that because they'd been born male they'd been blessed with superior intellect and character. Well, the women had set them straight very quickly. Very quickly indeed.

However, it wouldn't do to revive that silly rivalry. Mrs. Jeffries had a feeling they were all going to have to work together on this case. If, in fact, there was a case. It could well be that Mr. Barrett had been skewered by a member of his own household, someone who had already been overcome with remorse and confessed to the police.

But she didn't think it likely. A sword thrust through the back of a chair didn't smack of a killing done in a fit of rage. More like someone had deliberately tried to sneak up and kill the victim while he was unaware. "If Wiggins will drop a note off to the Crookshank household on his way out tomorrow, we'll all meet back here for the midday meal. We can fill Luty and Hatchet in then."

"Are you goin' to wait up for the inspector?" Betsy asked.

"Indeed I am." Mrs. Jeffries rose to her feet. "But the rest of you should get to bed. You're going to need your rest."

The kitchen of the Barrett household was ablaze with light. The servants were huddled in the butler's pantry, whispering among themselves and waiting their turn to be questioned. The police surgeon and the uniformed officers were upstairs examining the body and searching the study.

Witherspoon nodded at Barnes, and a moment later the constable ushered Hadley into the cozy room. "Do sit down," the inspector said, thinking to put the fellow at ease. He didn't want him to start mumbling to himself again; it was very distracting. "And pour yourself some nice, hot tea."

"Thank you, sir," Hadley replied with a heavy sigh as he sat down and reached for the teapot. "This has all been a terrible shock to us, sir. Absolutely terrible. You can't imagine how awful it's been, sir. Mr. Barrett upstairs dead with a sword poking through him, police everywhere, place colder than a tomb in a January graveyard. Horrible, sir." He stopped talking long enough to take a long, slurping drink of tea.

"Yes, I'm sure you're all most upset." Witherspoon cleared his throat. He always hated this part the most. Getting started. Trying to decide what to ask and what not to ask. He didn't know why it was so difficult, but it jolly well was. "Now, what was the last time you saw your employer?"

"Like I told you sir, it was when he went into his study around five o'clock."

"You didn't see him after that?"

"No, sir. As I told you earlier, Mr. Barrett didn't like being disturbed. He had me bring him some stamps and his stationery, closed the door and told me he'd ring the bell if he needed anything more.''

"And you're absolutely certain there were no visitors to the household, no unexpected guests?''

"Absolutely, sir.''

"The front door was open all day, is that correct?'' Witherspoon prodded.

"Yes, sir.''

"Then how can you be sure Mr. Barrett had no visitors?'' the inspector asked. "Isn't it possible someone could have come in and gone up to Mr. Barrett's study without being seen by any of the servants?''

"It's possible, sir,'' Hadley admitted. "Mind you, with the front door being open it was cold. I did spend most of my time downstairs today.''

"Where, exactly, were you?''

"In the kitchen,'' Hadley said. "Most of us was in the kitchen. Like I explained, Mr. Barrett had the doors and windows wide open and the house was cold. The kitchen was the only place where you could get a bit of heat.''

The inspector frowned. "The doors and windows were open because Mr. Barrett was having the third floor painted, is that correct?''

"And having the ceilings tinned and some carpentry work done as well.'' Hadley nodded enthusiastically. "Mr. Barrett was going to work in his study, there was workmen tramping up and down the stairs and getting under our feet, so we left them to it and stayed in the kitchen. All exceptin' Fanny, that is, and she was doin' up the drawing room.''

Witherspoon sighed. Anyone could have gotten into the house and up those stairs without being spotted by a servant. No doubt the maid in the drawing room had the doors closed to keep the cold November air out. Drat. This was going to be another difficult case. "Did Mr. Barrett have any enemies?"

Hadley hesitated. "Not that I'm aware of, sir."

"Has anything odd or unusual happened to Mr. Barrett lately?" The inspector pressed.

"What do you mean 'unusual'?"

"Oh, anonymous letters, threats against him, that sort of thing?"

"Not that I know about, sir." Hadley smiled apologetically. "Mr. Barrett wasn't one to talk about his private business."

"Was he well liked by his household?" The inspector remembered that his housekeeper had once remarked that one could gain insight into a person's character by finding out how those dependent on that person felt about him.

"Well liked . . ." Hadley hesitated again. "I shouldn't like to say, sir."

"Come now," Witherspoon persisted. "I'm not asking you to speak ill of the dead. But this is a murder investigation."

"But none of us killed him," Hadley yelped. "None of us would have gone into that study. Not with him telling us he didn't want to be disturbed."

"I'm not accusing any of you of murder. I merely want to know if he was a good employer or a—"

"He was a right old bastard," Hadley finished. Then he glanced at the door as if he was afraid of being overheard. "He didn't pay much, treated us like we was dirt and squabbled with everyone. His neighbours couldn't stand him. He didn't have many friends, and I, for one, won't shed any tears at his funeral."

Taken aback, the inspector stared at the man. Hadley's face was flushed, his hands trembled, and he was gulping air like he'd just run a footrace. Gracious.

"But that don't mean any of us killed him," the butler continued. "We were all in the kitchen until almost eight o'clock."

"The sword . . . er . . . was it Mr. Barrett's?"

Hadley nodded slowly. "Looks like the one he had hanging on the study wall. He pretended like it was a family memento, but he only got the blooming thing last year. Bought it from a family he'd turned out of their home."

That sounded like a good line of inquiry. "What was the name of this family?"

"Bennington, sir. But they didn't do it. After Barrett foreclosed on their home, they emigrated to Canada to live with relatives."

"What did you mean when you said Barrett squabbled with his neighbours?" Witherspoon asked.

"Exactly that." Hadley took another gulp of tea. "Around this garden, he's about as welcome as a case of typhoid fever. Mr. Barrett can be quite rude, abusive even. I'm not accusing any of the neighbours of murder, but he wasn't particularly well liked. He had a nasty row with one of them just this afternoon." Hadley realized what he'd said and flushed guiltily. "I'm sorry, Inspector, I know you asked me if anything unusual happened today, but well . . . it's so undignified. I really hate repeating such a sordid incident. A man like myself, sir, having to take employment with a man like Barrett!" He shook his head in disgust. "It's humiliating, sir. That's what it is. Did you know I once worked for the younger son of Lord Lynfield, sir."

"No, you didn't mention that," Witherspoon replied. "But do please tell me what happened today with Mr. Barrett and his neighbour."

"And I was trained in Lord Lynford's house, sir. Indeed I was!'' Hadley exclaimed, waving his arms around for emphasis. ''But those days are behind me, sir. I've been reduced to working for someone who gets involved in fisticuffs with his neighbours.'' He sighed. ''Mr. Barrett had a row with Mr. Spears. He lives next door. Spears's dog was found dead in Mr. Barrett's portion of the garden this afternoon. Mr. Spears accused Mr. Barrett of killing the animal. Words were exchanged and they got into a brawl.''

Witherspoon stared at the butler. ''What time was this?''

''About four-thirty, four forty-five, something like that.'' Hadley hung his head as though he were personally responsible for his employer's behaviour. ''It was shameful, sir. Absolutely shameful.''

The inspector tried asking a few more questions, but for some odd reason, Hadley decided he'd said enough. Witherspoon got nothing more out of him. He hoped he'd do better with the parlour maid, Fanny Flannagan.

She was a petite, dark-haired girl of about nineteen or twenty. She was also very pretty; large blue eyes, a small, straight nose and a perfect complexion. Witherspoon smiled kindly at her as she curtsied and motioned her into the chair the butler had just vacated. ''Do sit down and have some tea, Miss Flannagan,'' he offered.

''Thank you, sir.'' Her voice was low and rather musical.

''Now, I understand you were cleaning the drawing room late this afternoon?''

''Yes, sir,'' she replied, toying with the rim of her teacup.

''Wasn't that an odd time to be cleaning?'' Witherspoon couldn't remember any of his servants cleaning a drawing room at that time of day. Surely those sort of chores were done in the morning hours.

"Usually I did it of a morning, sir," she said slowly. "But I couldn't this morning. So I had to do it before supper, you see."

"Why couldn't you do it this morning?"

"Mr. Barrett was entertaining. He had a guest. I could hardly be in there polishin' and dustin' in front of a lady, could I?"

"A lady," Witherspoon repeated. "Do you happen to know this lady's name?"

"No, sir, I'd never seen her before." She dropped her gaze to her lap and bit her lip.

The maid was clearly nervous. "Is there something you'd like to tell me?" the inspector prompted softly.

"Well, I'm not sure if I should." She looked up at him and her eyes swam with tears. "Oh, sir, I don't like to think ill of the dead and I'm not a bad girl, but I couldn't help overhearin'."

"There, there." He reached over and patted her awkwardly on the shoulder. Egads, what if she started crying? "I'm sure you're not a bad girl at all. And sometimes it is impossible not to overhear. Now, why don't you tell me all about it."

She swiped at her eyes and gave him another dazzling smile. "I'd come up to clean about eleven o'clock, sir. Mr. Barrett didn't say he was havin' a guest, so how was I to know he was in there?"

"No, of course you didn't know," he murmured sympathetically. "What happened?"

"I opened the door and started in. All of a sudden Mr. Barrett's screamin' at me to get out. He were standin' in front of the fireplace. There was a woman standin' there, too, but she had her back to me, so I didn't know who she was. But I think she was cryin'. Her shoulders were shakin' and she was all hunched over like she was tryin' to hold herself together.''

"Did you see her face?"

"No, sir."

"Is that all that happened?" he queried. Drat. If only the girl had seen the woman's face.

"Yes, sir."

"Oh, dear, it's a pity you didn't get a good look at the woman."

"Yes, sir, it is."

"Did you see or hear anyone coming or going out the front door when you were cleaning the drawing room this afternoon?"

"I thought I heard one of the workmen going down the stairs at about a quarter to six."

"Wouldn't the workmen have used the back stairs?" Witherspoon asked.

"Not this time, sir." Fanny replied with a grin. "You see, the painters had gotten into a row with the carpenters. They was squabblin' and arguin' and gettin' in each others way that it like to drove us all mad. Mr. Barrett finally said the painters was to use the front door and the others the back. That's why I didn't think nothing of it when I heard them footsteps in the hall this evenin'.'' She shrugged. "And I had the door closed to keep out the cold, so I didn't see no one."

"Mrs. Jeffries, you are truly an angel of mercy," the inspector said several hours later. He reached for the glass of sherry she'd placed on the table beside his favorite chair and prepared to unburden himself. His dear housekeeper had waited up for him, providing him with two things he desperately needed: a glass of good Harvey's and a sympathetic ear.

"I take it there really was a body in the study?" she said softly.

"Unfortunately, yes." He paused and took a sip of sherry. "And I don't think it's going to be an easy case, either." Witherspoon sighed and told her everything that had transpired that night. It was so good to be able to talk to someone about these difficult cases.

Mrs. Jeffries nodded and smiled sympathetically as he told her about the corpse with the sword sticking out its chest and how anyone, absolutely anyone, could have done the foul deed. The doors were unlocked most of the afternoon and all the servants except for one were in the kitchen.

"Oh, dear," she said.

"Precisely," he agreed miserably. "I don't know how I'm going to solve this one."

"Perhaps you won't have to, sir," she said. "After all, isn't Inspector Nivens . . . er, chomping at the bit, so to speak?"

"He is, indeed," Witherspoon said gloomily. "But I've a feeling I'm going to get stuck with this one. You know how the chief is, he won't want to bring in Nivens now. Frankly, there's nothing I'd like more than to let Inspector Nivens have a crack at this one. It's going to be jolly difficult. The killer could have been anyone."

He went on to tell her how the servants didn't like their employer but he didn't seem any worse than many employers in London and how the victim wasn't a particularly popular man with his neighbours. She shuddered when he told her about how Barrett had been accused of killing a neighbour's dog.

"But that's dreadful, sir."

"That it is," he agreed.

"Did the police constables find anything when they searched the house?"

"Nothing out of the ordinary," he replied, taking a sip of his sherry. "And none of the neighbours had seen or heard anything, either. The killer was either extraordinarily clever or lucky."

Mrs. Jeffries sagged against her chair in relief. So far, no one reported seeing Smythe leaping out that window. "I can see why you think it might be difficult," she finally said. "I take it no one confessed?" She held her breath.

He shook his head. "No. Worse luck."

"If his staff didn't like him. . . . " She hesitated, not wanting him to think she was suggesting one of the servants might have killed the man. However, if they didn't like him, they might be feeling guilty and shocked. It would be easy to miss an important clue if that were the case, but the inspector interrupted her.

"Oh, it's not likely to be one of the servants," he said morosely. "All of them were in the kitchen at the time of death."

"Oh, you know what time he was killed?"

"Not precisely. Barrett was last seen alive at five o'clock this afternoon. However, he shouted at the workmen at sometime around a quarter to six, so we know he was alive then."

"I knew I'd get this one," Witherspoon moaned softly to Barnes. He peeked over the railing to make sure Inspector Nivens wasn't lurking about.

"Not to worry, sir," Barnes said. "The coast is clear. Nivens got called out on a house burglary this morning."

"Thank goodness." He started down the stairs. "Not that I'm afraid of facing the fellow, but he does rather make me feel guilty."

Barnes snorted. He didn't think much of Inspector Nivens. None of the uniformed lads did. "It's not your fault you're good at homicides, now, is it? If Inspector Nivens has a problem with your gettin' this case, he'd best take it up with the chief, hadn't he?"

"Well, yes, I suppose you're right." Witherspoon still sounded doubtful. "But we've work to do. Come, Constable, let's find a hansom."

Luty Belle and Hatchet arrived a good half hour before lunch. "I couldn't stop her," Hatchet explained as he handed Mrs. Jeffries their heavy coats. "Once she heard the word 'murder,' she was bound and determined to get here."

"Nell's bells, Hepzibah!" Luty yelped. "You shoulda sent fer us last night. The killer could be halfway to New York by now."

"Only if he sprouted wings and flew," Hatchet said.

"Please sit down. I'll tell you everything we know before the others get back."

By the time Smythe ambled in for his noonday meal, Luty and Hatchet were fully appraised of everything that had transpired the night before. Mrs. Goodge, who'd been setting the table as Mrs. Jeffries talked, had frequently added her opinion as well.

Betsy and Wiggins showed up next, and by the time the cook had the vegetables and meat on the table, they were all seated and eager to begin.

"Hear you had yerself a mighty fine adventure last night," Luty said to Smythe.

"More of a trial than an adventure," Smythe replied with a cocky grin. "I was pleased to find out from Mrs. Jeffries this mornin' that none of the neighbours had seen me leapin' out of Barrett's window." His grin faded.

"But I did find out a bit more about that argument Barrett had with his neighbour yesterday afternoon. There was more to it than what the inspector 'eard."

"Mrs. Jeffries already said he wasn't popular with the neighbours," Betsy pointed out. She was annoyed. She'd spent half the bloomin' morning trampin' up and down the high street in that area and hadn't learned a bloomin' thing. Now that she knew Smythe wasn't goin' to be carted off by the police for breakin' into a dead man's house, she didn't mind tweakin' his nose a bit. Kept him from getting such a big head.

"My ears work, lass. But bein' unpopular ain't the same thing as havin' someone threaten to kill ya."

"Someone threatened to kill 'im!" Wiggins exclaimed.

"Man named Adrian Spears. Bachelor, lives in the house next door to Barrett's." Smythe spread a thick slab of butter on his bread.

"Mrs. Jeffries already told us all this," Betsy pointed out.

"I know, lass. But I'm repeatin' it just so Luty and Hatchet will know everythin'. Anyways, as I was sayin' before I was interrupted." Betsy snorted delicately but the coachman ignored her and went right on. "Seems Barrett didn't like Spears's dog. Barrett was always chasin' it off and throwin' stones at it. Claimed the animal dug up his plants. Yesterday Spears couldn't find the dog at all. He and his servants went outside and they searched the garden. They found the animal outside Barrett's house in some bushes. His head had been bashed in with a hammer. Spears went crazy. He screamed for Barrett to come out and face him like a man. Well, of course, with Barrett's doors and windows wide open, the whole ruddy household come out to see what the ruckus was. When Barrett showed up, Spears went for him. He would have ripped his throat out right there if it hadn't a been for the servants steppin' in and breakin' them apart. But Spears was heard to threaten Barrett, said if 'e found out for sure that Barrett had killed the dog, 'e'd wring his neck.''

"That awful man!" Betsy exclaimed.

"Who?" Smythe asked curiously. "Barrett or Spears?"

"Barrett, of course. Anyone who'd take a hammer to an innocent dog deserves what he gets."

"But we don't know that Barrett killed the animal," Smythe pointed out reasonably. "It could have been someone else."

"That's very odd," Mrs. Jeffries said.

"What is?" demanded Mrs. Goodge.

"When Barrett's butler told the inspector what had happened, he said nothing about Spears issuing a death threat. His account of the whole incident was far more casual that what Smythe has just told us."

"Maybe the butler didn't hear the death threat," Hatchet suggested. "Or perhaps he was in such a state of shock, he forgot to mention it. What's the man's name?"

"Hadley," Mrs. Jeffries answered. "Reginald Hadley. Do you know him?"

"No." Hatchet frowned slightly. "I don't think so, but perhaps I'll ask about and see what I can learn about him."

Smythe leaned forward. "That's not all I found out. Seems that Barrett and Spears 'ave been squabblin' for months. The two men don't like each other. Course, from what I 'eard, not many round that neighbourhood much liked Barrett."

Mrs. Jeffries looked thoughtful. "Any idea what they'd been quarreling about?"

"Didn't have time to get many details," Smythe admitted. "But I'll keep at it."

"Excellent, Smythe." She looked at Betsy.

"I didn't learn a bloomin' thing," the girl admitted honestly. She fiddled with the skirt of her blue broadcloth dress. "None of the shopkeepers knew anything and all the shops were so busy this morning, I didn't really get much of a chance to talk to many of the assistants."

"Not to worry," the housekeeper said smoothly. "It's early days yet."

"Don't feel bad, Betsy," Wiggins said. "I didn't find out anything, either. No one from the Barrett 'ouse so much as stuck their nose outside today." He glanced at Mrs. Jeffries. "Do you want me to keep at it?"

"Of course, Wiggins." She decided that both the maid and the footman could use some encouragement. "Both you and Betsy must keep at it. You're both far too clever and far too valuable to us to stop now."

"I found out something," Mrs. Goodge announced. She waited till she had everyone's attention. "It seems Mr. Barrett isn't much of a gentleman."

"Course 'e's not," Wiggins interrupted. "Gents don't go about bashin' dogs on the 'ead." He reached down and stroked Fred, a mongrel who'd been adopted into the Witherspoon household some months earlier. Fred's tail thumped against the floor.

"We don't know for sure that Barrett did bash the dog," Smythe argued. "Accordin' to what I 'eard, he denied he'd touched the animal."

"We're getting off the point," Mrs. Jeffries said calmly. "I believe Mrs. Goodge was about to tell us something."

Mrs. Goodge's eyes narrowed ominously. "*If* everyone's finished, I'll continue. Now, as I was sayin'. I found out that Barrett is no gentleman.'' She paused and waited till there was utter silence. Even Fred had stopped banging his tail against the floor. Then she said, "He did the worst thing a man could do to a woman."

"Murdered her?" Luty asked.

"Ravished her?" Betsy guessed.

Mrs. Goodge shook her head at both these suggestions. She smiled triumphantly. "He left her at the altar."

"Nell's Bells!" Luty cried. "Is that all? Gettin' left at the altar ain't the *worst* that can happen to a body. Why, I can tell ya dozens of worst things than that; gettin' scalped, gettin' shanghaied, gettin' stuck in a blizzard and freezin'—"

"I think we get the point, madam," Hatchet interrupted smoothly.

"I think being left at the altar in front of a church full of people is quite enough," Mrs. Goodge snapped. "Imagine the pain, the humiliation, the disgrace . . ."

"Disgrace," Luty snorted. "Why should *she* be disgraced? He's the one who acted like a no-good skunk-bellied polecat."

"I suppose being jilted in such a public manner could be a motive for murder," Mrs. Jeffries mused.

"Murder! Humph!" Luty shouted. "If'n that woman stuck a sword through the varmint's heart, it weren't murder. It was justice."

CHAPTER 4

Inspector Witherspoon wished that Adrian Spears would stop pacing. But he could hardly say so. After all, it was the man's home. "Now, Mr. Spears," he began for the third time, "we're questioning everyone who lives on these Gardens."

Spears stopped and stared at him. He was a short, middle-aged man with thick black hair liberally sprinkled with gray, dark brown eyes and a large misshapen nose that looked as though it had been broken a time or two. "I don't expect you'll find out very much. People have a natural reticence about speaking ill of the dead. Especially as we're talking about a murder here. But rest assured, Inspector, regardless of what others say, I wasn't the only one of his neighbours who loathed Barrett."

"We're aware of the fact that most of Mr. Barrett's neighbours didn't care for him," the inspector replied. "His own staff admitted that much. But—"

"Neighbours!" Spears exclaimed. "His neighbours were the least of his problems. The man was being sued by practically everyone who'd ever done business with him. If I were you, I'd stop wasting my time questioning us about our petty squabbles and get on to the people who had real motives for wanting him dead.''

''And who would that be?'' Barnes asked softly.

''Thornton Astley for one,'' Spears replied, pacing again. ''He's filed a lawsuit. Barrett cheated him in a business deal. He actually stole money.''

''Why would this Mr. Astley kill him if he was getting ready to take him to court?'' the inspector asked.

Spears lip curled. ''To save himself the cost of a solicitor. No doubt once he heard how much it would cost him to take Barrett to court, he decided to take matters into his own hands.'' He clamped his mouth shut, closed his eyes and sighed. ''Forgive me, Inspector. I didn't mean that. Thornton Astley is an honourable man, I know him socially. He wouldn't murder someone, no matter how much he deserved it.''

Witherspoon started in surprise. Deserved it? He didn't think anyone *deserved* to be murdered, and he certainly was rather shocked to hear a seemingly respectable man say such a thing. ''Could you tell us about your dispute with Mr. Barrett?''

''Which one?'' Spears asked. ''Barrett's been a thorn in my side from the day he moved into the Gardens. He's been a thorn in everyone's side.''

Witherspoon made a mental note to come back to that issue. But for right now he was most interested in another incident. ''I'm referring to the death of your dog,'' he said.

''You mean his murder,'' Spears said softly, his voice suddenly shaky. He blinked rapidly to hold back tears. ''Poor King, he never had a chance. Barrett slaughtered my dog, Inspector, and for that act alone, I'm glad the bastard's dead. Anyone capable of killing a helpless animal deserves to die.''

Witherspoon didn't approve of killing dogs. He could certainly understand Mr. Spears's sentiments, but goodness, he hoped the man would bring himself under control. It would be very difficult to question a man who was blubbering, very difficult, indeed. "Er . . . why did Barrett kill your dog?''

Spears turned his back and stared at the brass candlestick on the carved mantel. He took a long, deep breath before answering. "He never liked King,'' he said softly. "Barrett had the gardener plant bulbs over in the beds outside his house. He accused King of digging them up. Claimed the dog barked at all hours and was generally a nuisance. But it wasn't true. King was well trained.'' He whirled around and gestured with his hands. "Oh, occasionally he barked—what dog doesn't? But he didn't go near Barrett's wretched plants.''

"Were the flower beds dug up?'' Witherspoon was sure that was completely irrelevant, but he was curious and he wanted to keep Spears talking.

"Of course not,'' Spears gestured impatiently. "Oh, there were a few spots here and there where the dirt had been disturbed. But that doesn't mean it was King that had done it. The garden is full of cats and dogs.''

"But apparently, Mr. Barrett was convinced your King had done the digging?'' the inspector prompted. "'Why? Why single out your animal for that kind of revenge.''

"He's hated me for a long time. He was always looking for an excuse to be unpleasant.''

"And why was that, sir?'' Barnes asked, looking up from his notebook.

"Because I bought this house right from under his nose,'' Spears said with a note of triumphant in his voice.

"Barrett had offered on it, but his offer came in after mine did and I was willing to pay more to get it. Barrett was furious. Threatened to sue the estate agents and myself. Naturally, he'd not a leg to stand on. He ended up buying the house next door to me, but, of course, he never forgave me for getting this one."

Spears paused and gazed round the drawing room, an expression of intense pride on his face. Witherspoon could well understand why the man was proud.

Dark, rich wood panelling accented the lower half of the walls. The upper half was painted a deep forest green. Paintings of the English countryside and several well-done portraits softened the masculine decor. Unlike many drawing rooms, this one wasn't overly furnished. A settee, several comfortable chairs and a table or two, and that was it. A carved marble mantel and a polished hardwood floor gave the exquisitely furnished room an air of wealth and dignity. An air that was distinctly missing in the Barrett house.

"Barrett," Spears continued after he'd finished his slow perusal of the room, "wasn't one to forgive and forget. After he moved in here, he was less than neighbourly. I did my best to be civil, of course. We were frequently at the same social gatherings."

"These social acquaintances you had in common?" Witherspoon queried, somewhat hesitantly. He was guessing on this point, but sometimes he'd found a guess could pay off tremendous dividends. "That's somewhat confusing. If, as you say, Barrett was habitually unpleasant . . ."

"He was never overt when he was a guest in someone else's home," Spears replied. "I tell you, the man was an utter hypocrite. He had no compunction about stabbing you in the back one minute and then acting as though you were a long-lost friend the next. It was appalling. But what was even worse was how successful it was. Take the Astleys for instance. Here they were suing Barrett, yet he fully intended to show up at their dinner party last night.''

"Why did the Astleys invite him?" Witherspoon asked.

"They invited him some time ago. Maud Astley had planned this dinner for months. Naturally, when they brought suit against him, they expected he'd send his regrets. But the man actually had the gall to send Maud a message last week telling her he was looking forward to seeing her." He shook his head in disgust.

"I see," the inspector said slowly.

Barnes cleared his throat. "You were going to tell us about yesterday afternoon," he said to Spears. "About your dog, sir."

Anguish flared briefly in the man's eyes and he quickly turned away. Witherspoon threw Barnes an appreciative nod. Sometimes he quite forgot where he was when he was questioning people.

"Yesterday afternoon I noticed King was missing." Spears spoke so softly both the policemen had to lean toward him to hear. "I was worried."

"Were you worried for any particular reason?" the inspector asked. "Or merely because Barrett had been so generally unpleasant?"

"I had a reason. Barrett had thrown stones at the poor dog only the day before. One of them had hit him quite hard in his forepaw, and I was concerned about him being outside and unprotected." He smiled sadly. "King was such a sweet-natured animal that he wouldn't think to run if Barrett came out and began abusing him. In any case, no one in the household had seen the animal, so I called out the servants and we started to search for him out in the gardens." His voice dropped to a whisper. "You know what I found. King was lying in the foliage behind Barrett's house. His head had been bashed in with a hammer.''

"I thought you said there were flower beds behind Mr. Barrett's house?" the inspector asked, puzzled.

"There are both. Each house has two planting beds bisected by a small path that leads to the communal garden. Most of the owners have generally agreed to plant the same sorts of things, give the gardens an air of continuity, or refinement. But not Barrett. He hadn't been here more than two weeks before he had the gardeners putting bushes and shrubs in one of his beds and those blasted bulbs in the other. That's one of the things the other neighbours didn't like about him. He didn't give a fig for what the rest of us wanted. Those were his wretched beds and by God, he'd put what he liked in them whether it made the garden look ridiculous or not." Spears made a derisive sound. "Believe me, Inspector. It did make the gardens look ridiculous too. Not that Barrett had the good taste to notice. He was actually proud of what he'd done, was showing those silly beds off to one of his acquaintances the day before yesterday. That's when he threw the rocks at poor King. And all the dog wanted to do was be friendly. I tell you, Barrett was a dreadful man. Positively dreadful."

"How unfortunate," the inspector murmured. He thought it an odd way to behave. But he hardly saw a quarrel over flower beds as a motive for murder.

"What time did you go lookin' for your dog, sir?" Barnes asked.

"Late in the afternoon, about four-thirty or five o'clock. I don't remember exactly. But it was getting quite dark."

"And you immediately went to Barrett's house?"

"No," Spears admitted. "I was so enraged I stood

there and bellowed for the blackguard to come out and face me. The bastard had the sheer effrontery to demand we get off his beds!''

''Was he angry?''

''He was always angry,'' Spears said with relish. ''But this time I was enraged. When I yanked the bushes back and showed him poor King's body, he acted as though it were my fault. Completely denied he'd had anything to do with the dog's death. I knew he was lying, of course. We quarreled.''

''We understand you did more than quarrel,'' Witherspoon said bluntly. ''According to witnesses, you attacked Mr. Barrett.''

''I did,'' Spears confessed. ''And I'm not the least bit sorry.''

Witherspoon sighed silently. This case was getting more ridiculous by the minute. Not that the death of a beloved pet was absurd, he could understand that. He'd be most upset if someone harmed his beloved Fred. What truly amazed him was the way two seemingly adult men had behaved over the entire episode. ''Had anyone seen Mr. Barrett in the garden? Did you have any witnesses that Barrett had actually been the one to kill King?''

''Barrett claimed he hadn't been out there all day.'' Spears laughed derisively. ''But what else could he say? He didn't want to admit to being such a savage in front of everyone. Ye Gods, Inspector, there were dozens of people watching us. My servants, his servants, some neighbours, even the workmen who were redoing his house came out to watch.''

''Did you threaten to kill him, sir?'' Witherspoon asked. As a motive, vengeance over a murdered pet might seem farfetched to most people. But as a policeman, the inspector knew that even wealthy intelligent men like

Adrian Spears were capable of committing heinous crimes if sufficiently provoked. And Spears certainly must have been provoked. But angry enough to murder? To take a human life?

"I didn't mean it, of course," he muttered. "But yes, I did threaten him. Pembroke, my butler, had the good sense to intervene before things got too heated." He smiled sadly. "Pembroke's been with me a long time and he knew how much King meant to me."

"I see. Was that the last time you saw Mr. Barrett?" Witherspoon asked.

"Yes, thank God. At least I was spared the sight of the man over the dinner table."

"Where were you between six and seven yesterday afternoon?"

Spears looked surprised by the question. "I went for a walk. For God's sake, man, I'd just found my dog with his head bashed in. . . . I needed to get it out of my system. So I went out to be on my own for a while and came home about six-twenty or so. I was due at the Astley house at seven."

"Where did you walk?" the inspector pressed.

Spears hesitated before answering. "I'm not really sure. . . . I was most upset, Inspector. As well as I can remember, I walked 'round the gardens to Kildare Terrace and out onto Talbot Road."

"Did anyone see you?"

"Of course not. It was quite dark by that time. I walked for about an hour, came home, poured myself a good-sized whiskey and got ready to go to the Astleys'. The last time I saw William Barrett, he was alive and well."

"Oh, no, what am I going to do?" Mrs. Goodge wailed. She shook her head as she stared at the telegram in her hand. "I can't leave now! We're on a murder."

"But you must go," Mrs. Jeffries insisted. "You'll never forgive yourself if your aunt . . . uh, passes on and you didn't go to see her."

"Bloomin' Ada!" Mrs. Goodge cried, for once so upset she didn't care if she used strong language. "Why now? Aunt Elberta's never had a sick day in her life."

"Well," Mrs. Jeffries said soothingly, "she is getting along in years. And it has been dreadfully cold lately. It's no wonder the poor old dear has pneumonia."

"I've got to go, don't I?" Mrs. Goodge shook her head sadly and tucked the telegram into the pocket of her apron. "She's got to be eighty-five if she's a day. What do you think the inspector'll say when he gets back and finds me gone? Do you think he'll mind?"

"Of course he won't mind," Mrs. Jeffries assured her. "Inspector Witherspoon would be the first to tell you you must go. Why, your dear aunt may be failing—he'd never forgive himself if he kept you from her sickbed."

"Do you think I can get a train today?" Mrs. Goodge asked, looking anxiously at the clock. "It's already gone two."

"You go get packed," Mrs. Jeffries told her firmly. "I'll check my timetable and see when the next train for Devonshire leaves."

"But who's going to get the goods on Barrett?" Mrs. Goodge wailed. She looked at the tray of fragrant brown buns cooling on the kitchen table, her expression mournful. "Who's going to question my sources? I've got half of London due in here this afternoon and tomorrow."

"Now, now. Don't worry," Mrs. Jeffries said as she gently shoved the cook toward the stairs. "I'll take care of your sources. Go get packed. I'm fairly certain there's a late afternoon train today. But you must hurry, you don't want to miss it.''

Muttering mutinously about crotchety old ladies taking it into their heads to get ill at the worst times, Mrs. Goodge trudged off to her room.

Mrs. Jeffries thought it amusing that Mrs. Goodge wasn't in the least concerned about who was going to cook for them.

Betsy smiled at the young man walking beside her. He was no more than sixteen, red-haired, with a pale complexion sprinkled with freckles and spots. Underneath his overcoat he wore a footman's uniform.

''I 'eard there was murder in that 'ouse,'' she said, nodding towards the Barrett home with her chin. ''Cor, it fair gives me a queer feelin' it does, just walkin' by the place.''

She deliberately mangled her speech, and she was smiling so hard her cheeks hurt. But she couldn't afford to miss this chance. The shop assistant at the fishmonger's had pointed the young man out. He worked at the Spears house. When Betsy saw the way he stared at her, she'd tossed her curls and given him her boldest smile. Let him think she was loose and had no morals; she didn't care. The footman worked next door to Barrett's. Not as good as actually talking to someone from the victim's house, but close.

''Don't worry, miss,'' he said, puffing out his chest. ''I'll walk you to the end of the street. No one'll bother ya if you're with me.''

''Do you work 'round 'ere, then?'' she asked, flashing him another smile.

''Right next door to where the murder happened,'' he said.

"Oh, you must be ever so brave," she replied. "Why, I couldn't sleep knowin' there'd been murder done so close." It never hurt to butter them up a bit, Betsy thought. She'd noticed that men would believe the most outrageous flattery.

"Don't bother me none," he said, slowing his footsteps as they neared the house.

"But what if it's one of them maniacs?" she persisted.

"Nah, it were someone who hated Mr. Barrett," the footman said easily. "I don't expect they'll come back and kill anyone else."

"Whyever not?"

"It was Barrett they was after. Mind you, I'm not surprised. If anyone was askin' to get done in, it was 'im. My own master had a row with him yesterday, not that Mr. Spears would ever do murder, but it just goes to show what kind of man this Barrett was. A real brute if you ask me."

As Betsy already knew about Spears's altercation with Barrett, she didn't need to hear about that. She wanted to go back to Upper Edmonton Gardens with something new. "Did this Mr. Barrett have a lot of enemies?"

"Just about everyone who knew him." He jerked his chin toward the late unlamented Mr. Barrett's house. "My guv hated him. Course I don't much blame him. He killed Mr. Spears's dog. Nice dog it was too, real friendly old feller. Course that's put everyone in an uproar."

"Well, an animal gettin' killed is pretty awful," she said quickly, "but—"

"Oh," he continued blithely, "it weren't just King gettin' done in that's got everyone all het up. Janie, that's one of the maids, is scared she's goin' to lose her position and Matilda's shakin' in her shoes as well. Course I told 'em, if they keeps quiet, no one will know that Janie left the door open. That's how King got out, ya see.''

She didn't care how the dog had gotten out. She wanted more information. ''Did—''

He continued on as if she hadn't spoken. Betsy wondered if he was deaf. ''And now Matilda, that's one of the upstairs maids, is wonderin' if she'll be sacked 'cause she didn't tell Mr. Spears that it were Janie that left the door open in the first place.''

''Did you hear anything about the murder?'' she asked, interrupting him and knowing it was rude. But they were almost at the end of the road and she was desperate.

''Huh?'' The boy stared at her in such shocked surprise that she thought she might have made a big mistake.

She gave him a big smile. ''I mean, I hope you don't mind my askin', but someone like you, you seem so smart an' all. I thought you might have found out somethin' even the police don't know.''

''Well . . .'' He blushed to the roots of his hair. ''I've always prided myself on knowing what's what, if you get my meanin'.''

''I do.'' She couldn't believe it. He believed every word she said.

''Well, I don't rightly know much about the actual killin','' he said. ''But I do know that he was havin' some kind of a row with a woman the night before he died. Don't likely think a woman could have killed him, but that just goes to show that he weren't really a gentleman.''

''What woman?'' Betsy asked softly. She had to be careful here. She had him talking; she didn't want to make a mistake.

''Don't know what her name was,'' the lad replied. ''But she and Barrett were havin' a fierce row the night before last. I heard them arguin' when I took out the ashes to the dustbin.''

"Maybe he was just havin' a row with 'is missus," she suggested.

"Barrett weren't married."

She sniffed. "Well, you're right, then. No gentlemen has a row out in public."

"They wasn't in public," he said, laughing. "That's why I thought it was so strange. They was in the gardens and it had gone on eight o'clock. But there they was, standin' behind some bushes hissin' at each other like a couple of cats."

"Did ya 'ear what they was on about?"

"Nah, but I could tell they was squabblin'. He weren't out there with the lady to steal a kiss or anythin' like that."

"Wonder who the woman is?" she mused. "Course we'll never know. With this Mr. Barrett bein' dead, it would take someone really clever to find out who he'd been squabblin' with." She glanced up at him through her lashes to see if he'd taken the bait. By the thoughtful expression on his face, she thought he had.

"I reckon someone could find out," he said slowly. "But why are you so interested?"

She shrugged. "Everyone's interested in murder. That's why they put it in the newspapers. I'm just curious, that's all."

They'd come to the end of the Kildare Terrace. Betsy stared out at Talbot Road. She could feel his gaze on her and she shifted uncomfortably. He was a nice lad and she was taking shameless advantage of him to get information.

"Uh, do you work 'round here?" he asked hesitantly.

"Not far," she replied.

He looked around suddenly. "I'd best be gettin' back. They only sent me out to get a newspaper."

"Oh." She contrived to look crestfallen. "It was ever so nice of you to walk me this far. I don't usually get lost." She had given him a silly tale of getting lost trying to find a shortcut while out on an errand for her mistress. "But I must say, havin' you with me made me feel ever so much safer. Thank you."

"Uh, look, if'n I could be so bold—" He paused and took a deep breath.

"Yes," she prompted. Betsy knew she'd hate herself later. The lad obviously was taken with her. She was far too old for him and she wasn't interested in him. But this was murder, so she wasn't above flirting a bit to get the information she needed.

He opened his mouth to speak just as a four-wheeler clattered past, one of its wheels creaking so loudly she didn't hear a word the lad said.

"Uh, if'n I can be so bold," he repeated, blushing furiously. "I'd like to see ya again."

"I'd like that," she replied, ignoring the nasty voice of her conscience. "You seem like a nice chap. Tell you what, I'll be along here tomorrow about this time. Maybe you can slip out and we can have another walk."

"Tomorrow?" He looked puzzled. "But I thought you said you only come this way 'cause you was lost?"

She thought fast. "I am lost." She laughed coquettishly. "But I go out every afternoon to get my mistress her chocolates. She likes them fresh. I'll make certain I get lost this way tomorrow."

A slow, pleased smile crept over his face. Betsy couldn't believe it. Men would believe any old load of rubbish you told them, as long as it was *them* you was butterin' up! She was torn between wanting to box his ears for believing such a silly tale and thanking her lucky stars he was so gullible.

"Well, in that case, I reckon I can find an excuse to get out. By the way, my name's Noah. Noah Parnell."

"I'll see ya tomorrow, then, Noah." She started across the street, then stopped and looked back at him. "Oh, and I do say, I think it's ever so clever of you to know so much about that murder."

"I'll tell you more tomorrow," he promised.

Betsy dashed across the road and started down the other side.

"Hey!" he yelled. "What's yer name?"

Thornton Astley was a man of about fifty, still youthful looking, though there was plenty of grey streaked through his dark auburn hair. Clean-shaven, his eyes were a clear, cool grey. His face was relatively unlined, though there was the hint of sagging flesh beneath his chin.

His wife, seated next to him on the overstuffed burgundy settee, was stunningly beautiful and a good thirty years younger than her husband. Small, blond-haired and blue-eyed, Maud Astley reminded the inspector of one of those lovely china dolls he'd seen in the window of a shop on Regent Street.

A third person, a thin, rather attractive young man with a full mustache, dark brown hair and deep set hazel eyes sat a respectful distance away from the Astleys. He was Mr. Astley's private secretary, Neville Sharpe.

"I don't think we can tell you anything about this unfortunate business," Thornton Astley said. "We haven't seen Barrett for some time."

"I believe he was due to have dinner with you last evening?" Witherspoon replied.

"He never arrived," Mrs. Astley said coolly. "We held dinner as long as we could, but finally Cook was getting most upset, so we went in."

"Didn't you wonder why Mr. Barrett hadn't come?" the inspector asked. Surely, he thought, they'd be somewhat curious when an expected guest failed to turn up.

Astley shrugged. "Not really. Barrett wasn't exactly what one would call a gentleman."

"Then why did you invite him to dine at your home?"

The Astleys exchanged a quick, furtive glance.

"Barrett was a business acquaintance," Astley said. "We'd extended the invitation some time ago. He might not have been a gentleman, but I am."

"When did you decide to sue Mr. Barrett?" Witherspoon watched him closely, but Astley's expression didn't change. The inspector realized that the man was prepared for the question. Drat. He'd so hoped to take him by surprise. Sometimes one could learn so much by a person's reaction to an unexpected question.

"So you know about that." Astley replied. "I'm not surprised. I've made no secret of my opinion of the man. Naturally, as I was suing the bounder, I'd hoped he'd have the decency to stay away from my home. But he actually had the gall to send my wife a note saying he was looking forward to seeing her. Unbelievable, really. But that was the kind of man he was. As to when I decided to sue him, it was some weeks ago." He turned to his secretary. "Do you recall exactly when, Sharpe?"

"You contacted your solicitor two weeks ago," he answered. "Sometime around the fourth or the fifth."

"That's right," Astley agreed. "However, Inspector, you should also know, I had decided to drop the lawsuit. Frankly, it would have cost me a great deal more than I could ever hope to recover from Barrett."

"That's true, Inspector," Mrs. Astley added.

Witherspoon was really puzzled now. "Precisely what

was it Barrett had done to you?'' he asked.

"Stolen a great deal of money.'' Astley grimaced. "And it was my own fault. You see, there'd been rumours about the man for ages. But I ignored them. Didn't place any credence in them at all.''

"You're too hard on yourself, dear,'' Mrs. Astley interrupted. "You couldn't be expected to take gossip and innuendo seriously.''

"Yes, but I should have been more careful,'' he replied. "I needed a partner for one of my business ventures. A building company. I've a number of business ventures and frequently take in partners because I can't run them all.''

"And Barrett ran this building company?'' the inspector prompted.

"Oh, yes. We weren't making huge profits, but I thought nothing of it—it was a new concern and growing. Then my secretary''—he glanced at the young man sitting behind him—''brought some invoices to my attention. Invoices the company had paid. He told me I ought to investigate them. I did so. Barrett had been paying false invoices to accounts that did not exist. Further investigation revealed he'd been doing this virtually since we went into business together.''

"So you were going to take him to court?'' Barnes asked softly.

"Yes, more fool I.'' He shook his head in disgust. "I knew there was talk about Barrett, I'd heard the rumours. But I was in a bind, Barrett had ready cash to go into the business, and I thought he had the ability to run the company. It was a rather good opportunity and I didn't want to let it slip away. So instead of investigating him as I should have, I blindly plunged ahead.''

The inspector nodded sympathetically. "What kind of rumours, sir?''

"Let me see, well"—he frowned slightly—"supposedly he'd left some poor woman standing at the altar."

"Really, Thornton," Maud Astley said quietly. "I don't think that's the kind of rumour the inspector is interested in."

"But it shows the man's character, Maud," he argued. "Shows what he was capable of doing. And then there was that awful business with that poor chap who hanged himself. Of course, that was fifteen years ago. Now, what was the man's name. Blumm, Borden . . ."

"Blunt, sir," Neville Sharp said. "Thomas Blunt."

"Oh, yes." Astley nodded. "And there are all sorts of rumours about Washburn."

The inspector was thoroughly confused but determined not to show it. "Washburn?"

Astley smiled tightly. "His current business partner. One of the reasons I went into business with Barrett was that he was already overseeing what I thought was another thriving business. Washburn and Tate. They're also builders, but they do commercial property outside of London, so there wouldn't be any conflict of interest or competition between the two firms. Then, of course, I heard about Owen Washburn."

"What about him?" Witherspoon hoped Barnes was taking excellent notes. This was getting most confusing.

Astley hesitated briefly. "Some say that Barrett blackmailed the man to do business with him."

"Really, Thornton!" Maud looked embarrassed. "You must be careful what you say."

"Why? One can't libel the dead, and if Barrett weren't dead, these men wouldn't be here."

"I mean you mustn't say anything about Mr. Washburn," she corrected. "That family has coped with enough disgrace."

"Disgrace?" Witherspoon queried.

"I really mustn't say more," Mrs. Astley said, her porcelain cheeks flaming. "It would be most unkind."

The inspector smiled sympathetically. "I appreciate your position, Mrs. Astley," he said softly. "But this is a murder investigation."

She looked at her husband, who nodded, encouraging her to go on. "Very well, then. It was Mr. Washburn's sister that Mr. Barrett left standing at the altar. It was so humiliating for the poor woman. He'd not even the decency to come to the church himself. He sent a cabbie in with a note. Poor Miss Washburn fainted—and in front of the bishop too!"

"How dreadful!" Witherspoon exclaimed. Gracious, sometimes it was so very difficult to have much sympathy with the victim. William Barrett sounded like a most disagreeable person. Imagine leaving a poor woman standing at the altar in front of all her relations, friends and acquaintances.

"It was," she agreed. "Most dreadful. No one could quite understand why Mr. Washburn continued to do business with Barrett after that. But if the rumours we've heard are correct, I don't really think he had all that much choice."

"Of course he did," Thornton Astley corrected. "He should have refused to have anything more to do with the blighter. I know I certainly did when I caught him cheating me. I immediately took action."

"How did you do that, sir?" Witherspoon asked curiously.

Astley blinked. It was Neville Sharpe who answered. "Mr. Astley instructed his solicitors to dissolve the partnership."

"Yes, but precisely how does one do that?" the inspector persisted. He hadn't the faintest idea how one dissolved a partnership, especially as there seemed to be money involved.

"My solicitors drew up papers formally dissolving it," Astley replied stiffly. "They also put my half of the company on the block."

"Does that mean that Mr. Barrett bought you out?" Barnes asked.

Astley's eyes grew cold. "He would have, eventually."

Witherspoon leaned forward. "If you weren't going to sue the man, how could you have persuaded him to buy you out?"

"Barrett didn't know I was dropping the suit," Astley explained. "He was quite upset about it as well. I suspect that's why he was planning on coming to dine with us. No doubt he wanted to find out just where he stood. Believe me, Inspector, I wasn't going to let him off the hook until I got his agreement to buy me out."

"I see," the inspector said, though he wasn't sure he did. "Mr. Astley, where were you yesterday afternoon between six and seven o'clock?"

Astley's jaw dropped.

"Really, Inspector," Sharpe said angrily. "I hope you're not implying that Mr. Astley—"

"I'm implying nothing," Witherspoon replied. Gracious, this was so tedious. How did people think homicides got solved if the police didn't ask simple questions?

Astley clamped his mouth shut. "I was working at my office in the city."

"Did anyone see you there?"

"No, the staff had gone home. I worked here for most of the afternoon and didn't get to the office until about half past five. I stayed for about a half an hour and then came home to get ready for dinner.

"Was Mr. Sharpe with you?"

"No."

"I went to the dentist," the secretary hastily explained. "Mr. Astley kindly gave me some free time so I could take care of a tooth that had been bothering me."

"How long have you worked for Mr. Astley?"

Sharpe smiled slightly. "Six months. I had a position in Birmingham before I came here."

"I assure you," Astley snapped, "my secretary barely knew William Barrett. His private business isn't any of Scotland Yard's concern."

"Nevertheless," Sharpe said quickly, "I'll be happy to tell you the name of my dentist. It's Pellman. He's got offices on the Richmond Road."

"Thank you, Mr. Sharpe." Witherspoon had the feeling there was something he was forgetting to ask. But he couldn't, for the life of him, think of what it was. "Mrs. Astley, did the other guests at your dinner party know William Barrett?"

"What has that got to do with anything?" Astley asked harshly.

"I'm merely wondering if the other guests were concerned when Mr. Barrett failed to arrive?" He knew he'd asked what seemed like a pointless question, but as Mrs. Jeffries frequently said, sometimes it was those kinds of questions that gave you the right answers.

Maud Astley shrugged helplessly. "I don't know how to reply, Inspector. No one was in the least concerned when he didn't arrive. Why should they be? None of them were overly fond of the man, and I know for a fact that Minerva Kenny absolutely loathed him."

CHAPTER 5

Smythe glanced over his shoulder, hoping that no one he knew would happen to come into the bank. "If you don't mind, Mr. Pike"—he turned his attention back to the white-haired banker—"I'm in a bit of a 'urry 'ere. Could ya get on with it, please."

Mr. Bartholomew Pike narrowed his eyes slightly. He was not of the nervous nature of his predecessor, a man Smythe had easily intimidated into leaving him alone. Mr. Pike was not going to be bullied. They had serious business to discuss here. Money. Decisions had to be made. "This matter is most important, Mr. Smythe," Pike said calmly. "You made enormous profits off the selling of your interests in those American cattle ranches. You must do something with it."

"Can't ya just leave it in my account?" Cor blimey, Smythe thought, wasn't that what bloomin' banks was for, hangin' on to cash? "I don't have time to make any decisions now, I'm in the middle of—" He clamped his mouth shut. He'd almost said he was in the middle of investigatin' a murder. Cor, the old boy would probably 'ave a stroke if he'd let that slip. "Something important."

Pike appeared not to hear him. "I strongly advise you that leaving that amount of money in a general account is most foolish. There are any number of investments you should consider."

"And I told ya, I don't 'ave time," Smythe snapped, losing his patience. The business about his money was becomin' more than an irritation. It was becomin' a ruddy pain in the arse.

It were bad enough he had to hide the fact that he was a wealthy man from everyone he cared about in this world. Now this bloomin' banker was takin' to pesterin' him about every little detail. "I'll 'ave to come round next week and we'll discuss it then."

"You said that last week," Pike reminded him. "Mr. Smythe, we're talking about thirty thousand pounds. By most estimates, that's a small fortune."

"I know how much it is," Smythe said sharply. "Now, if you don't mind, I'll have that cash I asked ya to 'ave ready fer me."

Pike's mouth hardened into a thin, flat line, then he lifted his hand and gestured toward the young bank clerk. Holding a pouch, the clerk scurried forward and handed it to the stiff-necked banker. "Here you are, Mr. Smythe." Pike handed him the pouch. "I'll send you a letter early next week reminding you to come in. We'll make an appointment at your convenience."

Smythe shoved the pouch into his coat pocket. He wasn't sure gettin' letters from banks was a good idea. Then again, people 'ad bank accounts. Even Wiggins 'ad opened a post office account. But Mrs. Jeffries was gettin' suspicious. He could see it in her eyes every time he bought a little gift for one of the household. Not that they knew the gifts come from him. They didn't 'ave a clue and that's just the way he wanted to keep it. But the housekeeper was gettin' close. "That'll be fine, Mr. Pike."

Smythe pondered the problem of his money as he hurried out of the bank. He turned in the direction of the Bishopsgate Underground Station, dodging around a cooper's wagon and a costermonger to cross the street. He knew that one day he'd have to tell them the truth, but not yet. He couldn't stand the thought of them treatin' 'im differently. Of not bein' one of them.

It was all Euphemia's fault, he decided. God rest her soul. He should never 'ave gone along with pretendin' to be 'er ruddy coachman when he came back from Australia . . . but, at the time, it seemed like a grand idea. Then she'd up and died, makin' 'im promise to stay on and keep an eye on her nephew, Inspector Witherspoon. Euphemia had been convinced either a fortune hunter or a confidence man would separate her Witherspoon from his inheritance. He'd stayed on, not just to look out for the inspector but to make sure Wiggins had a place in the household too. By the time he'd realized the inspector was innocent but not stupid, Mrs. Jeffries, Mrs. Goodge and Betsy had come. They was investigatin' murders and lookin' out for each other and actin' like a family of sorts. No, he couldn't stand the idea of givin' all that up. Not yet. Not until he knew for sure there was no hope for him and Betsy havin' a future together.

"Really, madam, you're not being very subtle," Hatchet hissed as soon as he was alone with his employer. "These things call for tact and diplomacy."

"I got plenty of tact," Luty shot back. She glared at her butler. "You're just jealous 'cause I got old Tilbert to spill his guts and you ain't found out nothin' yet."

"I would hardly call one vague reference to the victim, 'spilling his—' " Hatchet broke off as the door opened and an elderly gentleman, a large bound volume tucked under his arm, moved slowly into the room. "Excuse me for taking so long, Luty," he said. "But it took a few moments to remember where I'd put this."

"May I help you with that, sir?" Hatchet asked. Unlike Luty, he wasn't sitting down in front of a tea table but stood stiffly at her back. That was the only way he could get in to hear everything that went on. Generally butlers were banished to the servants' hall during social calls. However, Luty being an eccentric American, insisted on keeping him close. Most of the people she called upon had gotten used to him hanging about.

Old Tilbert gratefully handed the heavy volume to him. "If you'd be so kind as to spread it open on the settee, Luty won't have to move. You'll see it's my clippings." He smiled proudly. "I've been collecting them for years. Now, what was that name again, Luty. Parrett?"

"Barrett," Luty corrected. "William Barrett."

She'd come to see her old friend because he had once been someone important in the City. But that had been years ago. Now he was old, alone and spent most of his time cutting out newspaper articles about anyone and everyone who did business in London. When it came to gossip in the business community or in the City, Tilbert could be counted on to know it all. "Have you ever heard of him?"

"You needn't repeat yourself, Luty," Tilbert said patiently. "I'm not completely senile yet. I remember what you asked. As I told you, the name does sound familiar. Give me a moment or two to think on it. In the meantime, amuse yourself by looking at my clippings. Perhaps you'll find something useful there."

Luty nodded. From behind her, she heard Hatchet stifle a snicker. Luckily, Tilbert was slightly deaf, so he didn't hear a thing. She leaned forward and began turning the pages.

"Barrett, Barrett, Barrett," Tilbert muttered softly. "Shipping agent, I believe. For one of the South American companies. Or was that another Barrett?"

Luty turned more pages, her eyes skimming stories about share prices, bond slumps, investment opportunities in Malaysian tea plantations and bankruptcies.

"No, no, I believe it was William Barrett," Tilbert said loudly. "That's right. He was in partnership in a shipping firm up in Liverpool a few years back. Yes, yes, now I recall it well. Barrett sold his interest in the agency right before it went under." Tilbert laughed loudly. "How clever I am—'went under' and it was a shipping agency. Sinking ships."

Luty gave him a weak smile. Nell's Bells, Tilbert was gettin' worse all the time. Course he always did make bad jokes. "That was mightly clever, Tilbert. So you're sayin' William Barrett sold his interest in this agency right afore it went bankrupt?"

"That's right. There was some speculation that Barrett had been stealing money from the firm . . . but no one ever proved anything. He disappeared for a while after that."

"Who else was involved in the bankrupcty?" Luty asked. Maybe someone had skewered Barrett because of old grievances. Wouldn't be the first time someone had bided their time before takin' a little revenge.

Tilbert smiled sadly. "I'm sorry, Luty. I can't remember the names of the people involved, but I do know that there were whispers that Barrett had gotten his own money out and left the other partners to pay the piper so to speak."

"So first he bled the firm dry and then he yanked his own cash out?" Luty asked. Behind her, she could hear Hatchet clearing his throat. She grinned. Having to keep quiet was almost chokin' the man.

Tilbert cocked his head to one side, his wrinkled face tight in concentration. "That's what people said," he replied. "But remember, it was a long time ago." He straightened suddenly. "Chidwick!" he cried.

Luty tossed Hatchet a quick look over her shoulder. "Huh?"

"Lester Chidwick!" he yelled excitedly. "Talking about it has brought it all back. That's the name of one of the partners who went bankrupt . . . and there was someone else—" He broke off, concentrating again. After a few moments he slumped down in the chair. "I can't recall the name. But I think that one of the partners was totally ruined. There was a suicide. That's right. One of them threw himself off a bridge."

"When was this exactly?" she asked sharply.

"Oh, it was years ago." Tilbert waved his hand in the air. "Fifteen at least. Like I said, it happened in Liverpool. There's not much else I can tell you about this Mr. Barrett except that he's involved in a number of ventures. Let me see, he's partner in a building firm or two, and he's got interests in an ironworks and a rubber company." Tilbert shook his head. "He's got his fingers in a lot of pies, if I may use one of your more colorful expressions." He laughed again.

Owen Washburn was short, slender, dark-haired and sported a mustache. He motioned Inspector Witherspoon and Constable Barnes into the two straight-back chairs sitting in front of his desk. "What can I do for you, Inspector?"

"I take it you have heard of the death of your partner, Mr. William Barrett."

"You mean his murder." Washburn smiled faintly. "Of course I've heard, it's been in every newspaper."

Witherspoon nodded. "I understand you did business with Mr. Barrett?"

"Yes. As you mentioned, we were partners."

"How long had you been in business with Mr. Barrett?"

Washburn leaned back in his chair. "About six months. My former partner, James Tate, passed away last year. I didn't have the capital on hand to buy his share of the firm from his widow. Barrett did."

"Did Mr. Barrett take an active hand in running the business?"

"Yes, he did," Washburn replied. "But he had many business interests."

"When was the last time you saw Mr. Barrett?" Witherspoon asked. Drat, he was going to have to be most delicate here. But he was decidedly curious about Washburn. How could he have continued to do business with the man who'd publicly humiliated his own sister?

"The day before yesterday in the afternoon," Washburn answered promptly. "I stopped by Barrett's house to bring him some papers that required his signature."

"While you were at Barrett's that afternoon, did anything unusual happen?" Witherspoon asked.

"Unusual? Not really." Washburn thought about it for a moment. "The house was in a bit of a state. He had workmen on the third floor, and they were making such a racket with their banging and pounding that we went out into the garden to talk."

"Did anything happen while you were out in the garden?"

Washburn looked puzzled for a moment. "Oh, the dog. I see you've heard about that. It was rather disgusting, really. This little black-and-white spaniel came bounding over when we were standing by the terrace. Friendly little thing. Barrett picked up a handful of stones and began heaving them at the poor animal. Revolting, really. The dog wasn't doing anything. But Barrett claimed it was ruining his flower beds." His lip curled in disgust. "But then again, he wasn't a very nice man."

"Mr. Washburn, forgive me for bringing up a painful or embarrassing subject—"

"I know what you're going to ask," Washburn cut him off. "And Mr. Barrett's abominable treatment of my sister has nothing to do with his death. She was home all day yesterday."

"I wasn't accusing her of anything," the inspector said. "I was going to ask you why you continued to do business with Barrett after what he'd done."

"Unfortunately," Washburn replied, "I'd no choice in the matter. When Barrett bought into the firm, he brought a substantial amount of operating capital with him. When Tate died, some of our creditors, fearing that with Tate gone, the business wouldn't be as successful, demanded immediate payment. It put a strain on the company coffers. I needed Barrett's cash to keep the business operating."

"So Mr. Barrett really held the upper hand in the company?" the inspector said speculatively.

Washburn's eyes flashed angrily. "No one held the upper hand," he insisted. "We were partners. Furthermore, I'd managed to raise the money to buy him out. That's why I went to see him a couple of days ago. I took him the necessary documents to start the process. So you see, Inspector, I wasn't planning on continuing the relationship with the man.''

''Would you mind telling me your whereabouts yesterday afternoon between six and seven?'' The inspector fully expected Washburn to protest. They always did. But surprisingly, the man answered the question without hesitation.

''I was here, working in my study.''

''Did anyone see you?''

''Well, it was the servants' afternoon out, but my sister was home.''

The inspector drummed his fingers on the armrest. ''May we speak to your sister?''

''I'd prefer that you didn't,'' Washburn protested. ''Eliza is very nervous. What with the wedding being cancelled in such a shocking manner and Barrett's murder, she's been dreadfully upset.''

''Why?'' Witherspoon asked quickly. ''Did she still have feelings of affection for him?''

''Certainly not!'' Washburn snapped. ''But she was engaged to him. For God's sake, they were supposed to marry only last month. Barrett might have behaved disgracefully, but my sister isn't an unfeeling monster. She certainly didn't hate him enough to want to see him brutally murdered.''

''Mr. Washburn,'' Witherspoon said gently, ''I fully appreciate how upset Miss Washburn must be. But as you said, Barrett was brutally murdered. I really must speak with your sister. Rest assured, I will be as discreet and delicate as possible.''

Washburn glowered at the two policemen for a few moments then nodded curtly, stalked over to the bellpull hanging next to the door and gave it a hard yank.

A few moments later a maid hurried in, her white cap bobbing and her apron fluttering. "Yes, sir. You rang?"

"Could you ask Miss Eliza to join us," Washburn instructed. "And bring us some tea, please."

As soon as the maid left, Washburn resumed his seat.

"You've known Mr. Barrett for six months, is that correct?" Witherspoon asked. He couldn't think of anything else to ask, and sometimes it had proved helpful to get as much background information as possible.

"No, I said I'd been in business with him for six months," Washburn corrected. "I actually met him a little over a year ago."

"And where did you meet?"

"At the Astleys'. Mrs. Astley is a good friend of my sister's." Washburn closed his eyes for a brief moment. "Thornton Astley had just gone into business with him. Barrett seemed eminently respectable and appeared to have excellent prospects, so I had no objection to his courtship of my sister. We got to know him." He smiled bitterly. "I introduced him to my sister, and I was the one who suggested he contact James Tate's widow to buy into the company. God, I was a fool. The man brought us nothing but grief."

Witherspoon shot a quick look at the closed study door. There was one thing he wanted to ask before Miss Washburn arrived. "Did Barrett give you any reason for what he did to your sister?"

Washburn also glanced at the door. "He told me he realized he didn't love her."

"Did he tell Miss Washburn the same thing?"

"Oh, no, the note he sent her merely said she wouldn't make a suitable wife and that if they married it would be a grave mistake." Washburn slammed his hand against the top of the desk. "The bastard, I'm glad he's dead."

*   *   *

Mrs. Jeffries was exhausted. She'd coped with half a dozen people trooping into the kitchen looking for a nice natter with Mrs. Goodge, helped get the cook bundled off to Paddington Station, and she still had to do something about getting a meal ready.

She jumped as she heard footsteps coming down the hall. Lady Cannonberry's head popped round the corner. "Hello, Hepzibah, I do hope I'm not intruding. May I come in?"

"Of course, Ruth." Mrs. Jeffries started to get up, but her guest waved her back in the chair.

"I just thought I'd come round and give you a report," Ruth said, dropping gracefully into the chair next to her.

"A report?" Alarmed, Mrs. Jeffries stared at her. Goodness, did every living soul in London yearn to be a detective?

"About Barrett's murder. I've found out ever so much." Ruth gave her a cheerful smile. "First of all, Minerva was at the Astleys' last night for dinner, and of course, Barrett didn't arrive. Naturally, you know that. He was already dead. But what was interesting was that no one said a word, not one *word* about him! Well, don't you think it strange? I mean if one of my dinner guests didn't appear, I'd certainly comment on the situation."

"I suppose that could be considered unusual." Mrs. Jeffries glanced at the clock. Gracious, it was getting late.

"Exactly my thinking," Ruth said. "From what Minerva told me it sounded as though everyone at the Astleys' was avoiding the subject of Mr. William Barrett. She said it was the most peculiar evening. Everyone was nervous and jittery. Mr. Spears kept dropping his cutlery, people kept having to repeat themselves to Mr. Astley because he didn't appear to be listening to anyone, and

Mrs. Astley dropped a glass of red wine all over her good damask tablecloth. Minerva said it was the most uncomfortable dinner party she's ever attended.''

"Who all was there?" Mrs. Jeffries asked. She really didn't wish to be rude, but heavens, she had so much to do.

"Adrian Spears—he lives right next door to Barrett," Ruth explained. "And according to Minerva, the two absolutely loathed each other."

Mrs. Jeffries already knew that so she didn't pursue the matter, she just nodded. "Who else?"

"Both the Astleys and Mr. Astley's secretary, Neville Sharpe. Owen Washburn was supposed to come, but he'd sent his regrets. His sister, Eliza, had been invited too, but Minerva says she never goes anywhere these days, so no one expected her to come."

As Mrs. Jeffries already knew about Eliza Washburn, she didn't want to waste any precious time discussing it. "And who else?" she prompted before Ruth could repeat the gossip about Barrett leaving Miss Washburn at the altar.

Ruth paused. "Well, Minerva was there and some elderly gentleman who was visiting from Australia. I thought it might put your mind to rest to know that Minerva has an alibi."

"An alibi?"

"She was shopping." Ruth beamed proudly. "She was shopping all afternoon, and then she stopped for tea at Lyons. She didn't get home till almost seven. Her maid was most put out. She had to rush to get her ready for the dinner party. Naturally I didn't come right out and ask Minerva where she'd been. I was very subtle."

"I'm sure you were," Mrs. Jeffries said. "Wasn't she in the least curious as to how you'd managed to get the china bird from a dead man?''

"Not really." Ruth shrugged. "I merely told her a friend of mine had helped."

Mrs. Jeffries closed her eyes as a sudden realization hit her. They'd made a dreadful mistake. She should never have let Lady Cannonberry give that wretched china knickknack back to Minerva Kenny. Not until after this case was solved. "Oh, dear," she murmured.

"What is it?"

"We've done something very foolish and it's all my fault."

Alarmed, Ruth stared at her. "Your fault? What are you talking about?"

"I should have told you not to give the bird back to Miss Kenny."

"But whyever not?"

"Because the police are bound to talk to her. If she tells them anything about Barrett having that knickknack in his possession on the day he was killed, we're all in a great deal of trouble."

"Is that what's worrying you?" Ruth laughed softly. "Minerva won't say a word, I promise you. She'd rather die than have people find out about her uh . . . problem. Take my word for it, she'll not mention the bird at all."

"But what if someone else does?"

"Who else could possibly know about it?" Ruth said calmly. "Other than Minerva, the only person who knew she'd stolen it was William Barrett and he's dead."

Mrs. Jeffries sincerely hoped no one else knew about it. She knew Smythe hadn't killed Barrett, but he was in the house only moments after the murder had been committed. And he was there to steal. It might be in a good cause, but she didn't think the authorities would see it that way. "Do you mind if I have a chat with Miss Kenny?"

"Not at all," Ruth replied. "She's expecting you to call 'round. She's ever so grateful for your help. Of course, now she must think of a way to smuggle the bird back into the Astley house."

"I expect she'll come up with something," Mrs. Jeffries said. She glanced at the clock again and realized she'd better get the tea ready. They were all due back in less than half an hour, and after that, she'd have to cook some kind of supper.

Lady Cannonberry, correctly interpreting the housekeeper's expression, got up. "I'll run along now, Hepzibah. But do keep me informed as to your progress. I'll keep my ears open as well. One never knows when a clue will pop up."

"Thank you, Ruth." Mrs. Jeffries smiled weakly. "You've been a great help." She waited until her guest had disappeared and then she leapt into action. Domestic chores occupied her for the next half hour. She couldn't help thinking, as she sliced the bread, that if women didn't have to stop three or four times a day and feed a household, they could get ever so much more done.

Inspector Witherspoon was surprised by Eliza Washburn's appearance. She was quite lovely. Small and dark-haired, with the clearest blue eyes he'd ever seen. He didn't know why he was so taken aback by her appearance. Possibly because the mental image of a jilted woman was so at odds with the elegantly gowned and graceful lady sitting on the settee and pouring tea.

"Miss Washburn," he began, "er, I'd like to ask you a few questions."

"So I assumed, Inspector. Tea?" She arched one perfectly formed eyebrow and handed him his cup when he nodded an affirmative. "You'd like to speak to me about William's murder, correct?"

"That's correct," Witherspoon agreed. Perhaps this wouldn't be so difficult after all. She hadn't blushed or become hysterical at the mention of the man's name. That was certainly a good beginning.

"There's not really much I can tell you," she continued as she handed another cup to Constable Barnes. "I've had no contact with William Barrett since he broke off our engagement."

"When was that, exactly, miss?" Barnes asked.

"Last month." She cocked her head to one side and smiled. "I suppose you've heard the story. William Barrett left me at the altar. He humiliated me in front of everyone. Frankly, I'm not in the least bit upset that someone killed him."

"Eliza!" Owen Washburn gasped. "You really mustn't say things like that."

"Why not?" She shrugged. "It's perfectly true. The man was a cad, a bounder and a cheat. Eventually it had to catch up with him."

Witherspoon was rather surprised; she looked like such a gentle, delicate woman. Furthermore, she wasn't at all like the upset, nervous creature her brother had described. "Would you mind telling me where you were yesterday afternoon?" he asked.

"I was here."

"Alone."

"No. Owen was here as well. He was working in his study and I was taking a nap."

"I understand your servants were gone?" Witherspoon pressed. It never hurt to make doubly sure of the facts.

"It was their day out," Eliza said. "But Cook was here all afternoon."

"I didn't know that!" Owen exclaimed. "I thought she'd gone out as well."

Eliza Washburn smiled at her brother. "She wasn't feeling well, Owen. I think she may have that wretched influenza that's been going about. She spent the afternoon resting in her room."

"And where exactly is her room in the house?" the inspector asked. It would be so much simpler if the cook could verify that both the Washburns were safely at home at the time of the murder.

"On the third floor," Owen said. "She shares the box room with the maid."

"I'd like to speak to your cook," Witherspoon said. He put his teacup on the table next to him and rose to his feet.

"I'll get her," Owen said, starting to get up.

"That won't be necessary," the inspector said hastily. "If you'd be so kind as to point us in the direction of the kitchen, we'll have a quick word with her." The last thing the inspector wanted was one of his suspects hovering over the domestic who might be providing the alibis. Not that Washburn was yet a serious suspect. Unfortunately, Witherspoon thought, as yet he had no real suspects. Merely a number of people who seemed to loathe the victim.

"Very well." Washburn shrugged. "The kitchen's downstairs."

"Oh, do go with them, Owen," Eliza chided. "Mrs. Gantry will be frightened to death if two policemen come stumbling unannounced into her kitchen."

Before the inspector or Barnes could protest, Owen Washburn was leading them down into the kitchen.

"Mrs. Gantry," he said as they entered the room. "These men would like to ask you some questions.

They're from Scotland Yard. This is Inspector Wither-spoon and Constable Barnes.''

"Coppers are they?" Mrs. Gantry, a tall, grey-haired woman wearing a cook's apron, wiped the flour off her hands. "Now, what do you want with the likes of me?"

"We'd merely like to ask you some questions." With-erspoon's stomach grumbled and his taste buds tingled. He and Barnes had had only time for a quick bite at lunch-time, and the tangy smell of simmering meat coming from the oven reminded him he was hungry.

"I expect you'd like to speak with Mrs. Gantry alone," Washburn said, excusing himself. "Have her bring you upstairs when you've finished."

Witherspoon smiled and nodded. Then he turned to the cook. "Were you here all afternoon yesterday?"

"Oh, yes." Mrs. Gantry went back to kneading the slab of dough on the table in front of her. "It were my day out, but I was feelin' poorly, so I stayed in and had a nice sleep."

"And how are you feeling today?" the inspector asked politely. He'd found that getting people to talk about themselves often proved most helpful.

"Much better." She slapped the dough one last time, picked it up and flopped it into a waiting bowl. "Miss Washburn insisted I have a nice glass of sherry yesterday afternoon. Right decent of her, I thought. Put me right out, it did. Just what I needed too, a good sleep. I got up this morning feelin' right as rain."

"Can you confirm that Mr. and Miss Washburn were in the house yesterday afternoon?" Witherspoon asked hopefully.

"Miss Washburn went to take her rest right after she give me the sherry, and Mr. Washburn was workin' in his study," Mrs. Gantry said easily. "And they was both still here when I woke up."

"What time was that?" Witherspoon spoke loudly; his stomach was starting to make embarrassing noises.

"About half past six. Dulcie, that's the maid, woke me when she come in."

Witherspoon nodded. "What time did you go to sleep?"

"About half past two. Went right out, I did, and slept like the dead till Dulcie come in."

"What do you mean, Mrs. Goodge is gone!" Wiggins wailed. "Who's goin' to cook?"

"Isn't that just like a man," Betsy snapped. "Always thinkin' of their stomachs. What about poor Mrs. Goodge's aunt? It's not like the poor woman wanted to take sick. Mrs. Goodge had to go to her."

"But who's goin' to feed us?" the footman persisted. "We'll starve to death if she don't come back soon."

"Don't make such a fuss, Wiggins," Mrs. Jeffries said calmly. "I'm sure that in a houseful of adults we'll manage to keep our stomachs full."

"I'll send some vittles over," Luty said quickly. "It'll give Antoine somethin' to do."

Smythe grinned. "I'll do a bit of the cookin'."

"You?" Betsy gasped.

"Why not? I've done it before. Nothing fancy, mind you, but I can do a fry up and cook beefsteak."

"Thank you, Smythe," Mrs. Jeffries said calmly. "As for tonight's meal, I've already taken care of that. Now, does anyone else wish to volunteer to try their hand?"

"I'll have a go at it," Betsy said softly.

"Don't look at me," Wiggins put in. "I've never even boiled an egg." He reached down and patted Fred, who was sleeping by his chair. "And I'm not sure I want to learn how now," he mumbled to the dog.

"Anyway, enough about yer bellies," Luty stated. "With Mrs. Goodge gone we've lost us a good source of gossip. I propose to take on that task myself. Is that all right with everybody?"

Mrs. Jeffries smiled. "That would be wonderful, Luty. Mrs. Goodge's inquiries have been invaluable to us in the past."

"I ain't sayin' I'll get as much as she does," Luty warned, "but I'll do my best. Now, I'd best tell you what I found out today."

"I?" Hatchet said archly. "Don't you mean 'we'?"

Luty waved her hand dismissively. "All right, what 'we' found out today. Not that I heard you askin' any questions, Hatchet." She ignored his snort and continued. "But that's by the by." Luty told them everything she'd learned from her friend Tilbert. "So you see, seems to me this here Barrett feller ain't no more than a cleaned-up scallawag. I think it'd be a good idea if I kept on learning what I could about him."

"Yes, I think you should," Mrs. Jeffries said. She told them about Lady Cannonberry's visit, taking care to give them all the details. Then she turned to Betsy. "Did you learn anything?"

Betsy sighed. "Not much. I had a chat with the footman from the Spears house. He was a right old chatterbox too. Kept goin' on about Janie and Matilda bein' scared of losin' their postions because they'd left the ruddy door open when Spears's dog got out. But I finally managed to get a bit of useful information out of him. He saw Barrett outside in the gardens the night before the murder, and he was havin' a row with some woman. Noah couldn't hear what they was sayin'—"

"Noah?" Smythe interrupted softly.

"Yes, Noah," Betsy said impatiently, annoyed at being interrupted. "It's his name. Anyways, like I was sayin', he couldn't hear what they was sayin' but he could tell they was quarrelling. He said they was hissin' like a couple of cats. And they was tryin' not to be seen—Noah said they was hidin' behind the bushes."

"How very interesting," Mrs. Jeffries said.

"Did this young man see what the woman looked like?" Hatchet asked.

Betsy shook her head. "He didn't say, but he was fairly sure it weren't a neighbour. I'm seein' him again tomorrow and I'll try and find out more then."

"Don't bother," Smythe put in quickly. "If she weren't a neighbour I can probably find out who she was from one of the hansom drivers."

"But you don't know that she come there by hansom," Betsy protested. "Besides, Noah might have more information." She glared at the coachman.

"I'm only tryin' to save you some time and trouble," Smythe said defensively.

"Well, thank you very much, but I'd like to do my own investigatin'."

"Now, Betsy," Mrs. Jeffries interjected. "Smythe was only trying to help. However, I think you're right. Perhaps you should talk with this young man again." She turned to the coachman. "Were you able to learn anything?"

Smythe stopped frowning at the maid. "Not much. But I did find out that there was lots of hansoms comin' and goin' from Kildare Gardens yesterday."

"More than usual?" Mrs. Jeffries asked.

"That's 'ard to say," he admitted, "but the jarvey I talked to said he'd talked to a couple of cabbies that had picked up unexpected fares. It's worth lookin' into. I thought I'd go out tonight and suss out a few pubs in the area, see what I can learn.''

"I think that's a very good idea, Smythe,'' Mrs. Jeffries said. "And do talk to those cabbies. One of them might know something.''

"I didn't learn nuthin','' Wiggins complained. "Me and Fred spent the whole afternoon tryin' to find someone from the Barrett 'ouse to talk to. Didn't see hide nor hair of nobody.''

"It's early days yet, Wiggins,'' Mrs. Jeffries said calmly. "And I've another chore for you. I think you need to try and find out if any of the workmen in the Barrett house that day saw or heard anything.''

"Won't the police be doin' that?'' Wiggins asked. But he looked delighted to be given something to do.

"They probably already have,'' she explained. "But what a workman will tell a policeman may be quite different from what you could find out. You know what I mean, Wiggins. Get them talking. See if there's some small detail that may be important that perhaps they've forgotten to mention.''

"What about Minerva Kenny?'' Hatchet asked, his expression thoughtful. "No disrespect meant to Lady Cannonberry, but I do think it would be best if we ascertained that she really was shopping yesterday afternoon.''

"Are you thinkin' she might have killed him?'' Luty asked.

"I'm thinking that nothing is out of the bounds of possibility,'' he explained. "Lady Cannonberry has already told us she'd rather die than have anyone find out she . . . uh . . .''

"Steals,'' Luty supplied,

"Well, yes.'' Hatchet leaned forward. "And I'm wondering if she might feel compelled to kill to keep her secret.''

"It's certainly worth looking into,'' Mrs. Jeffries agreed. She glanced at the clock. "If there's nothing else, I expect I'd best get some supper started.''

"Are you cookin' tonight?'' Wiggins asked hopefully.

She nodded slowly. Poor Wiggins, he did so love his food. How unfortunate that she was such a bad cook.

CHAPTER 6

"Poor Mrs. Goodge," the inspector said sympathetically. "How very upsetting for her. She must be terribly concerned about her aunt. I don't suppose she's much family left?"

"No, sir, that's why I was sure you'd want her to go." Mrs. Jeffries was stretching the truth a bit. In fact, Mrs. Goodge had relatives (especially cousins) all over London. "I do hope I did the right thing, sir. But there was no way to track you down, so to speak. Furthermore, I don't like to burden you with household decisions when you're in the middle of an investigation. So I took the initiative and sent her off. But really, sir, considering Aunt Elberta's age, I thought it best to get Mrs. Goodge on her way as soon as possible."

"Don't give it another thought, Mrs. Jeffries," Witherspoon said. He reached for the glass of sherry sitting on the table beside his chair. "You were perfectly right to send Mrs. Goodge to her aunt. Family is important, and if the poor woman is dying, well, we'll just have to make do." He paused and a frown creased his forehead. "Per-

haps I should call around at one of those employment
agencies tomorrow and see if they can send us along a
temporary cook?''

''Oh, no, sir,'' Mrs. Jeffries said hastily. At his look of
surprise she forced herself to smile. ''That won't be necessary. You're far too busy for that sort of thing. Gracious, you shouldn't have to worry about temporary cooks
while you're trying to solve a heinous murder. The staff
and I will make do. We've all volunteered to have a hand
at the cooking.''

''But everyone has enough to do already,'' he protested. ''I won't burden the household with trying to cook
as well.''

Sometimes, Mrs. Jeffries thought, the inspector's
thoughtfulness could be a bit of a nuisance. ''Really,
sir—''

''No, I insist,'' he replied.

Truly alarmed, Mrs. Jeffries blurted. ''Then let me go
around to the agency, sir. You're very busy right now.
Your time needn't be taken up with silly details like
kitchen help.''

She absolutely refused to have a stranger take Mrs.
Goodge's place. Gracious, they were in the middle of a
murder, it was far too dangerous to have an outsider hanging about the kitchen and listening to their conversations.
There were already too many people who were privy to
their secret.

''Are you sure you don't mind?'' Witherspoon asked.
He looked at her over the rim of his spectacles. ''It *would*
save me some time. I've a full day tomorrow.''

''Not at all, sir. Now, I'm all ears. How did your investigation go today?'' She took a seat opposite him and
gave him a placid smile.

''Not too badly,'' he admitted cautiously. ''There is

certainly no shortage of people who hated William Barrett, but so far, I've no evidence that any of them murdered him.''

"How dreadful, sir, for someone to be that universally disliked.'' She clucked sympathetically.

"Yes, it does rather give one pause,'' Witherspoon said. "I shudder to think what the man's funeral will be like. I don't think there will be anyone in the church except the vicar.''

"What about his family, sir?''

"As far as we can tell, Barrett has no family. Ah, well, as the Good Book says, 'As ye reap, so shall ye sow,' or is it the other way around?'' He shrugged. "Well, it doesn't matter, you do take my point. Now, as to my day.'' He then told her about everyone he'd seen and talked with.

Mrs. Jeffries listened carefully. She waited until he was finished before she asked any questions. By the time Betsy stuck her head in the drawing room and announced that dinner was served, Mrs. Jeffries had determined precisely what she needed to do the next day.

"Oh, it's a cold supper,'' the inspector said as he stared at the block of cheddar cheese, joint of cold beef, pickled onions and fresh bread sitting on the dining table. "How nice.''

"You're being very good about it, sir,'' Mrs. Jeffries said appreciatively. "I know it's not a proper meal. But I'm afraid that by the time I got Mrs. Goodge to Paddington, I didn't have time to do any real cooking.''

Although he was dreadfully hungry, Witherspoon didn't wish his housekeeper to feel bad. "This will be fine, Mrs. Jeffries.'' He sat down, pulled his serviette on his lap and reached for the plate of beef. He stopped and looked up. "Mrs. Jeffries,'' he said curiously. The beef slipped onto the edge of the plate with a goodly portion of the flesh resting on the white linen tablecloth.

Mrs. Jeffries darted forward, snatched up a nearby serving spoon and rescued the inspector's beef. "Yes, sir."

"Uh, oh, dear, thank you. What are the rest of you eating tonight?"

"A cold supper like yourself, sir," Mrs. Jeffries admitted. She didn't bother to tell him she'd sent out to the baker's for some meat pies and cornish pasties. She didn't want to waste any more time worrying about their stomachs. There were one or two points she wanted to make about the murder. But she must be very careful here. "Sir, you didn't say if you'd spoken to any of the workmen who were at the Barrett house yesterday?" Might as well see if she could wangle a name for Wiggins to pursue.

"The uniformed lads took their statements," Witherspoon replied. "But none of the workmen saw or heard anything on the day of the murder. One of them had lost his hat the day before and another one had found one of his tools missing, but that's about the most interesting thing any of them had to say."

He tried to fork a pickled onion, missed and shot it out of the serving dish. It landed neatly next to his water glass. Mrs. Jeffries scooped it up and plopped it onto his plate. "Why?" He gazed at her curiously. "Do you think I ought to speak to the workmen?"

Mrs. Jeffries smiled brilliantly. "Oh, sir, I'm sure your lads did a wonderful job, it's just that . . . that—" she deliberately broke off.

"What?"

"Well, I don't quite know how to say this."

"Please, just go ahead and say it," Witherspoon prompted. His housekeeper sometimes had the knack of pointing out just the right thing. Putting him on the right track, so to speak. In the past two years, he'd learned a great deal of respect for a woman's intuition.

"It's not that I think the uniformed lads were in any way derelict in their duties, sir," she said slowly, "it's just that you're so very good at asking the right questions."

Witherspoon stared at her for a moment, then said, "What sort of right questions?"

"You know what I mean, sir. You're good at getting people to talk. Don't be so modest, sir. Not with me. We both know that one of your, shall we say secret weapons, is the way you get people to open up to you."

"Do you really think so?" he gazed at her hopefully.

"But of course, sir. You're good with people because you treat them with respect. Whether it's a washerwoman or peer of the realm, it's all the same to you." She shrugged in helpless embarrassment. "Oh, dear, I'm not saying this right. But I think if you'd questioned those workmen, you'd have gotten some very different answers than what the police constables obtained. You'd have asked them questions such as had they *heard* anything unusual on the afternoon of the murder."

Witherspoon's brow furrowed as he pondered her words. For one dreadful moment Mrs. Jeffries thought the jig was up. But then he smiled. "Of course, you're right. I would have asked that question. Naturally, it's important." He couldn't think why it was important, but he didn't let that worry him. These matters had a way of sorting themselves out. As Mrs. Jeffries often told him, his brain was a bit like a sponge. He soaked up all sorts of disparate information, and then, presto, like magic, he came up with the right answer.

Mrs. Jeffries relaxed. The workmen probably hadn't heard anything at all. However, at least now, the inspector would talk to each and every one of them personally. Who knew what tidbit he might pick up and pass on to her?

Smythe hoped a pint would ease the burning sensation in his stomach. He elbowed his way through the crowded pub to the bar. Them cornish pasties and that meat pie felt like they was made of lead and sitting smack in the center of his belly. He ordered a pint of bitter from the barman and turned to gaze around the room.

Smoke from the fire combined with the heavy scent of beer, gin and unwashed bodies and filled the room with an earthy, faintly acrid odor. Along the far wall men and women sat on the long benches, talking and laughing over their drinks. All of the round, rough-hewn tables were occupied, and the crowd at the bar was big enough to crush a lesser man than he.

He eyed the crowd carefully until he spotted a fat, red-headed man wearing a dirty rust-colored porkpie hat, a short checkered waistcoat and a white shirt with a bright red scarf hanging round his neck. The man looked up then and caught Smythe's glance. He raised his glass and Smythe motioned him over.

"Evenin', Smythe," he said, belching slightly.

"Evenin', Blimpey." He nodded toward an empty cor-ner. "Let's move over there."

"Got the ready?" Blimpey asked. He wasn't one to waste time on amenities when there was money to be had.

"Got the information?" Smythe retorted.

"Does a dog 'ave fleas? Course I got the story, it's what you're payin' me for, inn't it?" He wiped his nose with the sleeve of his coat, turned and stalked off toward the corner, leaving Smythe to follow him.

Two day laborers vacated a table as they made their way to the other side of the room. Blimpey sat down, ignoring the high-pitched squeak of protest as his backside made contact with the stool. Smythe cautiously sat down on the other one. He wasn't fat like Blimpey, but he weren't no feather, either, and these stools looked like they'd been here since Cromwell's time.

As soon as they were seated, Blimpey looked pointedly at the front pocket of Smythe's heavy pea coat.

" 'Ave I ever cheated you?'' Smythe demanded, getting irritated at Blimpey's blatant greed.

"Just bein' careful, mate.'' Blimpey gave him an ingratiating smile. What few teeth he had left were rotted and yellow stained. "Can't be too careful these days, you know. Times is hard.''

"Times is always 'ard,'' Smythe retorted, "but I ain't cheated you yet and I'm not plannin' to start now. So what did ya find out?''

"Well, they was three hansoms that will be of interest to you. Three, I mean, that was for the times ya give me. All of 'em went there between five-thirty and six-thirty on the day in question. Mind you, I 'ad to do a bit o' fast talkin' to get this information . . .''

"Get on with it,'' Smythe said impatiently. Blimpey wasn't just greedy, he'd talk a tree stump to death if he got half a chance as well. Tonight Smythe wasn't goin' to put up with it. He wanted to get home. His stomach rolled as he caught the scent of a particularly cheap cigar from the group of men at the next table.

" 'Ang on a minute,'' Blimpey said. "No need to rush these things. The first cabbie let the fare off at the top of Talbot Road, that's right up the end of the terrace from Kildare Gardens.''

"Why should that one be of interest? I'm payin' you to find out who went to bleedin' Kildare Gardens.'' Oh, Lord, Smythe thought, as a wave of nausea hit him, he'd never eat another meat pie again. No matter how hungry he got.

Blimpey smiled craftily. "Because the fare had asked to be taken to Number fifteen Kildare Gardens and then changed her mind."

"It was a woman?"

"Nice-lookin' one too." Blimpey nodded enthusiastically. "Real lady she was, accordin' to the driver."

"Where'd he pick her up at?" Smythe asked.

"Regent Street, and she offered to double his fare if he hurried."

"What did she look like?" Smythe asked. A description would be useful.

"She were young and slender, but he didn't really get a good look at her face. She was wearin' a veil."

"Then 'ow the bloody blue blazes did the driver know she was a good-lookin' woman?" Smythe snapped. That was the trouble with usin' Blimpey Groggins as an informant. He couldn't bloomin' well stop 'imself from addin' to the facts. Man was a natural born storyteller. He swallowed as another wave of nausea swept him.

" 'Cause of her voice and her figure," Blimpey said hastily. "Now, you want to hear the rest or not?"

"Go on." Smythe decided he'd better listen to what the old liar said—God knows he was goin' to be payin' for the information whether it was useful or not. "And just stick to what them drivers actually told ya."

"All right, all right, don't get your trousers in a twist," Blimpey took another swig of his beer. "Now, the second one was even stranger. It were another woman. She had the cab take her all the way to Kildare Gardens, got out and paid the bloke, then just as he's gettin' ready to drive off, she jumps back in and demands to be taken to Royal Oak Station." He emptied his glass, looked inquiringly at

Smythe, who nodded and then yelled to the barman, "Another one over here, mate!"

"Where'd this one get picked up?" Smythe took a sip of his own beer. A moment later he frowned as the bitter brew started to battle with the undigested meat pie in his stomach.

"Cabbie said he'd picked her up on the Richmond Road—" He broke off to nod his thanks at the serving woman who brought his beer. "But he couldn't say what she looked like. She was wearin' a veiled hat too and a big oversized wool cloak. He couldn't even tell if she were young or old. Woman was bundled up tighter than a spindle o'cotton, the cabbie told me. But I asked him, now"—Blimpey waved a finger at Smythe—"don't want ya thinkin' I wasn't doin' what you're payin' me for. I asked all them questions you give me."

"And the third hansom?" Smythe asked, pushing his unfinished pint away. If he didn't get out into the fresh air, he was going to be sick.

"This one was a man. Toff, dressed nice, top hat and real expensive overcoat. About five-fifteen the cabbic picked him up at the Great Western Terminus and took him directly to number fifteen Kildare Gardens."

"Did the cabbie see if the man went inside?" Smythe asked. He put his hand to his mouth as a soft belch slipped out.

Blimpey grinned again. "He saw him go in, all right. The toff was in such a hurry he hadn't closed the door. So Roland—that's the cabbie—had to climb down and shut it himself. By the time he got back up, he saw the toff walk right inside the house. Figured the fellow musta lived there. I mean, he walked straight in, bold as brass. Mind you, the front door was wide open. But this fellow went in like he owned the place."

Smythe reached inside his pocket and pulled out some notes. He handed them to Blimpey and then added an extra one more than they'd agreed. "What's the name of them drivers and where can I find 'em?"

"Mr. Spears is waiting for you in the drawing room," Pembroke the butler said to Witherspoon and Barnes.

As they followed the butler down the hall, Barnes whispered to the inspector, "That's odd. He made it sound like he knew we was coming here this morning."

"Perhaps Mr. Spears realized we'd be back since he hadn't an alibi for the time of the murder."

Adrian Spears was sitting on the settee waiting for them. "Please do sit down, gentlemen," he said, gesturing toward the chairs opposite him. "I expect you want to ask me more questions."

"Thank you." The inspector desperately wanted a cup of tea. His breakfast was sitting rather heavily on his stomach. Mind you, he really shouldn't complain, Mrs. Jeffries had done quite an admirable job. But he'd no idea that sausages could be so tough. And the eggs. Gracious, fried harder than rocks and swimming in fat. Well, he'd just hope that his dear housekeeper managed to find them a temporary cook as soon as possible. "First of all, Mr. Spears, we'd like to ask you for a few more details about your disagreement with the victim."

"Details?" Spears frowned slightly. "I'm afraid I don't understand?"

"Well," Witherspoon began. He wasn't sure what to ask. But at breakfast Mrs. Jeffries had said something about how convenient it was for the murderer that a neighbour had threatened to murder Barrett. Now how exactly had she put it? He suddenly remembered. "What I mean is, when you accused Barrett of throwing stones at your dog on the day before the murder—''

"I didn't accuse him of throwing stones," Spears interrupted, "I saw the man do it with my own eyes."

"Yes, I'm sure you did," Witherspoon said. "But what I want to know is did you threaten him at that time?"

Spears stared at him incredulously. "Threaten him? You mean physically?"

Witherspoon shook his head. "I mean did you threaten him verbally."

"I'm not sure I ought to answer that," Spears blustered. "Don't I have the right to a solicitor?"

"We're not accusing you of murder, sir," Barnes put in softly. "We merely want to know how many other people might have overheard your altercation with the victim on the day before the murder."

"Oh." He sank back against the seat. "You mean someone may have overheard our argument and then decided as I was conveniently screaming that I would kill the blackguard, that person might decide to do it themselves."

"Er, yes," Witherspoon said. He frowned slightly as a wave of heartburn raced up his chest.

"Well, then." Spears shrugged. "I'll admit it. I did threaten him. I told him if he didn't leave my dog alone, I'd wring his bloody neck. But for goodness' sakes, I didn't mean it literally."

Witherspoon heard footsteps in the hallway. He looked hopefully in that direction praying it was a maid with a tray of tea. It was the butler and he walked straight on past the drawing room. Drat, it was terribly difficult to concentrate when one's innards were on fire.

"Sir?" Barnes prompted softly.

The inspector cleared his throat. "Did anyone hear you threaten Mr. Barrett?" he asked. "I mean, were there other people out in the gardens who could have overheard you?''

"A number of people heard me," Spears admitted. "I was rather embarrassed afterwards, making a spectacle of myself and all. Frankly, I'm not sure who was out there. . . . '' He paused, his face a mask of concentration. "Let me see, Owen Washburn, Barrett's partner, heard me. He was with Barrett. The Astleys and Miss Minerva Kenny were having tea with me when the ruckus started. Thornton came outside with me and I'm sure he told Maud all about it. Miss Kenny is a dear lady, but rather inquisitive. I'm sure she got the whole story out of Maud Astley.''

Witherspoon momentarily forgot his discomfort. He stared at Adrian Spears. "Mr. Spears. Why didn't you tell us about this when we were here yesterday?''

Spears looked surprised by the question. "You didn't ask. I frequently have people 'round for tea. I saw no need to advise Scotland Yard of my social engagements. Furthermore, I didn't think it important.''

"Yes, well, is there anything else you neglected to mention?''

"Now, see here, Inspector.'' Spears got to his feet. "There's no need to be rude.''

"I do beg your pardon, sir.'' Witherspoon sighed silently. Gracious, people were so very sensitive. "I did not mean to cause offense.''

Spears closed his eyes. "None taken, sir. I'm afraid I'm not myself. It isn't very nice losing a beloved pet and becoming a murder suspect all on the same day. What else would you like to know?''

It was Barnes who spoke. "Did Mr. and Mrs. Astley and Miss Kenny know that Barrett had workers comin' and goin' from his house?''

Spears smiled wearily. "Yes. He was always bragging about the improvements he'd made to his home. I know the Astleys were aware of it because Thornton told me he thought Barrett was a fool to have work done this time of year. Takes ages for paint to dry in this damp weather."

"And did the Astleys know that the front and back doors were being kept open?" Witherspoon prodded.

"Possibly." Spears sighed. "It was hard not to see them open. The painters had their equipment and tools littering the front of the Barrett house."

"I see," Witherspoon said slowly. He wasn't sure what to make of this new information. But he wouldn't worry about it now. "Mr. Spears," he said suddenly. "Are you absolutely certain you saw no one who knew you when you went for your walk on the afternoon of the murder?"

Spears shook his head. "Absolutely. A workman coming down to get something saw me leaving my house, Inspector. That's the best I can do."

"And this was at five o'clock?" Barnes asked.

"As near as I can recall, but you must remember, I was very upset. It could have been four forty-five or it could have been five-fifteen. I didn't really look at my watch till I had gone some distance and only then because I knew I had a dinner engagement. Otherwise, I might have walked the streets all night."

"I do wish someone had seen you, sir," Witherspoon said truthfully. "It would make our task so much easier."

"Yes, I'm sure it would." Spears suddenly got up and walked toward the window. He stood for a moment staring out into the street.

Barnes and Witherspoon exchanged a puzzled glance.

"Before you ask me any more questions, Inspector," Spears said softly, hesitantly. "I've something to tell you.

Something which may be important.''

"Yes, sir, what is it?''

Spears turned and stared at them, his face a mask of anguish and turmoil. ''I . . . oh this is so very difficult.'' He glanced down at the floor and then raised his eyes to meet the inspectors. ''I don't believe in telling tales out of school, and I don't for one minute mourn the passing of that odious man, but this is a murder case.''

"Yes, sir. It is.''

Spears cleared his throat. ''I realize I'm a very likely suspect. I did threaten to kill Barrett, but that was in the heat of anger.''

Witherspoon didn't point out that shoving a sword through someone generally was considered a pretty angry act. ''You've admitted that, sir.''

"After I found King's body, I told you I went for a walk,'' Spears continued. ''And that is the truth. But what I didn't tell you was that I saw someone when I was leaving the gardens. Someone who also had a reason to dislike William Barrett.''

Witherspoon leaned forward. ''Who would that someone be?''

Again, Spears looked at the floor. After a moment he raised his gaze to meet the inspector's. ''This is much harder than I thought it would be. Perhaps I ought not to say anything. Perhaps she had a good reason for visiting Barrett that afternoon.''

"Please, Mr. Spears,'' the inspector said patiently, ''as you pointed out. This is a murder case. Regardless of how odious a person Mr. Barrett was, no one had the right to take his life. Now, whom did you see?''

"I didn't actually see her go inside the house,'' Spears hedged. ''But the hansom pulled up right outside and I saw her go up the walkway.''

Witherspoon straightened. "Her?"

He nodded, his eyes sad and troubled. "Yes, it was a woman. Someone who I know is a dear, kind lady who wouldn't hurt anyone. She's no more capable of murder than I am."

"Who is she?" Witherspoon pressed. "Please, you must tell us."

Spears drew a long, deep breath before he spoke. His voice was barely a whisper. "It was Minerva Kenny."

"Minerva Kenny? But why would she have a reason to dislike William Barrett?"

"I can't tell you why she hated him," Spears replied softly. "Only that I know she did."

"How do you know, sir?" Barnes asked.

Spears shrugged. "Because she told me."

"I told you I'd be here." Betsy smiled at the blushing young man and fought with her conscience. Was leadin' the boy on the right thing to do, even if they was investigating a murder?

"And I told you I'd tell you more about that murder house," Noah said proudly. He fell into step beside her. "But I don't have much time. I only slipped out when the butler turned his back. If he catches me gone, he'll 'ave me 'ead."

Her conscience rose up and almost strangled her. Either that or them awful sausages Mrs. Jeffries had fed them for breakfast. "You'll not lose your position, will you?" she asked in alarm. "I don't want you to get in trouble."

"Nah, old Pembroke's listenin' to them peelers through the keyhole, he'll not notice I'm gone."

"There's police at your house?"

Noah nodded and grinned. "They think Mr. Spears might 'ave done it. But they'd be wrong. Mr. Spears 'ated old Barrett, but he wouldn't hurt nobody. Mind you, he had cause. He and Barrett had been squabblin' for months. But Barrett fought with everyone 'round the gardens. Wasn't no one that liked the man.''

Betsy pretended to be shocked. "How awful to be always fightin' with yer neighbours. This Barrett sounds like a right old tartar.''

"Yeah, he was.'' Noah frowned slightly. "Course I don't know if he was as bad as everyone thought he was.''

"What do ya mean?''

"Barrett was a funny old bloke. He pretended he hated all the cats and dogs 'round there, specially King. But I don't think 'e did hate 'em and I don't think he killed the dog.''

Betsy frowned. "I still don't know what you mean.''

"Well,'' Noah said thoughtfully. "I was out there when Barrett was tossin' them stones at the dog, and I'll admit 'e did it. But funny thing is, it looked to me like he was aimin' to miss him. Truth is, I've seen Barrett out in them gardens with King and when he thought no one was lookin', he'd pet the dog, play with him like. Then someone would come out and he'd shoo the poor old thing off. It were odd, but I think that secretly he were a bit lonely. Does that sound daft?''

"Not to me.'' Betsy favored him with another brilliant smile. "People are always a lot more, well, peculiar than they seem, if you know what I mean.''

"I know just what you mean. Take Mr. Spears for instance, he were daft about that hound of his, treated it like a member of the family. Course, it's no wonder. He doesn't really have any relations. His wife died a few years back and he never had no children. That's why Janie's in such a state.''

"Janie's the maid?'' Betsy asked as they crossed the

road into Kildare Terrace. Betsy tried slowing her steps again, but if she walked much slower, she'd end up tripping over her own feet.

"Yeah and she's still frettin' that Mr. Spears will find out she left the door open and that's how King got out that day. She's been cryin' about it for two days now. Course she's a bit silly, Janie is. She claims she were just lettin' some fresh air into the kitchen, but we all knows she'd seen that painter she's sweet on in the gardens and that's why she went runnin' outside."

Generally, Betsy loved hearing about the romantic adventures of others. But not today. She wanted to get as much information as possible out of Noah. "Sounds to me like you're a right good judge of character, you are."

Noah's cheeks flushed and his chest swelled. "I do me best. I found out about that woman Barrett was havin' a row with the night before he was killed."

"You found out her name?" Betsy was genuinely impressed. She stopped and stared at him, her eyes wide with appreciation. This was better than she'd ever hoped. Smythe would be green with envy, she thought. Then she caught herself; she wasn't doing this to show up the coachman, even though he could irritate the very devil out of her. But sometimes he didn't irritate her, sometimes he made her feel all funny inside. She quickly shoved that silly thought to the back of her mind. "You must be really clever," she said.

"Nah." He blushed bright red and Betsy felt another prick at her conscience. He was only a boy. She had no right to be playin' the poor lad like this, even if they was investigatin' a murder.

"I'm just good at listenin'," he continued. "But I weren't the only one that saw them out there arguin'. Janie was out there too, and she was close enough to recognize the woman's voice." He broke off and glanced around him. "It was the wife of one of Mr. Spears's friends. A woman named Maud Astley."

"Goodness," Betsy gasped. She'd slapped her conscience into silence. "What on earth could a decent woman be doin' out havin' a row at that time of the evening?"

Noah laughed. "Well, I don't know if'n she's decent or not. For that matter, I don't really believe Janie was out for a nip of fresh air. More like a kiss with the painter from next door. But accordin' to what Janie heard, Mrs. Astley and Mr. Barrett was quarrelin' about some letters."

"Me name's Wiggins and this 'ere is Fred," he said to the tall, dark-haired young man.

"Pleased to meet you," the lad replied. He stared at Wiggins and the dog for a minute. "I'd invite ya in, but me mam don't allow animals in the 'ouse."

They were standing on the narrow door stoop of a small grey house in Brixton. The area was poor and working class. The homes were tiny and cramped with most of them broken up into flats housing whole families. The road was unpaved, and the air smelled of rotting garbage, grease and boiled cabbage.

But Wiggins noticed that this house was neatly painted and the door stoop scrubbed clean. The young man staring at him so curiously wore a clean but frayed white shirt. His hair was dark brown and his hazel eyes deepset in an angular, intelligent face.

Wiggins gave him a grin. "Sorry to be botherin' ya, but my guv sent me over. You was workin' on that Barrett house, weren't you?"

"You a peeler?" he asked angrily. "If you are, you can bleedin' well take yourself off. I already talked to you coppers, and I got nuthin' more to say.''

"I ain't no copper." Wiggins hated to lie, but then again, he hated being the only one who wouldn't have a bloomin' thing to report tonight if'n he didn't get this bloke to talk some. "Like I said, my guv sent me over. He saw the job you and your mates did at ole Barrett's 'ouse. He figured that since you ain't workin' there, he could get you to work for 'im.''

The young man's face cleared. "Oh, well, that's different, then, inn't it? You'd need to come in and talk to me brother. We works together and he's the oldest.'' He glanced at Fred, who picked that very moment to cock his head and sit down in a very polite manner. "He's a funny little feller, inn't he? Mum's gone for a while. I reckon you and your dog can come in. Me and Mick could sure do with the work. Me name's David. David Simms.''

"Aren't you goin' to finish Barrett's house?" Wiggins asked as he followed the young man inside.

"Can't," David said shortly. "The police won't let us in to finish the job 'cause they was searchin' the place, and besides, who would pay fer it? Hard luck too. We was countin' on the money from the Barrett job to make the rent this week. God knows when them solicitors will ever get around to payin' us what we're owed.''

He lead the way into a small, rather dark room. Despite the chill in the air, there was no fire in the grate. The windows were covered by thick, brown curtains. The settee was a lumpy mass of grey, and the carpet was threadbare in spots. But the room was clean with a faint scent of disinfectant soap lingering in the air.

"Wait 'ere," David ordered. 'I'll just nip up and get Mick.''

Alone, Wiggins stood stock still as the memories came back to him in a silent rush.

Memories of a small room much like this one and a slender, sweet-faced woman with dark brown hair, round cheeks and the prettiest blue eyes in the world. She was kneeling in front of him and wiping the tears from his face with a white handkerchief. He could still see that hankie. Her initial had been embroidered in pink thread in the corner. "Don't worry, lovey," she'd said. "We'll be together soon. It won't be for long. Just until I can find a position where I can have you with me."

He shuddered slightly and blinked hard to fight off the tears that sprang into his eyes. Fred, sensing something wrong, whined softly and licked his hand. Wiggins sniffed and wiped his eyes before the tears could roll any further down his cheeks. His throat hurt as he struggled for control.

This room was so much like the one from his childhood. So much so that standing here had brought it back to him like it had happened yesterday.

He'd been eight years old when he'd left her. Just a little lad sent off to live with relatives till his mum could find a position. But that day, the day she'd promised it wouldn't be for long and that she'd come get him soon, had been the last time he'd ever seen her.

CHAPTER 7

Miss Minerva Kenny was a small, thin woman with bright green eyes, dark hair heavily streaked with grey and a fluttering, twittery manner that reminded Witherspoon of a sparrow. As she was dressed in a gown of bronze and brown stripes, the image was further reinforced.

"Do sit down, gentlemen," she invited, gesturing at two stiff-backed chairs. "I suppose I ought to ring for tea," she muttered, more to herself than either of them, "but perhaps this isn't a social call."

"No, ma'am," Witherspoon said hastily. "It isn't. But a cup of tea would be most welcome."

"Of course," she said as she hurried to the door. "I'll just tell the maid."

Witherspoon took the opportunity to look around. The room was small and cluttered. Every available surface was covered with china figurines, delicate crystal, fringed shawls and inlaid boxes. Gracious, there was enough in this room alone to stock a shop, the inspector thought.

Constable Barnes cleared his throat and whipped out his notebook as Miss Kenny returned. "Tea will be ready

in a moment,'' she announced as she sat down on one of
the high-backed chairs. She fixed her gaze on the inspector.

''Thank you, ma'am.'' Witherspoon smiled politely.
Miss Kenny continued to stare at him. ''Now, we've some
questions for you—''

She interrupted. ''Is this about Mr. Barrett's death?''

''I'm afraid it is,'' Witherspoon began. ''As you know,
he was murdered—''

''I don't know a thing about it,'' she broke in again.
''So as soon as you've had your tea, I expect you'll want
to leave.''

''Leave? But that's impossible. We really must ask you
some questions,'' the inspector tried again.

''Why? I don't know anything.'' She smiled blandly.

Witherspoon nodded patiently. ''Miss Kenny, you
don't know if you know anything.''

''Well, if I don't know if I know anything, I don't see
how I can tell you about it,'' she replied reasonably.

''But that's the whole point,'' he countered. His head
was beginning to hurt now and the indigestion was getting
worse. ''You won't know what you don't know until we
ask you some questions.''

She cocked her head to one side and crossed her arms
over each other. ''Inspector, if you don't mind my saying
so, you're not making a great deal of sense.''

Witherspoon sighed silently. Of course he wasn't making any sense, but neither was she. However, he was far
too much of a gentleman to point that out to her.

''Forgive me, ma'am,'' he said, giving her another patient smile. ''But what I meant to say was perhaps you've
information that you don't know you have. I understand
you were visiting Mr. Spears the day before the murder,''
he said quickly, trying not to breathe so she wouldn't have

a chance to interrupt him. "And I understand you witnessed an incident between Mr. Spears and Mr. Barrett."

"Oh." She sagged against the back of the settee. "I did have tea at the Spears house, that's true. But I can't honestly say I witnessed any incident. Mr. Spears is always a perfect gentleman. He's hardly in the habit of having public quarrels with his neighbours."

Barnes looked up from his notebook. "The inspector didn't say he'd had a public quarrel," he told her softly. "He said he'd had an 'incident.' "

Miss Kenny's hand flew to her mouth. For a moment, she didn't reply, then she caught herself and straightened her spine. "Well, I assumed that's what you meant. How many different kinds of 'incidents' are there?"

Witherspoon sighed inwardly. This was not going to be an easy interview. "Miss Kenny, I believe you know what we're talking about. We shan't leave until you've answered our inquiries."

She gave him a long, calculating look before she answered. "I suppose I might as well tell you, then. I didn't see it myself, of course. I was in the drawing room with Mrs. Astley when it happened. But Maud told me about it."

"What did Mrs. Astley tell you?" Witherspoon prompted. He hoped the maid would hurry up and bring the tea.

"She said that Mr. Spears had caught that awful Mr. Barrett throwing stones at his dog. He and Mr. Astley had gone outside to smoke a cigar. Barrett didn't see them, of course. But when King went into Barrett's flower beds, Barrett started heaving stones at the poor animal." She paused as the maid brought in a tray of tea. They waited patiently while Miss Kenny poured. The inspector noticed her hand was shaking as she handed him his cup.

"I take it Mrs. Astley found out what had happened from her husband?" Witherspoon asked as soon as the maid had left.

"Not really." Miss Kenny gave him a strained smile. "Thornton thinks that's how she knew, but the truth is, she watched the whole thing from the window. As soon as she heard the raised voices, Maud dashed over and opened a window. Pembroke, Adrian's butler, was most put out. Of course, he could hardly order her back to her seat as if she were a schoolgirl, could he?"

"I see." Witherspoon took another gulp of tea. The brew soothed his raw stomach. "Did you get up and go to the window?"

She shook her head. "Oh, no, I stayed right where I was on the settee."

"And could you hear what was going on with the window open?"

"Not really and it was no good asking Maud, either." Her green eyes flashed with remembered irritation. "She kept shushing me every time I opened my mouth."

"When did she tell you what had happened?" Witherspoon was trying to picture the whole thing in his head. It was jolly difficult.

"Right before Adrian and Thornton came back inside. She said that she'd heard Adrian tell Barrett if he ever caught him hurting his dog again, he'd ring his wretched neck."

Witherspoon wanted to be absolutely clear about this. "So Mrs. Astley distinctly mentioned that she'd overheard your host threatening William Barrett, is that correct?"

"Yes."

Barnes and the inspector exchanged glances.

"Miss Kenny," Witherspoon said softly. "Would you

mind telling us why you went to William Barrett's house yesterday afternoon?''

The heavy footsteps in the hall shook Wiggins out of his reverie. "It's all right, boy," he whispered to Fred, "I'm fine. Just havin' some odd notions, that's all." Fred stared up at him intently out his big brown eyes. For a moment Wiggins was convinced the animal could understand everything. There was such sympathy, such devotion in those eyes that it was almost as if ole' Fred understood exactly how sad he'd been when he'd lost his mother as a little lad.

"This 'ere's me brother, Mick," David said as he and another man walked into the room.

Mick was a bigger, older and harder version of David. Wiggins smiled politely. "I'm Wiggins and this 'ere's Fred.''

Mick nodded but said nothing. He crossed his arms over his chest. Wiggins swallowed heavily as he saw the hard muscles bulging beneath the fabric of the thin, blue shirt the man wore. He had hands big enough to crush a man's skull as well, the footman thought.

"My employer sent me 'round.''

"And who would that be?" Mick asked.

Wiggins stared at him. He could hardly tell 'im the truth now. He had a feelin' this bloke didn't take kindly to people who worked for Scotland Yard inspectors. "Uh, I work fer an American lady. Name's Luty Belle Crookshank. She seen yer work when she was at the Barrett house and thought you might be willin' to do some paintin' for her. Last bunch she had in made a right old balls up of the walls.''

"A woman?" David said suspiciously. "But when you come in 'ere, you referred to your guv as a 'he.''

"I take my orders from the butler," Wiggins explained quickly.

Mick's frown turned into a narrow-eyed glare. "I don't think we want to work fer anyone who's a friend of that bastard Barrett."

Wiggins blinked at the man's tone. Fred's ears picked up. "She's not really a friend of Barrett's—"

Mick interrupted him. "She were at his house, weren't she?"

"Only because she had to be there!" Wiggins cried. He desperately tried to think of something to say.

"Look"—Mick stepped closer—"maybe you'd better shove off." He uncrossed his arms.

A low-pitched snarl came out of Fred's throat. Wiggins reached down and patted the dog's head. "It's all right, boy. We's only talkin'."

David came out from behind his brother. "Give the lad a chance," he said to Mick. "We may not be paid for the Barrett job and we need the work."

"We'll not be workin' for the likes of people like Barrett again!" Mick yelled, taking another step closer to Wiggins.

Fred jumped between them, snarling fiercely with his legs spread wide. They stood there for a moment, the dog's ears pinned back, the big man staring at him, and Wiggins wondering if he ought to make a run for it or brazen the situation out.

Then Mick started to laugh. He stepped back, holding his hand out in a placating manner. "It's all right, fella, I'm not going to hurt anyone."

Wiggins exhaled the breath he'd been holding and grabbed the dog. "Down, Fred," he soothed. Fred immediately flopped onto the floor and wagged his tail. He gave them a big dog grin.

"You've got a good dog, there," Mick said brusquely. "See that you treat 'im right."

"I will," Wiggins said quickly, sensing that the man had only backed off because he liked animals and hadn't wanted to have to kick Fred in the head if he attacked. "And my employer ain't no friend of Barrett's," he continued, suddenly inspired. "She were only at his house to threaten to sue him." That didn't seem to be stretchin' the truth too far. Seems like everyone who knew Barrett either wanted to box his ears, take him to court or stick a sword in him.

"That's not surprisin'." Mick jerked his head toward the settee. "Have a seat and we'll talk about this 'ere job."

Wiggins scrambled toward the lumpy couch. Fred was right on his heels. Now that he had the two men talking about Barrett, he didn't want to waste a minute. "Uh, seems like you didn't like Barrett much," he said.

"Like him?" Mick snorted. "The bastard were nothin' but aggravation from the minute we started workin' there." He jerked his chin at David. "I'da walked out the first day, when he started in on Davey here about takin' a tea break, only by that time we'd already bought the bleedin' paint. I knew if we didn't finish the job, we'd not see a bloody bob for our labour."

"Blimey." Wiggin's really was amazed. "Barrett didn't want you takin' a tea break?"

"He didn't want us stoppin' for nuthin'," David put in. "And he expected us to work seven days a week. We soon put a stop to that. Mum won't let us work on the Sabbath. Barrett couldn't make us, neither. By that time we'd put the word out to our mates about how miserable 'e was to work for. Barrett knew he couldn't find anyone else to do the job if he fired us, so 'e had to give us

Sunday off. He was in a right hurry to get the work done.''

"Wonder why?" Wiggins leaned over and scratched Fred behind the ears.

"He was tryin' to sell the 'ouse," Mick answered. "That's why he had us workin' twelve hours a day and them carpenters up there at the same time. It were bloomin' daft, too. We kept gettin' in each other's way. Finally old Barrett come up with a plan to have the carpenters use the backstairs and us use the front. Worked for a while."

"Like 'ell it did," David muttered. "One of them bloody carpenters knicked me hat and coat."

"They claimed they didn't," Mick said with a shrug. "Coulda been Barrett for all we know."

"Now, what would he want with a workingman's clothes?" David said reasonably. "He was a mean bastard, but I don't think he'd have much use for my old hat and overcoat. But them carpenters, now, they 'ad a reason to pinch me stuff. They was gettin' back at me 'cause they thought I'd taken their bloody hammer."

"Uh, was you there on the day of the murder?" Wiggins asked. He knew all about the petty squabbles people forced to work together could get into, and he didn't want to waste time listenin' to it now.

"Course we was," Mick said shortly. "Not that we seen anything."

"Oh." Wiggins desperately tried to think of something useful to ask.

"Mind you," Mick continued, for he was fond of the sound of his own voice, "I'm not surprised someone shoved a sword into Barrett. He was that kinda feller, if you know what I mean. Had his fingers in a lot of pies, had a lot of people dancing to his tune and bouncing around on his string.''

"What do ya mean?"

"I mean, he was a bit like a lad that plays with fire." He dropped his voice to a conspiratorial whisper. "He didn't half care who he made angry. Had some poor woman in tears the day he was killed. I could hear her beggin' and cryin' at him when I went down to get me paint."

"When was this?" David demanded. "You never said nuthin' to me about any woman."

"It slipped me mind until we started talkin'," Mick said. "It were the mornin' of the day he were killed. Barrett had this poor woman in his drawin' room, and he was threatenin' to do somethin' to her. I could hear her beggin' him to keep quiet, askin' him to please let her have it back—"

" 'Ave what back?" Wiggins interrupted.

Mick shrugged. "Don't know, couldn't really hear good by that time. The butler was comin' up the stairs and stompin' his feet loud enough to wake the dead."

"Cor blimey," Wiggins said, "I guess Lu—Mrs. Crookshank weren't the only one in town who didn't like him."

Mick threw back his head and laughed. "Not bloody likely, mate. Like I said, he had more enemies than you and I've had hot dinners. You'd think someone who was hated that much would have better sense than to leave a sword hanging on the wall. Whoever killed 'im didn't even have to bring their own weapon."

From the corner of his eye Wiggins saw David staring at him suspiciously. He thought it might be time to change the subject. "Uh, are you interested in another job?"

"This Mrs. . . . Kurshank—"

"Crookshank," Wiggins corrected.

"Is she a decent sort?" David interrupted. "I mean, is she likely to pay us?"

"Course she will," he replied honestly. "And she'll not expect you to work like dogs either. She's a good sort." Wiggins fervently hoped that Luty would have something that needed painting. He'd rather gotten to like these two.

"All right," Mick said. "We're interested. When's the job start?"

"Uh, not for a week or two," Wiggins said quickly. "Mrs. Crookshank only sent me 'round to find out if you was willin' to do it."

"We're willin'." Mick got to his feet. "You just call round and let us know where we need to go."

They walked him and Fred to the door. With each and every step Wiggins felt more and more depressed. These men really needed the work, and here he was raisin' their hopes. Bloomin' Ada, as Smythe would say.

"There's someone to see you, sir," the young constable said as soon as Witherspoon and Barnes got back to the station.

Witherspoon glanced longingly at the stairs leading to the second floor and the canteen. He was dreadfully hungry. "Who is it?" he asked the constable.

"Cabbie, sir. Name of Roland Moodie. He claims he's got information about the Barrett murder."

Witherspoon sighed. "Go on up to the canteen," he said to Barnes. "I'd best see what this chap has to say."

Roland Moodie was sitting in a straight-back chair beside the inspector's desk. He was a round, bald man wearing a houndstooth coat, several layers of scarves and holding a battered bowler hat on his knees. "You the copper that's in charge of that killin' on Kildare Gardens?'' he asked as Witherspoon approached.

"Indeed I am, sir.'' He introduced himself as he sat down behind his desk.

"Name's Roland Moodie,'' the cabbie said, "and I've got some information that might be useful to you.'' He put one hand in his pocket and fingered the fistful of pound notes that strange bloke had given him for coming here. Moodie didn't have much use for coppers. Always pushin' you off when you was lookin' for a fare. But the bloke and his lolly had convinced him to come and tell about the fare he'd dropped at Kildare Gardens. "I dropped a fare off in Kildare Gardens on the day of the killin'. Thought you might want to know about it.''

"How very good of you to come in!'' Witherspoon exclaimed, genuinely pleased. "It does one good to see one's fellow citizens doing their civic duty. You know, you'd be utterly amazed at the number of people who won't come forward with information. It's positively dreadful how people don't like to get involved.''

"Uh, yeah.'' Moodie didn't want to get involved, either. But the big bloke who'd been askin' him all them questions this mornin' had been real insistent. Mind you, he'd paid for Moodie's time. Moodie decided he'd better not say anything about the big feller. Wouldn't want this peeler thinkin' he was in here tellin' tales 'cause someone had greased his palm with silver. Besides, that big feller had paid him extra to keep his mouth shut about their conversation. Seemed like a decent enough bloke, but he was awfully big and, if the truth were known, a little mean-lookin' too. "Well, I likes to do me duty.''

"I'm sure you do, sir.'' Witherspoon paused to think what to ask first. He said the first thing that came into his head. "How did you find out about the murder?''

"It were in all the newspapers," Moodie replied, thinking it was an odd question. "And when I saw the address where it were done, I remembered I'd taken a fare there that very afternoon."

"Was the fare a man or a woman?"

"A man. Real gent he was too."

Witherspoon nodded. "What do you mean, 'a real gent'?"

"You know, a toff," Moodie said impatiently. "Had on a big black top hat, his boots were as shiny as new pennies, and he were wearin' quality clothes. I can tell, ya know. I picks up a lot of gents."

"I see." Witherspoon pursed his lips. "Where did you pick this person up?"

"At the railway terminal."

Witherspoon drummed his fingers on the desk. "Which one? London has a number of railways."

"The Great Western." Moodie might be in here talkin' to the copper, but he hadn't been paid enough to make it easy for 'em. They could bleedin' well work for what he had to say.

"What time was this?" Witherspoon's stomach growled. He swallowed heavily, thinking of the greasy fare in the police canteen. He hoped that Mrs. Jeffries had had some success in finding them a cook. The staff were doing their best, but really, he hadn't slept well last night, and this morning's breakfast had been almost inedible.

Moodie took his time about answering, his beady eyes squinted, and he scratched his nose. "About five-fifteen."

"And where did you take the man?"

"I told ya, to Kildare Gardens."

"Do you remember which number?" Witherspoon asked, trying hard not to sound impatient.

"Course I do," Moodie exclaimed. "Number fifteen.

That's the house were the murder happened, isn't it? Why the blazes do ya think I come in 'ere?''

Witherspoon closed his eyes briefly. "Of course. Now, could you describe the man?"

"I told ya, he was a gent wearin' expensive clothes."

"You described his clothes, sir." The inspector wondered if it was him or was this man particularly obtuse. "Now I'd like you to describe the man himself. What color hair did he have?"

"It were like a dark red, but it had a bit of grey in it. Mind you," Moodie explained. "I couldn't see how much he had 'cause he was wearin' a top hat. For all I know he might have been bald on top."

Witherspoon straightened. Dark red hair? Auburn perhaps? "Er, how old was this man?"

Moodie shrugged. "Maybe fifty, fifty-five."

"And how tall?"

"About six feet I'd reckon." Moodie rolled his eyes toward the ceiling as if he expected the right answer to be written up there. "Maybe an inch or two shorter."

The inspector forgot about his empty stomach and the police canteen. "Did you see him go into the house?"

Moodie grinned and nodded. "He walked straight in like he owned the place. I figured he lived there, you see. Even though the doors was open like, this gent didn't even bother to bang the brass. Just went on in."

"I see." Witherspoon asked him a few more questions and then wrote down his address. He wanted to be able to get his hands on this man when they went to court.

By the time Mr. Moodie had finished his statement, Barnes was back from the police canteen. He looked at the cabbie curiously, but said nothing until the man had taken his leave.

"Who was that, sir?" Barnes asked. He flicked a bit

of breadcrumb off his sleeve. "A witness?"

"A most valuable witness, I think," Witherspoon murmured. "He's a cabbie by the name of Roland Moodie. He took a fare to the Barrett house the afternoon of the murder. It was a man, Barnes. One of our suspects."

"Did the cabbie know his name?" Barnes asked eagerly.

"No. But from the description he gave me, I've no doubt who it was." Witherspoon paused dramatically. "Thornton Astley." He proceeded to tell the constable everything the cabbie had told him.

Barnes scratched his chin. "But why would Astley take a cab to Barrett's house? Especially from the railway station. Why not just walk there?"

"Why, to throw us off the scent," Witherspoon explained. "He couldn't risk being seen walking there. Much better to nip out somewhere, pretend to be going to an office in the City and then grab a hansom back."

"I see what you mean, sir," Barnes replied, but his expression was doubtful. "Then again, we only have Astley's word that he was droppin' the lawsuit. Perhaps he decided that would be a waste of money and wanted to get his own back by killin' Barrett. Wouldn't be the first time murder's been done over money."

"True," the inspector replied. "Of course, we don't know for certain it was Astley in that hansom, but it seems a reasonable assumption. Still, I mustn't jump to conclusions. Astley wasn't the only person to call upon the victim. Remember, Miss Kenny was there too."

Barnes shrugged. "But she claims she wasn't. She claims Mr. Spears is mistaken."

"That's why we've sent some lads round to Kildare Gardens," Witherspoon said patiently. "For goodness' sakes, someone other than Adrian Spears must have seen

Miss Kenny. Have you sent the PCs off yet?''

"Not yet, sir. I was going to do it after I had me tea.'' Barnes belched softly. "Sorry, sir. Bit of chop come back up."

The mention of food had the inspector's mouth watering.

"But I'll do it straight away," Barnes continued. "I'll have them check with the neighbours again and the local tradespeople and cabbies. If either Miss Kenny or Mr. Astley went to the Barrett house, someone is sure to have seen them." He started off and then stopped. "Will we be going back to the Astley house now?''

The inspector thought about it for a moment. He was torn between wanting to get something decent in his stomach and doing his duty. Duty won. "Yes, Barnes, give the PCs their instructions. I'll meet you downstairs and we'll see what Mr. Thornton Astley has to say for himself."

Barnes nodded and started off again. "Oh, forgot to tell you something, sir. Ran into one of the lads in the canteen, and he told me a bit of interestin' information. Seems that Astley's secretary, that Mr. Sharpe, the one who told us he was at the dentist the afternoon of the murder? PC Micklewhite says he weren't."

Witherspoon wondered why that was so interesting. He didn't see that Neville Sharpe had a reason to murder William Barrett. But he didn't wish to sound critical. "Excellent, Barnes. Do pass my compliments on to PC Micklewhite. What made him think to check the secretary's alibi?''

Barnes grinned. "He didn't, sir. But he were the one who took Mr. Sharpe's statement yesterday, and he noticed they went to the same dentist. Micklewhite's mother-in-law had a toothache late yesterday evenin', and he had to take her in. While he was there, he asked the dentist. The man had never heard of Neville Sharpe, and he insists he wasn't a patient.''

"How very odd," Witherspoon said. "I wonder where the man really was? Oh, well, make sure we ask him this afternoon.''

Betsy stared at the oven as if it were a snake. She weren't much of a cook and that was a fact. But tonight was her turn and she promised them she'd have a meal ready. She glanced at the clock and saw that it was getting close to teatime. She gave the oven another worried glance. Surely she'd done it right? Before she'd put the joint in, she'd put lots of salt on it, just like Mrs. Goodge always did. Maybe she'd put too much salt on it, she thought. But then again, maybe she hadn't. And what about them roast potatoes? Had she salted them too? She couldn't remember.

Betsy filled the kettle up and put it on to boil next to the big pot of cabbage she'd put on before putting the pork in the oven. Roast pork and potatoes and cabbage. That should make for a good dinner. She stared at the bubbling cabbage, the heavy steam rising off the open pan. Had she salted it? Betsy wasn't sure, but to be on the safe side, she thought, reaching for the salt cellar, maybe she'd add a bit more in.

Smythe leaned past the driver and pointed at the woman going into the Astley house. "Is that her?''

The cabbie's eyes narrowed. "Well, it could be. You've got to remember, I didn't get a good look at her face. She were wearin' a veil.''

"But you musta got a glimpse of her hair colour," Smythe pressed. "If it were that colour"——he pointed to the woman walking rapidly down the street—"you'da noticed, right?"

"Maybe . . ." he answered doubtfully. The cabbie frowned slightly as he watched the retreating figure. The woman's hair was a bright blond—even with that big hat on he could tell what colour it was. But he weren't sure she were the woman, and even though this bloke were payin' him to come round here and have a look-see, he didn't care how much money the feller had, he weren't goin' to say something was true unless he knew it fer sure. "I still can't tell," he finally said. "It were an overcast day the afternoon I picked the woman up, and it weren't half decent light, not like today."

Smythe sighed. There was no point in pesterin' the cabbie for an answer. The fellow simply couldn't tell if Maud Astley was the woman he'd picked up or not. "Would you tell me again what the woman was wearin' that afternoon?"

This time the cabbie sighed. "Listen, I ain't got all day."

"I'm payin' ya for yer time," Smythe snapped.

"All right, all right. She had on a dark hat with a big veil. The hat was black, if I remember rightly. She were all wrapped up in a big cloak. It was navy blue. I do remember that."

Smythe turned as he heard the *clip-clop* of another cab pull up behind them. A moment later the door opened and a slender, older lady stepped lightly to the ground, paid off the driver and then walked briskly up the walkway to the Astley home.

"I don't suppose you recognized that woman, did you?" Smythe asked the driver.

"Never seen her before," the cabbie said. "Why?"

"Just hoped she might be familiar to ya."

"Can I go now?"

Smythe reached into his pocket and pulled out the promised money. He handed it to the man and jumped down to the road. "Thanks for yer help," he called as the cabbie released the brake and then snapped the reins.

The man tipped his cap and the team shot forward. Smythe frowned. This case was costin' him a lot of lolly, not that he minded spendin' it. But he was payin' plenty out and not gettin' much in return. Just then another cab came down the square.

Smythe crossed the road so he wouldn't be facing the occupants when they went past. It wouldn't do to become too familiar a face in this neighbourhood, not with the police still hanging about.

He kept his eye on the hansom as he began walking toward Kildare Square. Maybe he'd get on back and have tea with the others. See what they'd found out.

The hansom stopped in front of the Barrett house. Smythe saw the door open and then a uniformed constable stepped into view. As soon as he saw who it was getting out of the cab, he ducked behind a lamppost and turned sideways. A second later the inspector stepped out.

Smythe held his breath and prayed neither man would glance this way. He could never explain why he was hidin' behind a bleedin' lamppost.

But the two policemen went into the Astley house without looking across the road.

"That was a ruddy close call," he muttered to himself as he started moving. There was no point in temptin' fate. If the inspector saw him hanging about, they'd all be in a right old mess.

Mrs. Jeffries dashed into the kitchen, tossing her coat and hat on an empty chair. "Are the others back for tea, Betsy?" she asked.

"They're due in a few minutes," Betsy said. She picked up the tray and carried it to the kitchen table. "Where 'ave you been? A man from the gasworks was here and a fruit seller stopped by. They was both looking for Mrs. Goodge. I reckon she must have put the word out that she was needin' information."

"Yes," Mrs. Jeffries muttered, looking distracted, "I expect she did. Did they tell you anything."

"Not really," Betsy said as she took a cloth off the Madeira cake she'd bought from the bakers. "Just passed on some gossip about Maud Astley. Do you want me to tell you now or should we wait for the others?"

Mrs. Jeffries thought about it for a moment. "We'd best wait."

They heard Wiggins and Fred come in the back door. "Come on, boy. Let's go see what there is for tea. 'Ello, 'ello," he said, hurrying to the table and licking his lips. His face fell when he saw nothing but bread and butter and one ever so tiny Madeira cake. He didn't even like Madeira cake. "Is this all there is?"

"That's plenty," Betsy protested. "I'm cookin' a big meal for tonight. You don't want to be spoilin' your dinner."

"What we havin?" Wiggins asked suspiciously. "I hope it ain't sausages. Them sausages we had for breakfast is still in my stomach."

"It's not sausages." Betsy glared at him and jerked her head toward Mrs. Jeffries, warning Wiggins to watch what he said. "Besides, there was nothing wrong with breakfast."

"Course there wasn't," Smythe agreed as he popped into the room. "If you was a starvin' man stuck in the middle of a ruddy desert," he added under his breath.

"Are we all here?" Mrs. Jeffries pretended not to notice their comments about this morning's meal. Goodness knows, she didn't claim to be much of a cook, and all in all they were being quite good about it. But really, it wasn't as though she'd meant to burn the sausages.

"Are we goin' to wait for Luty Belle and Hatchet?" Betsy asked. She put the big brown teapot on the table next to the bread.

"They said they'd be by this evening after dinner," Mrs. Jeffries said. "By the way, Betsy, something smells good."

Betsy smiled. "It's just a joint of pork and some potatoes," she said. "But I think it'll do nicely for supper." She'd put the cabbage in the cooling pantry. She hoped that letting it sit awhile in it's own juice might make it a bit more appealing. Funny, she'd never have guessed that cabbage went all mushy and green when you cooked it.

"Good," Mrs. Jeffries said. "Let's get right into it, shall we. First of all, something has happened. I went to see Minerva Kenny this afternoon."

"Is she a small, older woman with dark hair gone a bit grey?" Smythe asked, recalling the woman who'd stepped out of the hansom.

"Why, yes. How did you know?"

"I think *I* saw her this afternoon too," he said, reaching for the teapot.

"Really?" Mrs. Jeffries frowned. "Where?"

"Going into the Astley house."

"Oh, dear, I was afraid of that. She wasn't home when I called, and the maid didn't know where she'd gone."

"What are you so worried over?" Betsy asked, not liking the expression on the housekeeper's face. "It's only natural she'd go to see her friends, what with the murder and all. What's so terrible about her goin' to visit with Maud Astley?"

"There's nothin' terrible about it, exceptin' that Mrs. Astley isn't home," Smythe interjected. "She'd just gone out when Miss Kenny showed up."

"Oh, dear," Mrs. Jeffries muttered. "This is disastrous."

"What's a disaster?" Wiggins asked, just to keep up his end of the conversation. He wished Betsy had sliced the bread thicker. These slices was so thin you could read a ruddy newspaper through 'em!

"Because I'm afraid Miss Kenny may have gone there to put that silly china bird back in place," Mrs. Jeffries replied. "And that's the last thing we need. If someone sees her, it will only muddle things."

"Blimey, let's hope not." Smythe shook his head. "If the inspector walks in and catches her takin' that bird out of her pocket and shovin' it on a table, she'll have a lot of explainin' to do."

"The inspector!" Mrs. Jeffries cried.

"'Fraid so. I saw him goin' into the Astley house right behind Miss Kenny."

CHAPTER 8

"What's so awful about Miss Kenny puttin' the bird back?" Wiggins asked. "She's not likely to get caught, now, is she? I mean, she's been snatchin' things from her friends and returnin' 'em back for a long while now, and she ain't been caught by any of 'em."

They all stared at him.

"You know, Wiggins," Mrs. Jeffries replied thoughtfully. "I do believe you're right. She's apparently rather successful at her, uh . . . activities. As you pointed out, she's done it for years."

"That's right," Betsy agreed. "So what are we worried about? Miss Kenny won't get—"

"Aren't you all forgettin' somethin?" Smythe interrupted. "Seems to me the old girl's losin' 'er touch. The last time she 'ad sticky fingers, she did get caught! And the man who caught 'er is now dead. Someone shoved a ruddy sword through 'is 'eart."

No one said anything. Wiggins broke the silence with a loud groan. Betsy slumped back in her chair. Even Mrs. Jeffries looked disappointed.

"Then we'd better hope that Miss Kenny keeps her wits about her this afternoon," Mrs. Jeffries said softly. "Otherwise, we may all have a lot of explaining to do to the inspector."

"Do you think she's likely to say anything about how she got the bird back?" Betsy asked. She gave the coachman a quick, worried look. "It wouldn't be fair if Smythe got into trouble. We was *all* in on it."

"Sufficient unto the day is the evil thereof," Mrs. Jeffries said.

"What does that mean?" Wiggins asked.

"It means," Smythe replied, "don't go lookin' for trouble."

"Right," the housekeeper nodded. "Furthermore, even if Miss Kenny were to tell the inspector someone had retrieved the bird for her, she couldn't identify Smythe by name. Ruth never told her any of our names."

"But if he finds out it was Lady Cannonberry," Betsy countered, "how do we know she'll not say something? You know the inspector would ask her about it."

Mrs. Jeffries gave them her calmest smile. She was concerned too, but fretting over something that hadn't even happened was a waste of useful energy. Much better to concentrate on finding the real killer. "Let's keep our fingers crossed that Miss Kenny gets in and out of the Astley house without anything untoward happening. Now, we really must get down to business. Who wants to go first?"

"Better let me," Smythe said. "I may need to nip out before supper and talk to a cabbie."

"Very well." Mrs. Jeffries nodded. "Go ahead." She didn't have much of her own to report, and she was hoping that one of them had picked up something useful.

"I found out that there were three hansoms goin' to Number fifteen Kildare Gardens on the afternoon of the murder.'' He told them everything he'd learned, taking care not to mention Blimpey Groggins and implying that he had spoken to all the cabbies himself. Which, of course, he had, so on this matter at least, his conscience was clear. ''So you see,'' he finished, ''that's how come I know that Miss Kenny is at the Astley house.''

Betsy eyed him suspiciously. ''You mean you talked a cabbie into goin' all the way over to Kildare Gardens and then just sittin' there and waitin' till Maud Astley come out?''

Smythe was ready for that question. ''I was headin' over there myself, so I paid the fare.''

''Oh, dear, Smythe.'' Mrs. Jeffries clucked her tongue. ''Hansoms are dreadfully expensive. I know how devoted you are to the inspector, but really. No one expects you to spend your hard-earned wages on taking cabs just so you can get them to give you information.''

Smythe gave her a gentle smile. ''My feet were hurtin', Mrs. J., and I didn't relish fightin' the crowd on the omnibus or the underground. Besides, I've not much else to spend my wages on. Anyway, we now know that at least one of them three went into the Barrett 'ouse. The cabbie was sure the man did. Course, by my way of thinkin', any of the three of 'em coulda gone into the Barrett 'ouse and killed the man.''

''How do you figure that?'' Betsy asked.

''First of all, the woman that was dropped on Talbot Road coulda slipped in without bein' seen,'' Smythe explained. ''Seems to me that's why she 'ad the hansom drop her where 'e did; she didn't want no one connectin' her to Barrett's.''

''But the second woman went to Royal Oak Station,'' Mrs. Jeffries pointed out.

''And that's less than a ten-minute walk from Kildare

Gardens," the coachman countered. "Maybe that's why she jumped back in the hansom: She'd figured the cabbie would remember takin' her to Barrett's house."

"I wonder who the man was?" Wiggins said thoughtfully. He slipped Fred a bite of cake under the table.

"We'll know by tonight," Smythe said and then wanted to bite his tongue. They were all staring at him again. "I mean, I, uh, convinced the cabbie he really ought to go to the police."

"Very good, Smythe," Mrs. Jeffries said. "And I trust you made sure they wouldn't mention they'd spoken to you?"

"Course." He sank back into his chair.

Mrs. Jeffries glanced around the table. "Who'd like to go next?"

"I will," Wiggins said around a mouthful of bread. He told them about his visit to the Simms house. "They sure hated workin' for Barrett," he concluded. "Do you think they'll ever get paid?"

"I certainly hope so," Mrs. Jeffries replied. "Did they have any idea who the woman was in Barrett's study? The one they heard crying?"

"Neither of them got a look at her," Wiggins answered. "But tomorrow I'm goin' to see the carpenter. Mick thinks one of them might have got a look at her."

"Sounds like this is the same woman that Barrett's maid saw cryin' in his drawin' room," Smythe said.

"Must be. Even a man as miserable as Barrett wouldn'a 'ad two women weepin' on the same day. No one's that mean." Wiggins eyed another piece of cake. He really didn't like it, but he was so hungry he felt like his belly was touchin' his backbone. He started to reach for the cake plate and then snatched his hand back. No, he'd wait till dinner. Betsy was cookin' them a good supper and he didn't want to spoil it.

"Barrett wasn't real good with women, was he?" Betsy said, smiling blandly at the coachman. He grinned back at her. One of them big cocky grins that was so irritatin'. Well, just wait till he heard what she'd found out. That would wipe that silly smirk off his face. "Noah found out the name of the woman Barrett was havin' the row with the night before he died." She looked around the table. "It was Maud Astley."

"Miss Kenny," the inspector said to the woman standing on the chair. "Do you really think it's safe to be standing on that chair?"

Startled, she whirled around, lost her balance and toppled forward. Witherspoon made a lunge for her just as the chair slipped out from under her feet.

"Oww . . ." he moaned as Miss Kenny's weight sent them both tumbling through the air. They hit the carpet with a loud thud.

"Oh, heavens!" Miss Kenny cried. She tried throwing herself to one side and ended up shoving her elbow into the inspector's open mouth.

"Good heavens!" Barnes cried as he scrambled toward the two bodies seemingly locked in mortal combat on the floor.

Witherspoon tried to get a foothold on the floor so he could shove Miss Kenny to one side, but his boot got tangled in the hem of her voluminous skirts. He couldn't ask the constable for help; Miss Kenny's elbow was in his mouth. His arm shot out and smacked hard against Barnes's leg. The constable, who was leaning over trying to get a grip on Miss Kenny's arm, lost his balance and toppled forward, pinning both Miss Kenny and Wither-spoon to the ground.

"Ahh . . ." the woman screamed as the constable's full weight slammed on top of her.

"Uhhh," Witherspoon moaned as the breath was knocked out of him for the second time.

"I say, what on earth is going on here?" Thornton Astley's scandalized voice thundered into the room.

Barnes finally managed to roll off to one side and scramble to his feet. He managed to get a grip on Miss Kenny's waist. He lifted her off the inspector and set her on her feet.

"Oh, goodness," a breathless Miss Kenny murmured as she adjusted her hat.

"Are you unharmed, Miss Kenny?" The inspector asked as he climbed to his feet.

"I say!" Astley shouted. "Will someone please explain what is going on in here?"

"I'm fine, Inspector," Miss Kenny said, ignoring her outraged host. "You startled me, though."

"My apologies, madam," Witherspoon replied. "But when I saw you on that chair, I was afraid you'd fall and hurt yourself."

"Chair?" Astley yelled. "What chair?"

"Miss Kenny fell off a chair," Witherspoon explained. "Unfortunately, I tried to catch her as she fell and we both tumbled over. Constable Barnes was trying to help us up, but he lost his balance and toppled over as well. That's why we were all on the floor when you came in."

Astley stared at them, his expression incredulous. Finally he walked over and rang the bellpull. The butler, who Witherspoon was sure was eavesdropping outside the door, immediately appeared.

Astley ordered tea. "I think," he said slowly as soon

as the butler disappeared, "that we'd better sit down."

Witherspoon turned to Miss Kenny. "Are you sure you're all right?"

"There's no permanent damage, thank you," she replied politely.

"That was a right hard fall you took," Barnes said conversationally. "Would you mind tellin' us what you was doin' on that chair?"

Miss Kenny pretended she hadn't heard the question. "I do believe I'll sit down. I'm a bit shaken."

"Perhaps we'd all better sit down," Astley said loudly.

Witherspoon decided that was a good idea. His tailbone hurt and his knee throbbed rather painfully. He hobbled over to a nice, comfortable-looking wing chair and gingerly sat down. Barnes perched on the edge of the settee. Miss Kenny took the chair on the far side of the settee. It was as far away from them as she could get.

An awkward silence filled the room. Witherspoon cleared his throat. He felt like an absolute fool. Whatever must Astley think of him? But he could hardly have stood and done nothing while an elderly woman took flying leaps off chairs.

Barnes shuffled his feet against the floor and dug in his pocket for his notebook. He didn't start grinning until everyone's attention was diverted by the maid arriving with the tea tray.

Astley handed the tea 'round and then sat back, his expression still puzzled. "Minerva," he said gently. "Would you mind telling *me* what you were doing on a chair in my drawing room."

She stared down at her cup. "I . . . uh . . . wanted to get a closer look at those china birds on that top shelf," she finally said, her voice so soft that the inspector had to lean forward to hear her.

"I see," Astley said. "Well, next time, do say something to me and I'll have one of the servants take care of getting things down for you. You're far too valuable a friend to risk losing by a bad fall off the furniture." He looked at the inspector. "Why have you come here today?"

"I need to ask you some more questions," Witherspoon replied. He wondered if Constable Barnes had seen what he'd seen when they walked into the room. Minerva Kenny wasn't looking at those china birds, she was taking one out of the pocket of her dress and reaching up to the shelf when they had their accident. Why was one of Mr. Astley's birds in her pocket? But that question could come later, when he questioned Miss Kenny alone.

"I've told you everything I know about Barrett's murder," Astley said.

"Is Maud here?" Minerva Kenny asked timidly.

Astley smiled at her. "No, she's gone out. Shall I tell her you called?"

Minerva nodded and put her teacup back on the tray. "I'm so sorry for the upset," she said as she got to her feet. "Perhaps it would be best if I left. Please tell Maud I called."

"I'll ask her to call 'round and see you." Astley rose as well.

Miss Kenny turned and looked at the two policemen. "Good day, gentlemen," she said.

Astley escorted her to the door, talking to her in low soothing tones.

As soon as they were out of the room, Barnes leaned toward the inspector. "She's lyin'," he whispered. "I distinctly saw her take somethin' out of her pocket when we come into the room. She was puttin' somethin' up on that shelf."

"I quite agree," Witherspoon whispered back. "But I think it best if we ask her about it when she's alone."

"Right, sir." Barnes hastily sat back as they heard Astley's footsteps coming back down the hallway.

"Inspector," Astley said abruptly. "Will you please tell me what is going on?"

"Well, sir, it's as we told you," Witherspoon said. "We came by to ask you a few more questions."

"This has been a most unsettling day." Astley ran a hand through his hair as he sat down.

The inspector studied him carefully. Thornton Astley had dark circles under his eyes and his face was drawn, as though he hadn't been sleeping. "Murder is frequently unsettling. Mr. Astley, we've had a report that you were seen going into Barrett's house on the afternoon of the murder."

Astley's head jerked up and his mouth opened slightly. "I don't know what you're talking about," he protested. But his voice was thin and hollow, lacking conviction.

"The cabbie who took you to the Barrett house has already given us a statement," Witherspoon said softly. Really, it was almost embarrassing watching people try to lie their way out of a situation. "So please, just tell us the truth. It will be easier on you in the long run."

Astley stared at him a moment and then slumped back against the settee. "I suppose I've known all along you'd find out," he laughed bitterly. "Yes, I did go to the house."

"You went inside as well," the inspector stated.

"I'll admit I went upstairs into the study. But I didn't kill him!" Astley cried. "When I walked into that room, Barrett was already dead."

"What time was this?" Witherspoon pressed.

"About half past five. Maybe as late as a quarter to

six, I don't know. I didn't look at my watch.''

"Did you see anyone as you were going in or out?''
The inspector was confused. Astley sounded as though he
were telling the truth, yet one of the workmen had claimed
that he'd heard Barrett alive at six o'clock.

"No.'' Astley shook his head. "I could hear the painters and carpenters up on the third floor. There was a great
deal of pounding and shouting.''

"You saw no servants?''

"No one,'' Astley admitted. "Except for the cabbie, of
course.''

"Are you certain that Barrett was dead?'' Barnes asked.

"Yes. There wasn't much light in the room, the fire
had burned low and he'd not turned on the gas lamps.
But he was dead, all right. I checked for a pulse and there
wasn't one.'' Astley sighed. "Will there be no end to the
misery that man has caused? Even dead he finds a way
to torment people.''

The inspector asked, "Why had you gone to see Mr.
Barrett?''

"To tell him I was dropping my lawsuit.'' Astley explained. "I know it sounds odd. But Maud had been
pressing me to let it go. She claimed it would take months
to sort out and that with Barrett selling his house and
planning to go off somewhere, I'd never see a farthing of
the money he stole from me.''

"Mrs. Astley had talked you into dropping the lawsuit?'' Witherspoon asked. He wanted to make sure he
had all the facts right. "Is that correct?''

"I've just told you it is,'' Astley snapped. "My wife
is a very sensible woman. We probably couldn't have won
in court. Sharpe, my secretary, had come across some papers that shed a whole new light on the situation. It seems
that Barrett might not have been robbing me blind after

all. So you see, Inspector, I'd no motive for murdering Barrett.''

''Mr. Astley,'' Barnes asked quietly, ''how did Mrs. Astley know that Barrett was selling his house?''

Luty Belle Crookshank poured a cup of Earl Grey and handed it to her guest. She'd much rather have had a good shot of whiskey, but Myrtle was an old fussbudget, and she wanted to get the woman gossipin'. Not that it would be hard, she thought as she watched her neighbour delicately pick out a tea cake. Myrtle was about the biggest talker in London.

''Barrett, did you say?'' Myrtle Buxton shook her head. ''I've never heard of him.''

''Don't you read the papers?'' Luty asked. ''He got himself skewered with a sword a couple of days back.''

''Oh.'' Myrtle made a face. ''*That* Barrett. Well, I've still never heard of him. He was, after all, in trade.''

''What's wrong with bein' in trade,'' Luty snapped. From the corner of her eye, she saw Hatchet frowning at her.

Myrtle laughed. ''You Americans are so innocent! There's nothing wrong with it, exactly. It's just that people in trade aren't generally as—''

''I know what you're goin' to say,'' Luty interrupted her. She knew if she and Myrtle got into this argument, she'd be here all night, and she didn't have time for that. ''And I don't agree. So let's just leave it at that. So you're sayin' that you never heard of the feller until you read about him bein' murdered.''

Myrtle smiled coyly. ''Well, actually, now that you mention it, I do recall one bit of scandal. Did you know he left some poor woman at the altar?''

Hatchet coughed. Luty shot him a quick glare. He was

smirking. She knew exactly what he was thinkin'. All she was gettin' today was old gossip.

"I heard he left that Washburn girl at the altar," Luty sniffed. "If it'da been me, I'd a shot the varmit. But I reckon you English don't believe in settlin' scores the way we do back home."

"We're a bit more civilized than that." Myrtle smiled. "Of course, Eliza Washburn was practically ruined. Why, Octavia Haines told me that Miss Washburn was so distraught and nervous after being so publicly humiliated, her own brother took to slipping her sleeping draughts in her sherry."

"Seems to me she wouldn'a been so shaky if she'da taken a shot at the polecat," Luty replied. Honestly, women like Eliza Washburn made her itch to slap 'em 'round the side of the head. Any woman that couldn't stand up for herself and let a no-good bushwacker like Barrett walk all over 'em deserved what they got.

"Don't be absurd, Luty." Myrtle chose a napoleon from the silver tray in front of her. "Eliza Washburn is a lady. Of course, she virtually went into hiding after it happened. Everyone thought she'd gone abroad."

"She ain't," Luty said glumly. Myrtle had been here half an hour now and hadn't told her a blasted useful thing. Hatchet must be delighted. He'd been out this morning doin' his own snooping and had come back lookin' like a fox that had spent the night in the henhouse. And they were due at Upper Edmonton Gardens after dinner. She had to have something good to tell everyone.

"I know that," Myrtle said impatiently. "I said everyone *thought* she'd gone abroad."

Luty stared at her with renewed interest. From behind her, she heard Hatchet come closer to the settee. No doubt the old goat wanted to make sure he didn't miss a word.

"What do you mean by that?"

Myrtle gave her one of them superior, real irritatin'
smiles. "Because Eliza Washburn was seen a few days
ago. Mind you, according to Henrietta Oxton, that's my
friend. You may have heard of her, her aunt was a lady-
in-waiting to one of the royal princesses, I forget which
one." She frowned. "There were rather a lot of them at
Buck House before they got married off."

"Go on, Myrtle," Luty urged. Once Myrtle got onto
the subject of all her fancy friends with their fancy titles,
her mouth never stopped. That was fine with Luty, but
she wanted her talkin' about Eliza Washburn or William
Barrett, not some weak-chinned aristocrat who wouldn't
last a day back home. "What was you sayin' about the
Washburn girl?"

"Oh, yes. Well, Henrietta was ever so surprised. She
was riding past the Richmond Road, and there was Eliza
Washburn, hailing a hansom. Not that I was surprised,
mind you. The Washburns are in trade too. What else can
one expect."

"When was this?"

"Tuesday," Myrtle said promptly. "I remember because I saw Henrietta on Wednesday morning, and the
first thing she said to me was that she'd seen Eliza Washburn the day before."

"Did she say what time?"

"What time?" Myrtle repeated, looking puzzled.

"What time of the day was it when she saw the girl,"
Luty explained.

"Oh, it was late afternoon. Henrietta was on her way
back from having tea with Lady Worthington." Myrtle's
eyebrows drew together. "Why on earth do you want to
know?"

"Just curious." Luty grinned. The nice thing about

Myrtle was that she was such a gossip herself, she expected everyone else to be one too. "You know, I like to get all the facts straight."

"Yes, I know just what you mean." Myrtle laughed. "I always insist on knowing the details myself."

Luty gestured at the silver tray. Antoine had outdone himself. Napoleons, seed cake, delicate French pastries. Thank goodness the man liked to bake. She gestured at a cream puff. "Come on, Myrtle, try one of Antoine's puffs."

"Oh, I really shouldn't," but Myrtle was already reaching her plump hand toward the confectionary.

Luty wasn't certain, but if she remembered rightly, on the afternoon of the murder, Eliza Washburn was supposed to be restin' in her room. Now this was gettin' interestin'.

Neville Sharpe stood rigidly in front of the fireplace. "I don't know what you mean," he said to Witherspoon. "I was at the dentist."

Witherspoon shook his head. "But we know you weren't, Mr. Sharpe. We've checked with the dentist and he's never heard of you."

Sharpe glanced at the door of the drawing room. Thornton Astley had gone back to his study, and there were no servants lurking around. "All right, but please don't say anything to Mr. Astley. I don't want to lose my position."

"We'll not tell your employer any more than absolutely necessary," the inspector assured the young man. "Now, where were you on Tuesday afternoon?"

"I was walking." Sharpe shrugged. "You see, I'd told Mr. Astley that I had to go and see about my tooth. But that wasn't the truth. I've been thinking about changing my life, sir. I may have an opportunity to emigrate, and

I had a great deal of thinking to do. I needed to get out of the house. So I asked Mr. Astley for the afternoon off and went for a walk. Generally I work till half past five or six o'clock, but that day, I left at four-thirty."

"Did anyone see you?" Barnes asked. "I mean anyone who knows you."

"No. I'm afraid not."

Witherspoon didn't see much point in questioning the man further. Neville Sharpe had no reason to murder William Barrett. He barely knew the man. "All right, Mr. Sharpe. That's all for now."

"You'll not say anything to Mr. Astley?" Sharpe said anxiously. "I've decided not to leave England, and I really would hate to lose this position. He wouldn't take kindly to the fact that I'd lied to get the afternoon off on Tuesday."

The inspector smiled. "We've no reason to report your activities to Mr. Astley. I understand you found some evidence that purports to show that Mr. Barrett hadn't been stealing from Mr. Astley?"

"You mean taking money out of the business." Sharpe nodded. "Yes, I did."

"Exactly what did you find?"

"Invoices," Sharpe replied. "Invoices that showed the money we thought Barrett had skimmed into his own account had actually been paid for goods and services the company received. Not many of them, mind you. But enough to cast doubt on our assertion that Barrett was using that method to steal from the company."

"And when did you find these invoices?"

"Tuesday morning. I showed them to Mr. Astley right away."

Witherspoon and Barnes left shortly after their interviews. Barnes waited till they were out of the house before asking any questions. "What do you think of Astley's story?"

The inspector sighed. "I don't know what to make of it. He admits he was in the Barrett house."

"But we know that Barrett was alive at six o'clock," Barnes reminded him. "One of the carpenter's heard his voice. But Astley claims he was dead by then."

"Yes, it is a puzzle." The inspector didn't know what to think. He was dreadfully hungry, his head hurt and his knee was throbbing. Perhaps he'd wait until after dinner tonight and then sit down and have a good think about the whole matter.

"I say, Mrs. Jeffries, have you had any luck in finding us a temporary cook?" Witherspoon gazed at her hopefully.

"No, sir." Mrs. Jeffries sighed. "I'm afraid not. The agency is doing their very best, but the earliest they think they can find someone is next week."

"Next week!" The inspector cringed. He looked down at his plate. He really did hate to criticize. Betsy had done her best and actually, if you drank a lot of water and ate fast, the meal wasn't too bad. The joint *was* a bit salty of course, and the roast potatoes perhaps just a little hard. Of course, boiled cabbage had never been one of his favourites, so he really couldn't blame Betsy because he didn't enjoy it. "Oh, well, I suppose if that's the best they can do, we'll just have to make do."

"How very understanding you are, sir."

Witherspoon reached for his water and took a huge gulp. "I'm very tired this evening," he said, putting the glass down. "I think I'll go straight up to bed. I didn't sleep well last night at all."

Mrs. Jeffries nodded sympathetically. She felt very badly for lying to the dear man, but it simply couldn't be helped. They couldn't afford to have a strange cook in the house when they were investigating a murder. "I expect it's because you've so much on your mind, sir. This is a dreadful business with the Barrett murder. It's a wonder to me you've been able to sleep at all. But then, sometimes I forget that you're not like the rest of us."

He gazed at her curiously. "Er, in what way?"

"Well, sir. Once you're on the trail, so to speak, that brilliant mind of yours probably works night and day. I shouldn't be surprised if you were working out the solution even while you were sleeping."

Witherspoon smiled modestly. "Really, Mrs. Jeffries, I'm not that different." But it was so very good to hear her say it. Sometimes he felt overwhelmed by his responsibilities. But just when it seemed as though he would never determine what had happened, something came along and the solution popped into his mind like magic.

"You're far too modest, sir." She took a sip of water. "How did you get along today? I bet you found out an enormous amount of information."

"Actually"—he took another drink of water. Gracious, he was thirsty this evening—"I did."

"I was sure you would, sir."

Witherspoon went on to tell her everything he'd learned. He found that talking with Mrs. Jeffries sometimes helped him to think clearly. She had a way of making comments and asking questions that sometimes opened a whole new line of inquiry.

"So I take it you didn't get a chance to talk to any of the workmen that were in the house?" she said when he'd finished.

"Not yet. But I'm doing just that first thing tomorrow morning." He paused and yawned widely. "I say, I really must get to bed."

"Why don't you do that, sir? A good night's rest will do you the world of good."

As soon as the inspector had gone up the stairs, Betsy and Mrs. Jeffries hurriedly cleared up and dashed downstairs. Smythe, Wiggins, Luty Belle and Hatchet were already there.

"I'm sorry about supper," Betsy said as soon as they were seated in the usual spots.

"Don't be apologizin' now, lass," Smythe said kindly, even though his throat was dry as a bone. "You fixed a right good meal." It was one thing to tease the girl about their investigatin', but he wouldn't hurt her feelins about her cookin' for the world. Women could be awful sensitive about things like that. And supper had been truly awful. His back teeth were still sore from chewin' on them roast potatoes. For once, he was glad he had money. If one of his dreams come true and he and Betsy ever did end up man and wife, he'd be able to afford a cook.

"That's nice of you to say, Smythe." Betsy looked down at the table. "But it was terrible. I saw the way you was all drinking water to choke down that salty joint. And roast potatoes is supposed to be soft inside, not hard as marbles."

Wiggins, started guiltily and put down his glass of water. "It were fine, Betsy," he lied.

"You did a very nice job." Mrs. Jeffries patted her on the hand. "Goodness knows, it was certainly better than anything I could have cooked."

"Seems to me that none of you can cook worth a hill of beans," Luty put in. "I'll bring something over tomorrow fer yer suppers. We don't want to spend the rest of the evenin' talkin' about yer stomachs, do we?"

Mrs. Jeffries nodded, delighted to be off the subject of food. If Mrs. Goodge didn't get back soon, they were going to starve to death. Even Wiggins, who had a lead-lined belly, hadn't been able to choke down much of Betsy's dinner. "Luty's right. We'd best get on with it." She quickly told them what she'd learned from the inspector over dinner. "So you see, at least one of our suspects admits to being in the house. But he claims that Barrett was already dead when he got there."

"That's odd," Hatchet remarked. "But I expect we'll sort it out eventually, we always do."

"I'll go next," Luty announced. She didn't want her butler stealing her thunder. She told them about her visit with Myrtle. "She said her friend was sure it was Eliza Washburn she saw on the Richmond Road. So she couldn't have been at home restin' if she was out wavin' down hansom cabs."

"Was she dressed in a cloak and veiled hat?" Smythe asked.

Luty shrugged. "Myrtle didn't know. She hadn't asked Henrietta what Eliza Washburn was wearin'."

"Then we don't know if she's the woman who took the cab to Kildare Gardens," Mrs. Jeffries mused.

"But we don't know that she wasn't," Luty insisted. "We do know that she wasn't home restin', though."

Luty didn't have any more to add. She turned and cocked her head, frowning at Hatchet. "Better let Hatchet go next. I know he found out somethin' today 'cause he was out all mornin' and when he come back he looked like a cat that had just stole the cream."

"I've never resembled a feline in my entire life," Hatchet sniffed. "But as it happens, I did find out something rather important today."

"Well, go on," Luty urged. "Don't keep us waitin'. We've not got all night, and I want to have plenty of time to hear what the others have found out."

"Honestly, madam, you're so impatient." Hatchet stopped and took a deep breath. "As you all know, I've a number of acquaintances throughout our fair city. As it happens, one of them has some very good connections into the Astley household. Well, I've found out that Maud Astley was trying to get her husband to drop the lawsuit against William Barrett because Barrett was blackmailing her."

"Blackmailin' 'er?" Smythe asked. "What for?"

Hatchet coughed. "Well, I'm not sure I should say in front of . . ." He looked at Wiggins and then Betsy.

"Oh, stop bein' such an old woman!" Luty exclaimed. "Betsy's and Wiggins's ears won't fall off if you tell us. They're both grown-ups."

Betsy giggled. Wiggins grinned.

"All right. Barrett was blackmailing Mrs. Astley because he'd found out she was having an illicit relationship with Neville Sharpe, Mr. Astley's secretary. Furthermore, he was in possession of some love letters that Sharpe had written to Mrs. Astley."

"How'd you find out?" Luty demanded. She was fit to be tied. Damn that old straitlaced butler of hers. He had sources all over the city, and all she had was old Tilbert and that gossipin' Myrtle.

"Never mind how I found out," Hatchet replied. "The point is, if it's true—and my source was certain it was—then it appears that both Maud Astley and Neville Sharpe had a reason to murder Barrett."

"And the inspector told me tonight that Sharpe wasn't at the dentist at the time of the murder," Mrs. Jeffries added. "Add to that the fact that Mrs. Astley was out in the garden the night before the murder, arguing with Barrett—"

"But lots of people was squabblin' with Barrett,"

Smythe cut in. "And you've aleady told us Mr. Astley admitted to goin' into Barrett's 'ouse. For all we know, he could be the killer."

"For all we know," Betsy said firmly, "half of bloomin' London could have killed him. Seems to me that everyone who knew him wanted him dead."

CHAPTER 9

Mrs. Jeffries pulled her shawl tighter and sat back in her comfortable armchair. She stared at the dying flames in the fireplace and sighed. This case was so muddled, she was almost beginning to think they'd never make heads nor tails of it. And everyone was trying so very hard too.

She shook herself, refusing to give in to defeat. They'd solve this one, just as they'd helped solve many others. The Barrett murder might be complicated, but someone had walked into that study and rammed a sword into the victim's heart. That someone had to have made a mistake, left some kind of clue.

She frowned slightly. There was something about the murder, something about the way the entire thing must have happened that seemed . . . She tried to think clearly, to grasp the elusive something or other that had been bothering her almost from the first. The murder seemed what? Cold? Calculating? Yes, that's it. That's what had been nagging at the back of her mind. This was no impulsive killing, there was something about it that smacked of deliberation.

A burning coal flared brightly, filling the quiet room with a crackling hiss. Mrs. Jeffries reached for the glass of water she'd had the foresight to bring with her before retiring and took a sip. Poor Betsy. She smiled. The girl had tried so hard to cook a good meal. But the best one could say was that it had been barely edible. Perhaps, she thought, one of the reasons we're having such a difficult time is because everyone's famished. It was difficult to think properly when one was hungry. But she had to think.

She closed her eyes and forced herself to go over each and every bit of information they'd acquired. First of all, how well did Lady Cannonberry really know Minerva Kenny? Ruth admitted that Minerva would rather die than have anyone suspect she was a thief. Perhaps she'd rather kill than die. Miss Kenny had been at the Barrett house on the afternoon of the murder. And she could have been the woman whom the painters had overheard crying in the drawing room. It was perfectly plausible that Minerva had come to plead with Barrett first, and when she found he couldn't be moved by her distress, she could have come back and killed him. She had the motive. Becoming known as a thief would ruin the woman.

But there were so many other possibilities as well, she admitted silently. Betsy was absolutely correct. It did seem as though half of London wanted Barrett dead.

And no one seemed to be telling the truth. She straightened as she heard the sound of footsteps from down the stairs. Then she heard the door of the water closet open, and she sank back in her chair. Poor Inspector Witherspoon, she thought with a rueful smile. He'd drunk so much water choking down Betsy's meal, he'd probably make several trips to the water closet before the night was out.

Mrs. Jeffries watched the bright embers grow dark. She really ought to get to bed herself, but she wasn't in the least tired. There was so much to sort out. Hatchet's source claimed that Maud Astley was having an affair with Neville Sharpe. Mrs. Astley was overheard arguing with Barrett the night before his murder, and the secretary wasn't at the dentist as he'd claimed. But did that add up to a motive for murder? And why kill Barrett? If Barrett was planning on exposing them, it seemed to Mrs. Jeffries that *if* either of the lovers was capable of murder, they'd have killed Thornton Astley. Then Maud would have been a rich, young widow and could have told Barrett to go to the devil. And, of course, she mustn't forget Adrian Spears or the Washburns.

She took another sip of water. Spears was a lonely bachelor, devoted to his dog. Barrett killed the dog. Mrs. Jeffries knew that that particular piece of brutality could have pushed Spears over the edge. And who better to know that the front and back door was wide open and that workmen were banging around on the third floor? Who better to know exactly when the servants would all be in the kitchen having their meal leaving Barrett alone in his study? Who better to know that even if Barrett cried out in alarm, the sound of hammering and sawing would cover his cries for help? Adrian Spears was in a perfect position to know all of this. Furthermore, he didn't have an alibi. The inspector had told her that none of the PCs had found anyone who'd seen Spears on his walk.

She yawned. The Washburns weren't in the clear, either. Luty's friend insisted that Eliza Washburn was out hailing a cab on the Richmond Road the afternoon of the killing. She'd claimed she was home asleep. The Richmond Road wasn't far from Kildare Gardens. "Hell hath no fury like a woman scorned"—the quote popped into her mind as she stared at the dying fire. No, Miss Washburn couldn't be counted out of the running. For that matter, neither could her brother. If she wasn't at home that afternoon, then she could hardly be an alibi for her brother.

She got up and stretched, thinking about the three hansom cabs. Minerva Kenny was in one, Thornton Astley was in another, but they didn't know for sure who was in the third. All they knew was that it was a woman. But which one? Maud Astley or Eliza Washburn? More important, was one of them the killer?

The smell of sizzling beef greeted Mrs. Jeffries when she came down to the kitchen the next morning. Startled, she stopped in her tracks and gaped. Smythe, a long fork in one hand and mug of tea in the other, was standing in front of the stove.

"Mornin', Mrs. J.," he called.

"Whatever are you doing?" She moved closer and peeked around his broad shoulders.

"Cookin' beefsteaks," he replied. "Thought I'd do us a fry-up for breakfast. I've got eggs to go with this lot."

"Wherever did you get beefsteaks? I know we'd none in the cooling pantry, and the butcher isn't due to deliver till this afternoon."

"Popped out myself early this mornin'," he replied, flipping a long, thin strip of beef.

"Smythe . . ." Mrs. Jeffries clucked her tongue. "You mustn't spend your own money on household food." She started back toward the door. "Let me go up and get the money you spent."

"No need for that," he said, expertly turning the last few strips. "It didn't cost all that much, and I don't mind doin' my bit to fill our stomachs."

She started to protest and then thought better of it. She was fairly certain Smythe had no shortage of coins, and he seemed to have a great need to give to them. But that was another matter for another time. One of these days the two of them would sit down and have a nice little chat. Perhaps they'd discuss all the mysterious presents that turned up for each and every one of them from time to time. Or perhaps they'd discuss those letters he kept getting from his bank. But all in good time. Right now they had to catch a murderer.

"Something smells good," Betsy said. She stopped short at the sight of the big, brawny coachman cooking their breakfast. "Are you cookin', then?" she asked incredulously. She dashed over and peered into the frying pan. "And it looks good."

"It will be good." He gave her a quick grin and then reached for a large brown egg. "Watch this." He broke the egg in one hand as he cracked it into another frying pan.

Betsy laughed. "You didn't even break the yolk."

"Don't be too impressed, lass," Smythe replied, reaching for another egg. "You've just about seen it all."

Betsy gazed at him speculatively. "Where'd you learn to do this?"

Mrs. Jeffries paused as she reached for the rose-and-white bone china teapot.

"Oh, picked it up 'ere and there." Smythe shrugged. "Lived for me own a while in Australia. Got hungry for somethin' besides salted beef and beer, so I learned to do fry-ups and all."

"Even a fry-up is better than I can do," Betsy admitted honestly.

"There's more to life than cookin'," he said. "You're good at other things."

"Right, like cleanin' the stairs or polishin' floors." She sounded morose. "Never met a man yet that wanted a clean house over a good meal."

Mrs. Jeffries watched this exchange with interest. Finally the two of them were actually getting around to talking about something important to both of them. She put the teapot down softly so as to not break the mood.

"Since when 'ave you been carin' about what men wants? You thinkin' of gettin' married?" he queried, his voice so low Mrs. Jeffries could barely hear him. She cocked her head to one side as she reached for a teacup.

"Well," Betsy said slowly. "Every girl wants to get married some day. Mind you, I'm in no hurry—and that's a good thing too, considerin' the way I cook."

"Now, don't be worryin' about yer cookin', lass," Smythe said eagerly. "There's plenty of men about that can afford to hire you someone like Mrs. Goodge."

"Cor blimey, what's that wonderful smell!" Wiggins yelled as he burst into the kitchen. Fred trotted right at his heels. They both rushed over to Smythe.

Betsy, a blush on her cheeks, quickly turned away and began pulling plates out of the cupboard.

Mrs. Jeffries sighed and finished making the inspector's tray. "I'll take the tray up now," she called to Smythe. "Then I'll pop right back for the inspector's breakfast."

The inspector was sitting at the dining table. There were dark circles under his eyes, his face looked haggard, and his hair was mussed. "I'll just have a nice hot cup of tea this morning," he said to Mrs. Jeffries.

"Oh, but, sir"—she put his cup in front of him—"Smythe's doing a really nice breakfast."

"Smythe!" Witherspoon said, his voice horrified.

"Yes, sir—" she began, but he interrupted her.

"Oh, don't bother to bring me any," he said, grabbing

his cup and taking a huge gulp. "I've so much to do today I shan't have time for breakfast. No, indeed."

"But, sir—" she tried again.

"I really must be going!" Witherspoon stood up and took another quick gulp. "I'm sure Smythe will do an excellent breakfast, but I must be off." If the truth were known, it would take a whole regiment of the Queen's Guards to force him to eat anything *any* of them prepared. "I've got to talk to Barrett's banker and his solicitor, and then I must speak to the carpenters and the painters." He edged toward the door. "After that there's Miss Kenny and Mr. Spears to be interviewed again."

He broke into a trot, snatched up his coat and hat as he flew past the coatrack and charged for the front door.

"But, sir!" she yelled. "I'm sure it will be good this time."

Witherspoon flung the front door open. "My compliments to Smythe. I'm certain his culinary skills are excellent." He shuddered. "I'll pop back this afternoon for tea and you can tell me all about it."

"Don't forget Luty's bringing dinner tonight," she called out as he ran down the stairs. "It's a nice Mexican recipe."

But her dear inspector had disappeared.

Mrs. Jeffries washed the last of the dishes and put them in the wooden rack to drain. She'd dry them later if she had time. Everyone was in a much better frame of mind this morning. It showed what a good meal could do for one's disposition. Smythe's breakfast had been very good. Very good, indeed.

Now everyone was out gathering clues and digging up information. Smythe had gone off on some mysterious errand he refused to discuss with them. Betsy had gone

over to the Washburn house to see what she could learn
about Eliza Washburn's movements on the day of the
murder, and Wiggins had gone back to Kildare Gardens.

She'd no idea what Luty and Hatchet were up to. But
she had every confidence in their ability to turn up
something interesting. Mrs. Jeffries took off her apron. As
she didn't have to worry about what they were going to
eat for supper tonight, she was going out to do some
snooping of her own. It hadn't really been quite fair, this
case. She'd spent far too much time inside instead of out
and about as she usually did when they were on the hunt.

"Hello, hello," Ruth's voice called from the back door.

Mrs. Jeffries sighed. Much as she liked Lady Cannonberry, she really didn't have time this morning to chat.
"Hello, Ruth," she replied.

"I do hope I'm not interrupting," Ruth said as she
sailed into the kitchen. "But I've found out something
and I thought you ought to hear it straight away."

"Well, I was just on my way out," Mrs. Jeffries explained.

"This won't take long." She headed for the kitchen
table, her dark pink skirts rustling as she sat down. "And
it is important." Her blue eyes sparkled and her cheeks
were flushed with excitement.

Mrs. Jeffries stifled a groan. Lady Cannonberry had no
doubt been out snooping again. Now what was it! The
dear woman tried so very hard, but really, she'd turned
up absolutely nothing of any use. Not that any of them
would ever bring that fact to her notice, of course. But
Mrs. Jeffries was worried that her friend would get so
carried away she'd give them all away. Indiscreet questions were sometimes noticed. "I'm sure it is. Now, tell
me what you've learned."

"First of all, I must say I think the inspector has been

far too harsh to Minerva." Ruth paused. "Not that I'm accusing him of brutality."

"Brutality? The inspector?"

"I didn't mean that, exactly." Ruth frowned slightly. "It's just that Minerva's in an awful state. She's sure Inspector Witherspoon is getting ready to arrest her. Can't we do something about that?"

"Ruth," Mrs. Jeffries said gently. "I know you're concerned with your friend, but this is a murder investigation. Inspector Witherspoon is only doing his duty."

"Yes, of course he is and I'm sure he was a perfect gentleman towards Minerva." She shook her head ruefully. "But she's a bundle of nerves. Especially since the inspector almost caught her putting that wretched china bird back yesterday."

"We heard about that." Mrs. Jeffries glanced at the clock and drummed her fingers impatiently on the tabletop. "But even if he did see her putting it back, it doesn't necessarily follow that he's going to arrest her for murder."

"Of course, you're right. In any case, Minerva's been nervous for days now," Ruth said thoughtfully.

"Unfortunately her habit of . . . er . . . 'borrowing' things seems to be having a rather horrid effect on the poor woman," Mrs. Jeffries replied. "Perhaps it's all to the good, though. Barrett's catching her may help her to overcome this odd compulsion of hers."

"I certainly hope so." Ruth pursed her lips. "Mind you, I'm not altogether sure she can help herself. Do you know, she told me she was so angry that Barrett was screaming at her that day she stole some of his papers. Served him right, if you ask me—he actually struck her!"

Mrs. Jeffries stared at her, her mouth slightly agape. "Day? What day are you talking about?"

Ruth blinked. "Why, the day of the murder, of course."

"The day of the murder!" Mrs. Jeffries gasped. "You mean she told you she was there?" Gracious, sometimes dealing with Lady Cannonberry would try the patience of a saint. She should have given them this information immediately.

"Oh, yes, late yesterday afternoon after the inspector told her she'd been seen going into the Barrett house, she broke down and admitted to me she was there," Ruth explained. "But she didn't kill him. She only went there to plead with him to give her the bird back. She was most upset, but he didn't care. He actually took it out of his desk and began taunting her, called her a sticky-fingered thief and other horrible names. Some of them were so awful Minerva couldn't bring herself to repeat them to me."

"How dreadful for her. Do please go on," Mrs. Jeffries urged.

"Well, Minerva got so angry at Barrett, she tried to snatch the bird away, and in the process she knocked some papers off his desk." Ruth snorted. "But he, being no gentleman, got furious. He slapped her hand and called her a clumsy cow. Can you believe it? That dreadful man. It's no wonder someone murdered him."

"And then what happened?" Mrs. Jeffries prompted.

"Then one of the workmen accidentally banged into the door with a length of wood and that set Barrett off again." Ruth leaned forward. "He got up and flung open the door to scream at the workman and Minerva was so angry, she picked up some of the papers she'd knocked on the floor and stuffed them into her pocket. Then she left."

"Why didn't she take the bird?" Mrs. Jeffries asked curiously.

"He had it in his hand."

"Oh, I see. What kind of papers were they?"

"Nothing very interesting," Ruth replied. "Just some letters to a bank."

"Did Minerva open the letters?"

"Of course not." Ruth sounded genuinely shocked by such a question. "Minerva would never open someone else's letters."

"What time was she there?" Mrs. Jeffries asked.

"She wasn't quite sure," Ruth replied. "As I said, she was in a state. But she thinks it was sometime close to five o'clock."

Witherspoon hid a yawn behind his hand. He was dreadfully tired. He'd gotten no sleep at all last night. All those trips to the water closet. Well, tonight he could look forward to a good dinner. Luty Belle Crookshank's cook was one of the best in London. Thank goodness Mrs. Crookshank had taken pity on their plight. It was really a shame Mrs. Jeffries was having such difficulties finding a cook.

"This is Ted Metcalf and Eric Honts." Barnes nodded at the two men he'd brought to the inspector's desk.

"Do sit down," Witherspoon indicated the chair by his desk. "Constable, if you'd be so good as to pull up another chair."

As soon as the two carpenters were seated, Witherspoon said, "I'm sorry to bring you down here. I realize you've already made statements, but I've a few more questions to ask."

"It's all right," Metcalf, a tall, morose-looking man with thin brown hair and a pockmarked face, replied. "We weren't out on a job today. But I don't know what

else we can tell you. We didn't see nothin' when old
Barrett got himself murdered.''

Honts snorted. ''Didn't see nuthin' and don't know nuthin', so I don't know why you've made us waste our
time comin' down 'ere.''

The inspector looked at Honts. He was a short, blond
wiry man with deepset hazel eyes and a ruddy complexion. ''Both of you were working on the third floor that
afternoon, is that correct?''

''Right,'' Metcalf replied. ''The painters were up there
too, gettin' in our way and makin' a nuisance of themselves.''

''Wasn't it odd that Mr. Barrett had carpenters and
painters working at the same time?''

Honts answered this time. '' 'E was in a 'urry. 'E was
wantin' to sell the 'ouse. It were right stupid, though.
Barrett didn't want to give us time to do a job properly.
We'd just get a room finished and 'e'd 'ave them ruddy
painters in doin' it up. You couldn't go back and try and
do any finishin' work, Barrett wouldn' stand fer it.''

Witherspoon, aside from being dreadfully hungry and
tired, was also confused. ''What makes you think that
Barrett was in a hurry to sell the house?'' The inspector
didn't think that could possibly be true. He'd spoken with
Barrett's solicitor this morning, and the man had categor-
ically denied any knowledge that William Barrett was
moving house. Yet the painters had told the inspector the
same story.

''We overheard him tellin' that Mr. Washburn he was
sellin','' Metcalf said. ''And I know it were true 'cause
he told Miss Washburn the same thing that very mornin'.''

''Miss Washburn?'' Witherspoon gasped. ''Are you
sure?''

"Sure I'm sure. She come that mornin'."

"How did you know who she was?" Witherspoon pressed.

"Barrett called 'er by name, now, didn't 'e," Metcalf said, his tone was exasperated as though he were explaining something to a dull-witted child. "I was standin' right at the top of the stairs when she come waltzing in the front door. 'E asked her what she were doin' there and she says, 'Is it true? Are you selling your house and leaving?' About then he caught sight of me, and he hustled her into the drawin' room."

"Gracious, why didn't you tell the police constables this?" Witherspoon asked.

"They didn't ask." Metcalf shrugged. "Besides, this were hours afore Barrett was killed."

"Did you hear anything else?"

"No, I went back upstairs to work."

"Tell 'im about what we overheard when he was talkin' to Mr. Washburn," Honts urged.

"You were eavesdropping on Mr. Barrett and Mr. Washburn?"

"Eavesdroppin'!" Metcalf laughed. "We didn't have to do that. Washburn and Barrett was yellin' at the top of their lungs about it. A deaf man could of heard them two goin' at it."

"When did this argument take place?"

Metcalf rubbed his chin. "Let's see now, I reckon it were a few days afore Barrett was killed."

"Nah," Honts corrected. "It were at least a week earlier. I remember because we was workin' on that south wall when it happened, and we finished that job at least ten days ago."

"I do wish you'd mentioned these facts when the police constable took your statements," Witherspoon remarked worriedly. This information was undoubtably important. Not that he could see why just at the moment, but it would come to him. He hoped.

"No one asked us," Metcalf said.

"All the peelers asked was what was we doin' at the time of the murder," Honts put in. "None of 'em asked us anything else."

Witherspoon nodded slowly. Mrs. Jeffries had indeed been correct; it was a good idea that he spoke to the workmen himself instead of relying on the PCs statements. "Is there anything else you can think of that might be important?"

Metcalf and Honts exchanged puzzled glances, as though they weren't used to being asked their opinions.

"Well, let's see," Metcalf muttered. "You know about the ruckus over Mr. Spears's dog? The stones and all?"

"That was the day before the murder," Honts corrected. "I remember 'cause it was the same day that painter pinched me hammer and then 'ad the gall to accuse me of stealin' his ruddy hat and coat."

"That's what I'm sayin', you bloody fool. You gone deaf or somethin'?" Metcalf glared at his friend. "I'm talkin' about the day before when Mr. Washburn was there and he and Mr. Barrett threw stones at Mr. Spears's dog."

"I know what you're talkin' about," Honts shot back, "and I'm only tryin' to 'elp keep things straight."

"You're just confusin' everythin'! If you'd keep quiet and let me finish—"

Witherspoon closed his eyes. He dearly would love a cup of tea. The two carpenters were now engaged in a heated debate on what had happened when.

"You've gone daft, man!" Metcalf yelled. "I know

when things happened, and your hammer went missin' the day before the murder.''

"I'm daft?" Honts cried. "You've not got enough sense to come in out of the rain . . . and I know bloody good and well when my tool got pinched.''

"Gentlemen, please!" Witherspoon shouted. They both fell silent. "Now, let's start over, shall we?"

"Is the inspector home yet?" Betsy asked as she put the finishing touches on the table.

"He's having a glass of sherry in the drawing room," Mrs. Jeffries replied. "The poor man is so worn out, I probably won't get much out of him until breakfast. He was too tired to talk, but I did learn a few things. Barrett was going to sell his house, and Owen Washburn and his sister knew about it. Eliza Washburn is the mysterious woman he was quarreling with in his drawing room."

"Eliza Washburn! She were the one? That's a surprise. I wonder what she wanted?"

"I don't know," Mrs. Jeffries admitted. "I'll see how much more information I can get out of the inspector after he's had a good night's sleep."

They heard voices and footsteps at the back door.

"Yoo-hoo, we're here!" Luty Belle yelled.

A moment later Luty, dressed in a bright blue aqua gown, a gigantic hat festooned with plumes and lace and a matching parasol, came into view. Hatchet was right behind her. He was carrying a huge black kettle.

"Good evening," Hatchet said.

"We've brought supper," Luty informed them gaily. "And wait till you taste it. I made it myself. Just put the pot down on the center of the table," she told Hatchet. "We can dish it up right out of the kettle. No need to be fancy."

"This is so kind of you, Luty," Mrs. Jeffries said. Like everyone else at the table, her eyes were on the food.

Hatchet lifted the lid. Everyone leaned closer to get a better look. The kitchen was filled with strange and exotic smells. Inside the kettle, chunks of meat swam in a bright red sauce. "I had to use my special spices," Luty informed them. "Lucky I went back home this past summer. I brung back a whole load of dried chili peppers. They keep real well."

"Except for those few spots you had to cut out," Hatchet said. His face was straight, but his eyes were twinkling. "I can't wait till our friends taste this dish, madam. I'm sure they'll devour every single morsel." He gave them all a wide grin. "Madam spent all afternoon working on this dish. Do enjoy it."

Wiggins's mouth gaped open. "Cor, look at that, it's red."

"It's a special recipe of mine," Luty said proudly. "Learned it from my neighbour back in Colorado. Rosa Herrera was one good cook. Mind you, Antoine's nose is out of joint, he don't like me shooin' him out of the kitchen. But I wanted to cook this myself."

"I'll just take a plate up to the inspector," Mrs. Jeffries said as she reached for a dinner plate. "The rest of you go on ahead and eat. We've much to talk about tonight."

Mrs. Jeffries left them dishing up Luty's feast and hurried up the stairs with the inspector's dinner on a tray. He met her in the hallway. "Is that my supper?" he asked hopefully.

"Yes, sir, Luty cooked it this afternoon and brought it right over." She hurried into the dining room, the inspector right behind her.

"I say." Witherspoon sniffed as Mrs. Jeffries removed

the silver cover on the plate. "That does smell unusual, rather nice, actually."

"It's a Mexican dish," Mrs. Jeffries replied. "And I'm sure it's very good. Admittedly, it does look strange to us, but that's only because we're not used to exotic food."

"Well, it smells delicious." Witherspoon lifted his fork and poked at a piece of beefsteak. "Is Mrs. Crookshank still here?"

"She's dining with the staff."

The inspector took a huge bite. He was so hungry.

"If you don't mind, sir . . . as Mrs. Crookshank so kindly brought our dinner—" She broke off in alarm. "Gracious, sir. Whatever is the matter?"

Witherspoon's eyes bulged, his cheeks ballooned out, and his face was as red as the sauce on his plate. "Mouth burning—water!" He lunged for his water glass.

"Oh, dear." Mrs. Jeffries closed her eyes briefly.

He gulped half a glass of water and choked. Mrs. Jeffries pounded him on the back.

He caught his breath and sighed. "How much longer do you think Mrs. Goodge will be gone?"

A few minutes later Mrs. Jeffries made her way back to the kitchen. Poor man. He really was in a quandary. He didn't wish to hurt Luty's feelings, but obviously that dish she'd brought was hot enough to blister his tongue. She'd left him scraping the sauce off the meat and gulping water between bites.

When she came into the kitchen, she noticed Hatchet grinning like a playful puppy as he watched the others struggle to eat without actually putting any food in their mouths.

Wiggins was gulping water, Smythe was trying to chew and hold his breath at the same time, and Betsy's cheeks were flaming. Luty, on the other hand, was eating heartily.

"Do sit down and have some," Hatchet said, giving Mrs. Jeffries an evil grin.

"Thank you, I'm sure it's excellent." Actually, she rather liked spicy food. Her late husband had been great friends with an Indian gentleman, and they'd often eaten at his table. She took a liberal portion of the stew.

"How'd ya like it?" Luty asked, beaming at everyone.

"It's very nice," Betsy muttered. She used the edge of her fork to cut her meat chunks into sections small enough to feed a mouse. "But I'm really not all that hungry tonight."

"Go on, eat up. Young woman's got to keep her strength up." Luty chuckled. "Especially when we're tryin' to solve a murder. What about you, Smythe? How's it taste?"

"Uh . . ." Smythe gave her a weak smile. "Real good, Luty. Ain't had a dish like this in years." Not since he'd been forced to eat fried lizards out on the Australian bush. But that had only been disgustin', it hadn't made his mouth feel like he was chewin' on hot coals.

Luty glanced at Wiggins. He was still gulping water. "Guess it's a bit hot fer ya, huh?"

"A little," Wiggins rasped.

Mrs. Jeffries took a small bite. Her tongue smarted slightly, but the flavour was really quite good. She chewed delicately. "Now," she said, "let's talk as we eat." That would give the others an excuse to slow down and, if they were very lucky, would distract Luty from noticing the real effect her food was having on everyone.

Betsy dropped her fork. "I'll go first."

"All right." Mrs. Jeffries nodded. "What did you find out today?"

"Uh, well . . . uh . . ." She deliberately stumbled over her words. No point in telling her news too quickly. She'd have to eat more of this god-awful stew if she did. "It's not much, really. But I talked to a greengrocer's boy over near where the Washburns live."

"And?" Mrs. Jeffries prompted.

Betsy shrugged slightly. "He didn't say much exceptin' that he had a delivery to make to the Washburn house. But when he knocked on the back door, no one answered."

"And what did you conclude?" Mrs. Jeffries wondered if she was going to have to drag information out of all of them. Gracious, they'd be here all night.

"I thought that maybe that meant that no one was home."

"I'm not so sure," Mrs. Jeffries said thoughtfully. "If you'll recall, Lady Cannonberry told us that there were rumours that Owen Washburn had been giving his sister sleeping draughts for her nerves. Maybe she was asleep? The servants were out and the cook was napping as well. Perhaps no one heard the lad knock."

"But what about Owen Washburn?" Betsy persisted. "He was supposed to be workin' in his study. And what about Eliza bein' seen hailing that hansom on the Richmond Road?"

Mrs. Jeffries didn't know what to think. "There is that. You do have a point. I think perhaps you ought to see what else you can find out about how the Washburns spent that afternoon." She turned to Luty. "Is your friend absolutely certain it was Eliza Washburn she saw that day?"

Luty nodded. "That's what she said. But I found out somethin' real interestin' about Mr. Owen Washburn. My friend Tilbert come by this afternoon when I was cookin'."

"When?" Hatchet scowled. "You never said a word to me."

"I don't tell you every little thing, now, do I?" Luty snapped. "Anyways, as I was sayin', Tilbert come by and he give me an earful."

"What did he say?" Mrs. Jeffries asked.

"Seems Owen Washburn wasn't just partnerin' with William Barrett. The truth is, Barrett was bankrollin' the whole kit and kaboodle. Paid the suppliers, paid the workers and the drivers and kept the creditors off Washburn's back."

"So now that Barrett's dead, what happens?" Mrs. Jeffries asked.

"Probably means that Washburn is straight out of luck," Luty replied. "With Barrett gone, the estate will probably cut off the money."

"Who does get his money?" Wiggins asked. At this point he didn't really care. But askin' questions was a good excuse not to keep stuffing his mouth with food that was so hot it was growing blisters on his tonsils.

"The inspector said the bulk of the estate goes to some cousin that lives abroad," Mrs. Jeffries replied. That was one of the more interesting things she'd learned while the inspector sipped his sherry. "The rest of the estate goes to charity."

"Charity!" Betsy cried. "That don't sound like William Barrett."

"One must do something with one's money." Mrs. Jeffries shrugged. "Perhaps that was his way of trying to make up for all the grief he'd caused during his life."

"So if the money gets cut off . . ." Smythe mused.

"But we don't know for certain that it does," Luty interrupted. "Lots of businesses have survivorship clauses in their company contracts. That would mean that Washburn would still be entitled to whatever operating money Barrett had originally put into the business.''

"But if they didn't have such an agreement," Mrs. Jeffries said, "that means that even though Washburn and his sister might have hated Barrett, they would have no reason to kill him. Barrett was more useful to them alive than dead.''

CHAPTER 10

Witherspoon didn't know how much more of this he could stand. He felt worse this morning than he had yesterday. His clutched his stomach as he trudged down the stairs to the dining room and tried not to think about food. He wasn't sure his digestive system would ever recover, but he was sure the roof of his mouth was still raw. Gracious, did people actually enjoy such spicy food? He couldn't believe it. Though it had been kind of Mrs. Crookshank to provide them with a meal, he hoped she wouldn't do it again.

He stopped by the dining room door, steeled himself and went inside.

"Good morning, sir," Mrs. Jeffries said cheerfully. "I hope you slept well."

"Actually, I didn't," he admitted honestly, his gaze fixed on the table. He smiled in relief at what he saw. Lovely brown toast, coddled eggs and three rashers of bacon that looked absolutely perfect. "Goodness, *that* certainly looks good. Who did the honours this morning?" He hoped it hadn't been his housekeeper or Betsy.

"Smythe did," Mrs. Jeffries replied. "He spent some time in Australia living on his own, you know. He's quite a deft hand at cooking. Inspector, do you know that Luty told us the oddest thing last night."

Witherspoon yanked out his chair, sat down and dug right into his meal. "What?" he mumbled around a mouthful of egg. He closed his eyes in pleasure as the first bite slipped down his throat. It was wonderful, delicious. Not overcooked, oversalted or overspiced. Thank God.

"You know how she admires you, sir." Mrs. Jeffries raised her voice. The inspector was eating so intently she wanted to make sure he could hear her. "She follows all your cases. Well, naturally we mentioned this current case and do you know, she'd actually heard of William Barrett." She paused to see if he would react. But he didn't, he merely bobbed his head and spooned another bite of egg into his mouth.

"Of course," she continued, "we didn't say a word about the investigation itself, but as we chatted, it came out that a friend of Luty's knew quite a bit about Barrett's business dealings. This friend, I believe he's retired from the City, told Luty that Barrett wasn't just Owen Washburn's partner, he was actually providing the cash to keep the company going."

"How very interesting," Witherspoon replied. "Except for one thing: Washburn claims he was going to buy Barrett out."

"Do you think it's possible Washburn is lying?"

He took a sip of tea. "It's possible. Perhaps I should look into it further."

Relieved, for that's precisely what she wanted him to do, Mrs. Jeffries poured herself a cup of tea from the pot and sat down in her usual place. She had many items she needed to cover, and she had to be very careful of what she said. Oh, yes, indeed, she must take care, but by the time he was through with breakfast, she'd make sure he had a flea in his ear about a number of things in this case. Inspector Witherspoon was going to have a very busy day. Last night's meeting had turned up several intriguing possibilities.

Smythe walked toward his bank, frowning irritably with every step. That bloomin' Pike, 'avin' the nerve to keep pesterin' a body with them stupid letters! Another one had arrived with the first morning post, and luckily, he'd been in the hall when it had dropped through the letter box. He was goin' to have a few words to say to that ruddy banker when he saw him. Bloomin' Ada, he'd told the man he'd come in next week. That shoulda been good enough. But no, the silly old git had written him two letters remindin' him. Well, he'd soon put a stop to it. He wasn't goin' to let money run his life, and he wasn't goin' to let some banker do it either.

He reached the front door of the bank and pushed it open. Across the lobby Pike was sitting at his desk. As though he had a sixth sense, he looked up at that precise moment. Smythe paused in the open door and glared at him. The banker gave him a thin smile in return.

"Out of my bloody way!" an angry shout came from the street behind him. Smythe turned his head to see what was goin' on. A four-wheeler, with a driver screaming his head off, was caught behind a slow-moving dray. Smythe grinned as the driver of the dray wagon made a rude gesture at the driver of the wheeler. "I said to get that bloody thing outa the way!" the wheeler screeched at the top of his lungs. "Or I'll move it for ya."

"You and what army?" the dray shouted back.

Sounded like a right old tussle was startin'.

Smythe's smile faded as he saw a familiar figure walking on the other side of the dray. His eyes narrowed. Now, what was he doin' here? He watched the man hurry toward the end of the street and then turn the corner.

Smythe hesitated only a moment, shoved out the doorway and let it bang shut behind him. He leapt down the stone stairs and almost collided with a woman. "Sorry, ma'am," he mumbled, trying to dodge around her wide girth.

"I should hope so," she snapped.

"Mr. Smythe, Mr. Smythe!" Pike shouted from the door. "Aren't you coming in?"

"Later!" he yelled as he ran toward the corner where Owen Washburn had disappeared. He could still hear the banker blustering as he rounded the corner. Washburn was just disappearing into a bank.

It was a bigger, fancier bank than the one Smythe used. His footsteps pounded on the marble floors as he crossed the wide foyer. Several clerks looked up and he slowed down.

At the far window Owen Washburn was talking with an older man. Smythe reckoned he must be the manager. He was as tight-lipped and disapprovin' lookin' as old Pike was.

"May I help you?" a young clerk asked, leaning out of his cage.

"Uh, I'm thinkin' about openin' an account here," Smythe replied quickly. He didn't want some clerk tossin' him out before he could see what Washburn was up to.

The clerk sniffed. "A deposit account?" His tone implied he didn't believe Smythe even knew what a deposit account was, let alone have the money to open one.

Smythe nodded. "Right." Out of the corner of his eyes,

he saw Washburn and the bank manager chattin' away like they was mates.

"There are some forms you'll need to fill out," the clerk said, looking down his nose. "Will you need help?"

"Why should I need any bloody 'elp?"

"I meant do you need assistance reading them?"

Smythe yanked a pouch of money and a roll of notes out of his pocket. The coins jingled as he slapped it right under the clerk's nose. "I can read and write, ya silly git. Now get me the forms."

The clerk at the next window snickered as the first clerk turned a bright red. "Yes, sir."

Smythe turned his attention back to Washburn while the clerk fumbled with some papers on the other side of his cage.

The bank manager had disappeared. Washburn was just sitting there, but his spine was as rigid as a post, and even from this distance, Smythe could see the way he was fidgetin' with his hands.

"Here you are, sir." The clerk shoved some papers toward Smythe. "And please accept my apologies, I didn't mean to imply—"

"I know exactly what you meant me to think," he snapped, incensed on behalf of working people everywhere. Just because you weren't dressed in a ruddy gent's suit, people thought they could treat you like dirt. "I'll take 'em over there to fill out." Smythe jerked his head toward the other side of the bank. There was a long wooden waist-high partition separating the public from the employees. It was a much better spot to watch Washburn. "Don't like people lookin' over my shoulder."

"Bring them back here when you're through, sir," the clerk said nervously.

Smythe walked across to the partition, put the forms on

the top and pretended to read them. From this vantage point, even with his head down he could see what was happening. Washburn and the manager was no more than fifteen feet away from him. He cocked his ear to one side, hoping to hear a snatch of their conversation.

The bank manager reappeared and handed a thick, flat canvas bag to Washburn. They talked a few seconds longer, but Smythe couldn't hear what they was sayin'. Finally Washburn took the bag and left. Smythe waited a few seconds and then followed him out. He left the papers sitting on the partition.

"Sir, Mrs. Astley is here to see you," Barnes said to Witherspoon. "She's just outside. Should I bring her in now?"

The inspector looked up from the statements he was going over for the tenth time. "Mrs. Astley? Here?"

"Right, sir." Barnes shrugged. "She won't tell me what she wants. Insists on seein' you."

"Bring her right in, Constable." Witherspoon hastily began trying to tidy his desk. "And pull up another chair for yourself."

Maud Astley, followed by Constable Barnes, marched down the aisle to Witherspoon's desk. "Good morning, Inspector," she said politely. "I'd like to speak with you, please."

"Please have a seat, Mrs. Astley." He gestured at the chair beside his desk. "What is it you'd like to speak to me about?" he asked as soon as she was comfortable.

She fumbled with the handle of her umbrella. "I'm not quite sure how to begin," she said, her voice low and hesitant. "My coming here seems so disloyal."

"I take it what you have to say has something to do with Barrett's murder?"

She nodded and gazed down at the floor. "This is so difficult. But I really felt I had to come. My conscience simply wouldn't let me keep silent."

"Please, Mrs. Astley." Witherspoon didn't wish to press the woman, but he had so much to do today. Ever since breakfast he'd had so many new ideas about the case, and he wanted to get on with his inquiries before he forgot them all. "Just tell me what you think I ought to know."

Mrs. Astley took a deep breath, lifted her lovely chin and looked him squarely in the eye. "It's about Minerva Kenny. She's a very dear lady and a very good friend, but I happen to know she went to see William Barrett on the day he died."

"We're aware of that," the inspector replied. "May I ask how you found out?"

She looked surprised by his statement, but she caught herself quickly. "I found out from Adrian Spears. He came to see me yesterday after you'd spoken with him. He mentioned he'd seen her going into Barrett's home."

"I see." Witherspoon frowned slightly. "But if you knew Mr. Spears had already given us this information, why did you bother to come in?"

"Because there's something else you should know." She bit her lip. "It's about Minerva, Miss Kenny."

"What about her?"

"She had a good reason to dislike William Barrett. Actually, I think she hated him."

"Mr. Spears told us that as well," the inspector said. "But he declined to tell us what that reason might be. Will you tell me?" He was fairly certain she would; otherwise, she wouldn't have bothered to come all the way down here.

"She hated him because he'd found out that

she . . . she . . . takes things. Knowing Barrett, he was probably threatening to expose her. Minerva would be ruined socially.''

Witherspoon gaped at her. "Takes things? What kind of things?''

"Oh''—she shook her head—''I'm not explaining this right. We've all known about Minerva, at least the women have, for some time. Females tend to be a bit more observant than men in these kinds of circumstances. In any case, Minerva has a . . . problem. Actually, it's more like an affliction. She'll go into someone's home and see some trinket or knickknack she likes, and she'll put it in her pocket and take it home. But she always puts them back. As I said, several of her friends have known about her little habit. We've just looked the other way because it seemed such a harmless, childish thing to do.'' Mrs. Astley sighed. "But perhaps we should have said something to her, made her realize what she was doing. Maybe William Barrett would still be alive if all Minerva's friends hadn't looked the other way.''

"Are you suggesting that Miss Kenny murdered William Barrett?'' Witherspoon asked. His expression was grave and his voice somber. This was a most serious charge. He didn't like to think a gentle lady could be capable of murder, but he'd learned that the mildest of countenances could hide the most diabolical of hearts.

"I don't know what to think,'' Mrs. Astley murmured. "But I know that Barrett had found out Minerva was pinching things.''

"How do you know?'' Before he accused anyone of anything, the inspector was determined to have all his facts right.

"Because he told me himself. He told me he'd caught her in the act.'' Her cheeks flushed with embarrassment.

"Minerva had tried to put back the bird she'd taken from our drawing room last week. Barrett caught her. I think he was tormenting her in some way. She's been dreadfully upset and very nervous ever since. When we were having tea at Mr. Spears's house, I tried asking her what was wrong, but she pretended everything was fine. Minerva tends to live in a dream world. It's as though as long as she pretends everything is all right, then it is."

"Why did Mr. Barrett choose to confide in you?" Barnes asked quietly.

"He didn't choose to confide in me," Mrs. Astley declared. "We were having a dreadful argument, and during the course of that argument, he lost his temper and it slipped out."

"You were arguing about Miss Kenny?"

"Yes," Mrs. Astley replied firmly. "I suspected that Barrett was the reason for Minerva's nerves, so I confronted him."

"When did this argument take place?"

"The night before he was killed. I ran into him out in the gardens."

Drat, thought the inspector, that was one of the inquiries he was going to make today. Well, he wasn't going to inquire specifically about Mrs. Astley, but he had been planning on going back to Kildare Gardens and asking the servants if they'd seen or heard anything about Mr. Barrett in the weeks or days preceeding the murder. That idea had occurred to him while he was chatting with his housekeeper this morning. "And that's when he admitted he'd found out about Miss Kenny's . . . uh . . . activities."

"He admitted that he was tormenting her, Inspector." Mrs. Astley's pink lips curled in disgust. "Our exchange became quite heated. Mr. Barrett hated women. He was delighted that he'd found something out about Minerva that could put her in his power. I told him I didn't care about a silly piece of china, but he said what I thought didn't matter. He said that when he got through, there wouldn't be a decent house in London that would accept Minerva socially.''

"Do you think that Miss Kenny killed him?'' The inspector watched Mrs. Astley carefully. After all, as Barrett was dead, they had no one to corroborate her statement. For all he knew, she could be making the whole episode up.

"I don't know what to think.'' She clasped her hands together. "Minerva is a dear woman, a delightful person. I don't like to think she's capable of such a brutal crime. But she was there and she did have a reason for wanting him dead. He was going to ruin her. I don't think she could have stood that. Her social standing is very important to her.''

"Why, Inspector,'' Mrs. Jeffries said, "I didn't expect you home for lunch.''

"I hadn't planned on coming home,'' he said, "but as I was in the neighbourhood, I thought I'd pop in for a cup of tea.'' He was dreadfully tired, he really wanted to take a bit of a rest, and he could hardly do that at the police canteen. Besides, their food was almost as dreadful as what he'd been eating here.

Mrs. Jeffries forced herself to smile. Oh, bother, she thought. How much worse could today get? There wasn't a thing to eat, Lady Cannonberry would probably pop in any minute with those apple fritters she'd promised, and she'd run smack into the inspector. "It's quite a lovely day, sir,'' she said enthusiastically. "Why don't you have a seat outside in the garden and I'll bring you out a pot of tea. Are you sure that'll be enough? Would you like some bread and butter?'' She prayed he'd decline; they had exactly two slices of bread left.

Witherspoon smiled gratefully. A pot of tea and a short snooze in the sun—what could be better? ''That's quite a good idea. It is unseasonably warm today, and I might as well take advantage of it. Just tea will be fine, Mrs. Jeffries. I've been having a slight problem with my stomach, so I don't really want anything to eat.'' He started down the hallway and suddenly stopped. ''By the way, I don't suppose the agency's had any luck finding us a cook?''

''I'm afraid not, sir.''

He sighed softly. ''Right. Well, I expect they're doing their best. Oh, yes, before I forget, Constable Barnes is calling in for me at one-thirty. Do give me a shout when he comes.''

''Yes, sir.'' Mrs. Jeffries hurriedly brewed a pot of tea. She prayed that if Lady Cannonberry took it into her head to bring those fritters over now, she'd be very careful what she said in front of the inspector.

Ten minutes later Mrs. Jeffries picked up the loaded tray and walked out into the November sunshine. Balancing herself carefully, she shouldered the back door open and stepped outside. She gasped in shock at what she saw.

Inspector Witherspoon was bent forward, his chest and head flat on the table, eyes closed and arms splayed out to the sides.

''Inspector!'' she cried in alarm as she charged toward him. ''Inspector Witherspoon.''

''Hmmm . . . Whatdidya . . .'' He opened his eyes, saw his housekeeper running at him with a loaded tea tray and shot straight up in the chair. ''Good gracious, what is it, Mrs. Jeffries?''

''What is it?'' she repeated breathlessly. ''I thought you

were dead. You were lying on the table.''

"Oh . . . oh . . . I'm dreadfully sorry," he said, giving her an embarrassed smile. "I was so tired, I merely thought I'd rest my eyes for a few moments. I must have dozed off. Gracious, how silly of me. I didn't mean to frighten you."

"That's quite all right, sir." She took a deep breath and set the tray down. "I shouldn't have reacted as I did."

"It's all right, Mrs. Jeffries." He yawned. "I haven't been sleeping well and none of us have been eating—" He broke off as he realized what he'd almost said.

"Go ahead and say it, sir," she said. "None of us has been eating very well these days. It does take a toll on one's nerves."

"Breakfast was very good," he pointed out, not wanting her to feel bad about the situation. "So much so that I was actually able to get a lot of work done this morning. We've had a bit of luck in the case today. We found a neighbour who remembers seeing Minerva Kenny go into the Barrett house on the day of the murder."

"Really? Were they absolutely sure it was Miss Kenny going in?" she asked curiously.

"Oh, yes. They were sure it was her," the inspector replied. "And that's not the only corroboration we've had that she was there. Maud Astley came by and told me the reason Miss Kenny hated William Barrett. It's quite sad, really, the poor woman has a habit of—"

"Hello," Lady Cannonberry's cheerful voice rang out. "I do hope I'm not interrupting."

"Not at all, dear lady." Witherspoon gallantly rose to his feet. "I was just going to have some tea. Do join me."

Lady Cannonberry was holding a small cloth-covered basket in one hand. "Thank you, I'd be delighted." She handed the basket to the housekeeper. "Mrs. Jeffries told me about your cook being gone, so I made some apple fritters and brought them over. Perhaps you'd like some with your tea, Gerald.''

''I'll just go get another cup and some plates,'' Mrs. Jeffries said. She wondered how much Ruth had heard. The interruption couldn't have come at a worse time.

''Thank you, Mrs. Jeffries, that would be lovely.'' He turned to Lady Cannonberry. ''Apple fritters? I'm not sure what those are.''

She pulled the cloth back, and the tangy sweet smell of apples mingled with the crisp air. Dozens of dark brown, rather lumpy round objects lay nestled in the basket. ''It's an apple batter that's been deep fried,'' she explained, holding the basket out to Witherspoon. ''Do try one. I made them myself. A friend sent me the recipe from America.''

Witherspoon reached for one of the brown lumps; he hoped they tasted as good as they smelled. He took a big bite and almost choked as sticky raw batter filled his mouth.

''How are they?'' Lady Cannonberry asked eagerly.

''Mmmm,'' he mumbled. Gracious, did no one in London know how to cook?

''I'm so glad you like them.'' She smiled proudly. ''I wasn't sure how long to fry them, and I wasn't sure if the grease had gotten hot enough.''

Loathe to hurt her feelings, he managed to swallow what he had in his mouth. ''They're lovely,'' he stated, reaching for his teacup.

''Oh, Gerald, thank you. I wasn't sure they'd come out right at all. Cook was no help. I think she was quite put out that I was in the kitchen. But I did want to make these for you. Poor Mrs. Jeffries, she and the others seem to be trying so very hard. And cooking and baking is such hard work too.''

''Yes,'' he agreed hastily. ''They've been trying very hard.''

''Aren't you going to eat the rest of it?'' she asked, frowning at the half-eaten fritter in his hand.

''Oh, yes, yes, of course.'' Luckily, Mrs. Jeffries came back with the plates and serviettes.

''Here you are, sir,'' she said, ''but I'm afraid you won't have time to enjoy your fritters. Constable Barnes has just arrived. You're wanted back at the station.''

Witherspoon shot up from the chair. ''Then I must be off.''

''But, Gerald, you didn't get to drink your tea,'' Lady Cannonberry protested. ''And you didn't get to finish your fritter. Why don't you take it with you?''

''That's quite all right, I mustn't keep my superiors waiting.'' He started for the back door. ''I'm sure Mrs. Jeffries will save me some of those lovely fritters for after my supper tonight.'' The thought of eating another supper at Upper Edmonton Gardens made him stop in his tracks. ''Lady Cannonberry, would you do me the honour of accompanying me to dinner tonight? As you so kindly brought me those delightful, er . . . fritters, I would love to show my appreciation by taking you to Simpson's.''

Lady Cannonberry stared at him and then broke into a broad smile. ''I'd be delighted, Gerald.''

''Excellent. I'll call 'round for you at half past seven.''

''I didn't learn a thing!'' Luty exclaimed as she popped down next to Betsy. They were gathered 'round the table at Upper Edmonton Gardens. Supper, such as it was, was over.

''Don't feel bad,'' Wiggins mumbled. ''I didn't learn

nuthin', either. I spent the whole bloomin' day watchin' the Washburn 'ouse, and the only thing that happened was Miss Washburn throwin' somethin' into the dustbin.''

Mrs. Jeffries glanced around the table. Everyone's spirits were low. It was this case. It simply didn't make sense. She knew there was something she was missing, something small and important and right under her nose. But for the life of her, she couldn't think what it was. ''Well, the inspector came home for tea today, and he told me that Maud Astley had let the cat out of the bag about Minerva Kenny. The police now know she takes things.''

''How'd Maud Astley find out?'' Luty demanded.

''I don't know. And I won't get a chance to ask the inspector until either later tonight or tomorrow. He came home so late he only had time to dress before he took Lady Cannonberry to supper.''

''It's lookin' bad for Miss Kenny, isn't it?'' Wiggins said.

Mrs. Jeffries wasn't sure. ''It could be,'' she said cautiously. ''Unfortunately, not only did Maud Astley tell the police about her problem, but one of the neighbours saw her going into Barrett's house that afternoon.''

''Do you think he's going to arrest her?'' Hatchet asked.

''I don't know. The inspector is always very, very careful before he makes an arrest.'' Mrs. Jeffries was at a loss. Half of London may have hated William Barrett, but half of London hadn't been seen going into his house right before the murder.

''What about Thornton Astley?'' Betsy asked. ''He were there too.''

''That's precisely why Mrs. Astley decided to betray her friend,'' Mrs. Jeffries replied. ''No doubt Adrian

Spears had told Mrs. Astley about seeing Miss Kenny that afternoon. As Thornton Astley was also seen going inside, I'm quite sure Maud Astley decided to throw the poor woman to the wolves in order to take suspicion off her husband.''

"So she provided the motive," Smythe muttered. "Clever. That's the one thing the police didn't have. As far as they knew, Minerva Kenny might not have liked Barrett, but she had no reason to want him dead.''

"I'm surprised she bothered," Betsy said. She pursed her lips. "After all, Maud Astley was carryin' on with that secretary.''

"That's over," Hatchet added. "Neville Sharpe gave notice. He's leaving Astley's employ and striking out for parts unknown.''

"How'd you find that out?" Luty demanded.

Hatchet smiled serenely. "I have my sources, madam, and though it pains me to say this, I did promise they'd remain anonymous.''

Mrs. Jeffries said, "Has anyone else learned anything today?" Her own investigations had been fruitless.

"I talked to the Spears's maid, Janie," Betsy said. "But she didn't know anything. She's right depressed, though, because the workers from Barrett's house are gone. She was sweet on one of the painters, and she's still feelin' real bad about the dog.''

"Why's she feelin' bad?" Wiggins asked. "It weren't her fault that Barrett took a hammer and bashed the poor thing's head in.''

" 'Cause she's the one that let him out in the first place. She left the door open when she run outside that day," Betsy explained. "She thought she saw David Simms out in the garden, and so she dashed out to have a word with him. But when she got out there, he'd disappeared.''

Hammer. Dog. Something tweaked the back of Mrs. Jeffries mind. She went still, trying to snatch the elusive idea and force it to stay long enough for her to examine it.

"Well, I didn't do any better than the rest of ya," Smythe admitted. "But I did see Owen Washburn today at the bank—" He stopped as he realized what he'd said. "I mean, I followed him to the bank. But he didn't do nothing but pick up a bag."

"Where did he go after that?" Mrs. Jeffries asked. The idea was coming closer. She hadn't gotten her hands on it yet, but it was almost there, she could feel it.

"Went to his company offices, stayed there a few minutes and then went on 'ome," the coachman replied. "I stayed a bit and watched, but 'e never come out again. I waited till it started to get dark."

"Gets dark so early these days," Betsy complained. "I just hate it."

"Too bad that the inspector didn't get a chance to find out if there was a survivorship agreement between Barrett and Washburn," Luty said thoughtfully.

"There wasn't," Hatchet said softly.

"Now how in the dickens do you know that?" Luty glared at her butler. This was too much. Did the old goat have a crystal ball!

"As I said before, madam, I have my sources." Hatchet couldn't suppress a smile. "But in the interests of fair play, I'll tell you how I know. I found out from Barrett's butler."

"How does Barrett's butler know?" Mrs. Jeffries asked quickly. Luty looked as though she wanted to strangle her butler.

"It's simple," Hatchet explained. "Hadley overheard Barrett and Washburn arguing over that issue. Barrett refused to put that clause in the contract. Washburn maintained that as he'd already had one partner die which had caused great financial hardship on the company, he thought it a good idea. He was willing to sign a survivorship clause, but Barrett wasn't.''

"How long ago did this argument take place?" Smythe asked.

"As well as Hadley could recall, he thinks it was about a week or ten days ago." Hatchet leaned back in his chair. "I gather it was quite a shouting match."

"The killer could be anybody," Betsy said glumly. "I don't think we're any closer to solvin' this one than we ever was. Nothin' makes sense, everyone who knew the victim hated him, and half of London was in or out of his house that afternoon."

"Yeah, anyone coulda stuck that sword in 'im," Wiggins agreed.

"No, they couldn't," Mrs. Jeffries said firmly. "This case is not impossible. This was no impulsive murder; it was well planned and well executed."

"Who did it, then? Do ya have an idea?" Luty asked.

"Yes," Mrs. Jeffries replied, "I've a very good idea. As a matter of fact, there's only one person who could have killed Barrett. One person who had the motive, the means and the opportunity."

"Who?" they all demanded at once.

But she shook her head. "Before I tell you the name, there's something that Wiggins and Smythe need to do."

"Just tell us what it is," Smythe said.

"I want you to go to the Washburns and search through the dustbin. If my theory is correct, you'll find a working-man's hat."

"You want us to go now?" Wiggins yelped. "At this time o' night?"

"Come on, lad, I'll be with ya." The coachman was already getting to his feet. "I reckon we should be back in less than an hour."

"We'll be waiting right here," Mrs. Jeffries assured them.

"I hate it when they go out at night," Betsy said as soon as Smythe was safely out of earshot. "It's always a bit of a worry."

"Don't worry," Mrs. Jeffries said reassuringly. "Smythe can take care of himself, and for that matter, Wiggins has a good head on his shoulders. They'll be fine. Now, who's for more tea? We've got some of Lady Cannonberry's apple fritters to go with it."

"Be quiet," Smythe hissed. "You're makin' enough noise to wake the dead." He eased around the hedge with Wiggins right on his heels. "Where's the bin?"

"It's right over there." Wiggins pointed at the side of the house. "I were standin' beside the 'edge, that's how come I saw her tossin' somethin' in it."

"Stay 'ere," Smythe ordered. "And if anyone come out, you take off runnin', you 'ear?"

"All right. But you be careful now. I'll stay 'ere and keep watch."

Smythe eased his way across the small lawn to the front of the house. Ducking down, he scurried along the paved walkway, keeping his head low so that anyone inside the front room wouldn't see him. He couldn't hear any voices, but that didn't mean the room was empty. As he reached the edge of the brick building, he stretched up and peeked in the corner of the window. The lamps were brightly lit, and there was a fire in the grate, but the room was empty.

Easing around the side of the building, he ducked to

avoid another window, slowed his steps and tiptoed to the bin.

The bin was metal and dented on one side. There was no cover on it. Smythe looked up to make sure there were no faces at the window of the house next door. All they had to do was glance out and he'd be done for. But he saw no one.

He struck a match and held it over the bin. Inside, there were some tins, a half empty bottle of Sainsbury's Lavender Water, old newspapers and sticking out from beneath the side of one of the newspapers, a dark patch of something. Smythe stuck his hand inside and pulled out a flat wool working man's cap. He shook his head, grinned and shoved the cap in his pocket. That Mrs. Jeffries, she didn't half surprise him sometimes. Now how the bloody blue blazes did she know this cap was going to be right where she said it was?

"You'll have to take it back." Mrs. Jeffries instructed them after they'd all examined the cap.

"What—tonight?" Wiggins couldn't believe his ears. "But it's freezin' outside and I'm dead tired."

"We can take it back," Luty volunteered.

"No, that's all right," Smythe said quickly. "I don't mind goin', and the lad can stay here. It won't take two of us."

"I'm afraid it must go back," Mrs. Jeffries said apologetically. "It'll only be useful as evidence if the inspector finds it in the Washburn dustbin."

"Was it Eliza Washburn that killed him?" Luty asked hopefully.

"Oh, no, Luty." Mrs. Jeffries shook her head. "It

wasn't Eliza Washburn. It was her brother, Owen. But we're going to have a very difficult time getting the inspector to arrest the right person without exposing our part in the case. Very difficult indeed.''

CHAPTER 11

Mrs. Jeffries was suddenly very unsure. What if she were wrong? There could be another reason that cap was in the Washburn dustbin. No, she shook herself slightly, there couldn't. Given everything they'd learned, there was only one possible conclusion.

"Luty, do you think I can borrow Antoine tomorrow morning?" Mrs. Jeffries asked. "It's imperative we keep Inspector Witherspoon here as long as possible in the morning."

Luty, who was putting on her coat, gave her a curious stare. "Sure. I don't reckon Antoine will mind."

Mrs. Jeffries nodded her thanks and turned to Smythe. "How long do you think it will take you to get that cap back to the Washburns?"

"I should be there and back in less than an 'our."

"Owen Washburn," Hatchet murmured. "Whyever do you think he killed Barrett?"

"I'll tell you everything tomorrow," Mrs. Jeffries promised. "It will take far too long to make sense of it tonight, and I've got to go out."

"Go out!" Betsy and Smythe cried at the same time.

"Yes, yes." She brushed their concern aside. "I know what you're going to say, but I must speak with Lady Cannonberry before she retires for the night."

"Why don't I have Hatchet stay and go with ya?" Luty suggested.

"I'll do it," Wiggins said. "Hatchet's got to see you get home safely."

Luty patted her fur muff. "Long as I got my peace-maker, here"—she patted the muff again—"I don't much worry about bein' bothered none."

There was a collective groan. Luty carried a Colt .45 in her muff. They were all sure that one day she'd accidentally shoot herself, or even worse, one of them.

"Really, madam," Hatchet said frostily. "This is not the American West. There is absolutely no need to carry a firearm in a civilized city like London."

"Wiggins can escort me to Lady Cannonberry's," Mrs. Jeffries said quickly. "Tomorrow, however, I may need your help. Do you think you can stay when you bring Antoine over?"

"Wild horses wouldn't get me outa here," Luty said. "You know I like to be in on things at the end. If the inspector arrests Washburn, I want to be right here where I can git all the juicy details. What time do ya want us here?"

"Early, by seven if possible." Mrs. Jeffries filled them in on a few more details, and then they left. Smythe left right behind them. Betsy turned to Mrs. Jeffries and asked, "Do you want me to go with you to Lady Cannonberry's?"

"No, you'll need to stay here in case the inspector needs something. He would get very suspicious if no one in the household were here."

*   *   *

Wiggins and Mrs. Jeffries hid in the shadows outside of Lady Cannonberry's big three-story house at the end of Upper Edmonton Gardens. Flattened against the side passageway leading to her back door, they had a good view of the street.

Mrs. Jeffries pulled her cloak tighter. The rustle of the fabric sounded unusually loud in the quiet night. Wiggins, who was sulking because she'd made him leave Fred at home, was hunched forward, his arms folded over his chest as he tried to stay warm.

" 'Ow much longer, do ya reckon?'' he asked, blowing on his stiff fingers.

"Not too much, I hope." Her feet were freezing.

They heard a hansom turn the corner. A moment later the hansom pulled up and Inspector Witherspoon emerged. A second after, Lady Cannonberry came out. Witherspoon took her arm and escorted her out of the range of their vision, up the steps and to the front door.

"Now," Mrs. Jeffries said to Wiggins. They both scampered quietly down the passageway to the gate leading to the communal garden.

Inside the gardens, Wiggins picked up a handful of small stones. They waited for what seemed an eternity and finally, a light on the second floor appeared. Mrs. Jeffries nodded at the footman. He tossed the first pebble toward the window. It bounced against the glass with a gentle *ping*.

They waited. Nothing happened.

" 'Cor blimey, do you think she's in there?''

"Try again."

Wiggins threw a second and then a third. Suddenly Ruth Cannonberry appeared at the window. Mrs. Jeffries waved her arms, hoping that in the faint moonlight the woman would recognize her.

Ruth stared at her for a moment and then threw open the window. "Hepzibah! What is it? Is everything all right?"

"Everything's fine," Mrs. Jeffries whispered loudly, "but do please come down, we must talk to you."

It was several moments before they saw the small back door opening. Ruth stepped outside, leaving the door open a crack. "Goodness, you gave me such a start. What is it?"

"I know who the murderer is," Mrs. Jeffries began, "but the only way to catch him without revealing our involvement in this case is for you to convince Minerva Kenny to bring that letter she took from Barrett's office to Inspector Witherspoon."

"Who is it?" Ruth asked eagerly.

"Owen Washburn, but it's going to be very difficult to prove."

"I'm not sure that Minerva will do it," Ruth murmured.

"She must," Mrs. Jeffries said bluntly. "If she doesn't, the inspector will arrest her for Barrett's murder. She's got to bring him that letter, and she must do it as early tomorrow morning as possible."

"I'll pop 'round and talk to her right after breakfast."

"That'll be too late," Mrs. Jeffries said. "You must talk to her at the crack of dawn. She must get that letter to Inspector Witherspoon before he finishes breakfast."

Betsy was anxiously pacing the kitchen when they got back. "What took you so long? The inspector's gone to bed."

"Good." Mrs. Jeffries took off her cloak and laid it on

the chair. "Wiggins, why don't you go on up to bed. Betsy and I will wait up for Smythe."

The footman looked doubtful. But blimey, he was cold and tired. There was no sense in all of 'em losin' sleep tonight. "All right, but you come wake me if'n Smythe don't get back soon."

As soon as he went upstairs, Mrs. Jeffries put on the kettle. She knew that Betsy wasn't going to budge from this kitchen until the coachman was safely home. They might as well have a cup of tea while they waited.

Five minutes later they were at the kitchen table, a mug of tea in front of them. Betsy kept glancing at the clock. Mrs. Jeffries smiled to herself. The girl's feelings for the coachman were as plain as the nose on her face, and his feelings were equally obvious.

"Do you think he'll be all right?" Betsy asked anxiously. "I mean, he knows how to take care of himself, so I don't think anything will happen to him."

"He can take excellent care of himself."

But Betsy was trying to convince herself, not the housekeeper. "For all his cock-o'-the-walk-ways, he's a sensible man. He'll not be takin' any silly chances when he puts that cap back."

"I'm sure he won't."

"But then again, it's a cold, dark night out there and anythin' can 'appen." She bit her lip and looked at the clock again.

She was dropping her 'h's. Mrs. Jeffries knew that was a bad sign. Betsy was really worried about Smythe. The kind of fear that a woman felt when the man she really cared about was doing something that could get him in a great deal of trouble.

"Don't fret, he'll be fine," she said firmly. "Now, don't you want to know how I figured it out?" That should keep the girl's mind occupied.

Betsy didn't even hear her. "Course Smythe is clever, and even if he were to get caught, which I'm sure won't 'appen, 'e'll talk his way past it."

Mrs. Jeffries gave up and sipped her tea. For the next hour Betsy watched the clock and paced the floor. Finally, when even the housekeeper began to be concerned, they heard the back door open.

"What took you so bloomin' long?" Betsy snapped the moment Smythe appeared.

"Easy, lass," he said quietly, "I had to do a bit a snoopin'."

"What happened?" Mrs. Jeffries asked.

Smythe sat down across from her and poured himself a cup of tea. "I put the cap back, all right, but we've got us a problem. One of the reasons I'm so late was 'cause I peeked in the windows, wanted to see what was goin' on."

"You peeked in the windows!" Betsy hissed. "What for? We've been walkin' the floor, worried sick that somethin' 'appened to you, and you was out playin' about watchin' the Washburns through the windows. . . . "

"Yeah," he gazed at her speculatively. "I was and it's a good thing too." He drug his eyes away from Betsy and looked at Mrs. Jeffries. "As soon as I drink this tea, I think I should go back and keep an eye on the Washburn house."

"Why?" Mrs. Jeffries knew something was terribly wrong.

" 'Cause Owen Washburn and his sister is packin' up. I watched 'em loadin' up their trunks through one of the windows. They're fixin' to leave town."

* * *

Antoine, arrogant, French and decidedly put out, arrived with Luty and Hatchet very early the next morning. Mrs. Jeffries quietly filled them in on the latest development while the cook clattered around the kitchen making as much noise as possible to show his displeasure.

"Is Smythe keepin' an eye on the Washburns?" Luty asked.

"He's been there all night," Betsy replied. She stared curiously at the black-haired Gallic cook. "Is your cook upset?" she whispered.

"Oh, no," Luty replied. "He always acts like that."

Mrs. Jeffries gave them their instructions. Then she and Betsy hurried upstairs to the dining room.

Witherspoon came down right on time. "I say, something smells delicious." He sniffed appreciatively.

"It's poached eggs Florentine." Mrs. Jeffries lifted the lid of the serving dish. "Luty sent her cook over to prepare you a very special breakfast."

"Gracious." Witherspoon grinned widely as he sat down. "How very kind of her."

"She thought you needed a good meal," Mrs. Jeffries said as she edged out of the dining room and into the hall. She left him happily eating away at his eggs.

While Betsy ferried the various courses from the kitchen to the dining room, the housekeeper hovered by the front door. But Minerva Kenny didn't come.

Mrs. Jeffries went back to check on the inspector. He'd just finished a kipper and was pushing his plate to one side. "I do believe I'm finished. . . . "

"But Antoine made some croissants," Mrs. Jeffries protested.

"I don't think I could eat another bite," Witherspoon protested. "Though it has been thoroughly delightful."

There was a knock at the front door. "I'll get it!" Mrs.

Jeffries flew down the hallway, praying it was Minerva Kenny. She flung open the door.

Her prayers were answered. A middle-aged woman wearing a heavy cloak and a scowl stood on the door step. "My name is Minerva Kenny. May I speak to Inspector Witherspoon, please."

"Certainly, do come in, please." Mrs. Jeffries escorted her into the dining room.

"Goodness," Witherspoon said in surprise, "whatever are you doing here?"

"I've come to give you something." Minerva thrust a letter at him. "I took this letter from William Barrett's study the day he was killed, but I didn't kill him. I thought it might be important. Now that I've given it to you, I'll go."

With that, she turned on her heel and stomped out.

"Miss Kenny." Witherspoon leapt to his feet and started after her.

"I should let her leave," Mrs. Jeffries said. "After all, you do know where to find her if you need to. Why don't you read the letter, sir?"

"Do you think I ought to?"

"It's evidence, isn't it?"

"Yes, of course it is." He tore open the envelope, pulled out the letter and read it. "Gracious," he murmured a few moments later, "I'm not sure what to make of this. But I think it might be very important." He looked up at his housekeeper. "It's a letter from Barrett to his bank instructing the bank to immediately cease any and all payments to Owen Washburn or any other representatives of Washburn and Tate."

Mrs. Jeffries relaxed. She hadn't been wrong. The letter said precisely what she was sure it would say. "You mean he was cutting off the money, sir?" She didn't have time to play about. She wanted to make sure the inspector got the point as quickly as possible.

Witherspoon frowned. He looked most confused. "It certainly sounds like it. I believe that as soon as Barnes gets here, we'll nip over to the Washburn house and see what he has to say about this."

But that wasn't good enough. Mrs. Jeffries took a deep breath and started talking. By her estimation, she had about five minutes to drop hints and get the inspector thinking along the lines she needed.

"Clever of you to think of that, sir," Barnes said admiringly as they got out of the hansom in front of the Washburn house.

Witherspoon smiled modestly. "Not really. It's merely a matter of using one's reasoning powers. But it did occur to me that the murder had been meticulously planned. I had to ask myself who had the means of doing such planning"—he started up the walkway—"and the only possible answer was Mr. Washburn. He was the one who was there the day that Barrett was throwing those stones at the dog, you see."

Barnes wasn't sure he did, but he nodded anyway. They'd reached the front door. Witherspoon banged the brass knocker.

They waited. And waited.

He banged the knocker again. Suddenly the door was flung open. Owen Washburn stared out at them. "What do you want?" he asked rudely. His hair was mussed and his shirt wrinkled.

"May we come in?" Witherspoon asked politely.

"Do you have a warrant?"

"No," Witherspoon said softly. "But I can get one within the hour."

Washburn gazed at him for a long moment and then threw open the door. The two policemen stepped inside.

Valises, carpetbags and suitcases were stacked in the hallway. Witherspoon glanced at Barnes.

"Planning on going somewhere?" Witherspoon asked softly. Washburn ignored the question and stalked into the drawing room. His sister was piling books into a trunk.

Eliza Washburn gasped and dropped the book she'd been holding. "What are you doing here?" she cried.

"I'm afraid you'll have to postpone your trip," Witherspoon said gently. "We've some very important matters to clear up."

"You can't stop us from leaving," Washburn snapped.

Silently Witherspoon handed the letter to him. "Would you like to explain this, Mr. Washburn?"

His fingers trembled when he saw the address on the front. He tore it out of the envelope and read it quickly. "This proves nothing," he said to Witherspoon when he'd finished. "I told you, Barrett and I were thinking of dissolving our partnership. I was going to buy him out."

"But you couldn't buy him out, sir," Witherspoon replied. "You've no money. We know your creditors were pressing you, and with Barrett's withdrawal of funds from your company, you were ruined."

"That's ridiculous."

"I'm afraid it isn't." Witherspoon turned to Eliza Washburn. "Mr. Barrett ended his engagement to you because of your financial position—isn't that correct?"

"Certainly not," she protested.

"Mr. Washburn," Barnes said, "I'm going to call the police constables in, sir. We're goin' to search your house."

"And what precisely do you hope to find?" Washburn sneered.

Witherspoon smiled sadly. "A workingman's coat and cap, sir. But even if we don't find them, we've enough evidence to place you under arrest."

"I saw 'em find David Sims's cap," Smythe said, "and Eliza Washburn kicked up an awful fuss when they took her brother away."

"All right." Luty slapped her hands against the table. "Are you gonna tell us now?" she asked the housekeeper.

"Of course, I was merely waiting for Smythe to return." Mrs. Jeffries took a dainty sip of tea. "You see, I'd realized that the murder was well planned. Therefore, there was only one person who fit all the facts."

"What facts?" Wiggins asked. "Seems to me all we 'ad was a dead body with a sword stickin' out of 'is chest and 'alf a London wantin' the bloke dead."

"It might have appeared that way, Wiggins," Mrs. Jeffries explained, "but the truth was quite different. Once I found out that Barrett was planning on selling his house and, as far as we know, wasn't planning on buying another one here in London, I concluded that he was leaving the city. I started thinking that for most of the suspects in our little drama, Barrett leaving would be precisely what they wanted. Miss Kenny would have liked him out of the way, Maud Astley and Neville Sharpe would certainly liked to have seen the back of the man, and Adrian Spears would be positively delighted to find that Barrett wasn't going to be his neighbour. The same applies to Thornton Astley, especially as he knew that taking Barrett to court would be a waste of time. There was only one person who would be damaged if Barrett left. That was the man who depended on him for money. Once I realized that, the rest fell into place."

"I still don't see how," Hatchet grumbled.

"Don't you?" She smiled. "As I said, the killing was planned down to the last detail. There was only one person who could have planned it and that was Owen Washburn. I think he decided that Barrett had to die quite some time ago. I suspect that Barrett ended his engagement to Eliza Washburn last month because he'd found out how close to bankruptcy the Washburns were. I think Washburn realized he had a golden opportunity to kill the man and get away with it on the day he and Barrett were outside and Barrett threw stones at Spears's dog. With Spears shouting at the top of his lungs that he would kill Barrett if he touched the dog again, Spears became a very convenient suspect."

"You mean that Washburn killed the dog?" Betsy said.

"That's right," Mrs. Jeffries said. "That's how I knew he committed the murder. He stole the carpenter's hammer for that very purpose. He knew the front and back doors of the Barrett house were open because of the painting. Washburn stole David Simms's cap and coat, and the hammer, the day *before* the murder. And he did it deliberately to lure everyone out in the gardens, giving him a chance to slip inside the Barrett house without being seen. Washburn was the only one who could have taken them. The other suspects weren't in Barrett's house that day. On the day of the murder, he slipped into the garden, waited till the poor dog came outside and killed it," she closed her eyes briefly, thinking of that poor, defenseless animal being brutally used to set up a murder. "Washburn knew perfectly well that Spears would come looking for the animal. With all the doors and windows open, he was fairly certain there would be a huge ruckus."

"That's why Janie, the Spears's maid, thought she saw David out in the garden!" Betsy cried. "She caught a glimpse of Washburn wearin' David's cap."

"Correct, that's why Washburn pinched the hat in the first place. He wanted a disguise of sorts." Mrs. Jeffries took another sip of tea. "With the dog dead, I suspect he hid somewhere, waited until everyone from the Barrett household was outside watching the commotion and then slipped inside and hid in one of the rooms on the second floor. A few moments later Minerva Kenny came in through the front door, confronted Barrett and took the letter."

"Do you think that Washburn knew that Barrett had written that letter?" Smythe asked, remembering he'd seen Washburn at the bank.

"I think he hoped he hadn't," Mrs. Jeffries mused. "I suspect that's why he went to the bank yesterday, he wanted to make sure Barrett's funds were still available to him. But I do think he knew the inevitable was coming. The day before the murder, Washburn told the police he'd come by with some papers for Barrett to sign. That wasn't true. I suspect he came because Barrett wanted the meeting. He probably told him he was instructing his bank to stop the funds. That's why Washburn had to kill him and had to do it quickly."

"Git on with yer story," Luty demanded.

"Oh, sorry. As I was saying, Minerva Kenny arrived, and Washburn had to stay hidden until she left. That's where he made his biggest mistake. A mistake we should have seen right away, but didn't."

"What was that?" Betsy asked.

"The room was dark," Mrs. Jeffries replied. "That's what should have been obvious from the first. Both Smythe and the inspector said that none of the lamps had been lit. If Barrett had been alive at six o'clock, he wouldn't have been sitting there in the dark."

"But Barrett was alive at six," Hatchet countered. "He

shouted at one of the workmen as they were leaving.''

"Washburn yelled at the workman," Mrs. Jeffries corrected. "Barrett had probably been dead since right after Minerva Kenny left. I'm fairly certain that as soon as Miss Kenny left, Washburn slipped into Barrett's study, grabbed the sword and shoved it through the chair. It happened so quickly, Barrett didn't even have a chance to cry out. After that, Washburn had to wait in the study until it was safe to leave. He knew the servants went down for their meal at six o'clock, the same time the workmen left. So he sat there in the dark, waiting. A few minutes after six, he slipped out the front door. Just to be on the safe side, he wore David Simms's coat and cap, in case someone saw him leaving.''

"Who was the woman in his drawing room, the one the workmen heard crying?" Betsy asked. "I mean, we know it was Maud Astley who was in the garden the night before, havin' a row with Barrett, but who was the other one?''

"Eliza Washburn," Mrs. Jeffries said. "And it was Eliza Washburn who came back that afternoon in one of the hansoms too. But for some reason or other, she lost her nerve and didn't go into the house.''

"Why did she come to see Barrett?" Wiggins asked. "Seems to me 'e'd be the last man she'd want to talk to. 'E did leave 'er at the altar.''

"Probably she came to plead with Barrett on behalf of her brother." Mrs. Jeffries shrugged. "I'm only guessing, but I suspect she knew how desperate her brother was. No doubt he'd told her that Barrett was planning on cutting off the money. Without the funds, the Washburns were ruined.''

"It didn't do no good, though." Betsy shook her head.

"Why'd she bother? Barrett had already proved he was a heartless beast."

"Desperate people will do desperate things," Mrs. Jeffries said sadly. "Perhaps she felt he still had some vestige of feelings for her."

From upstairs, they heard the sound of the front door opening.

"The inspector's back," Mrs. Jeffries got to her feet. "I'll see what I can find out from him."

Witherspoon sipped at his sherry. "He won't confess, you know. And even with the cap and coat, we're going to have a very difficult time proving he did it."

Mrs. Jeffries smiled. They'd been talking for over an hour, and she was satisfied that the inspector now thought *he* had come up with the sequence of events leading to Washburn's arrest. She'd been worried all day.

There had been so little time this morning when she started dropping hints and talking fast. But perhaps she was underestimating him? Perhaps he would have come up with the solution on his own. She liked to think so. "But you do have some evidence that isn't circumstantial, sir. The coat and cap *were* found in Washburn's house."

"Yes, stupid of the man not to get rid of them, but there you have it." Witherspoon sighed. "Even the cleverest of people will often make a fatal mistake."

"You also have the letter that Barrett wrote to the bank," she added. "And the testimony of some of the residents from Kildare Gardens. The episode with the dog being killed and the theft of the hammer used to kill the poor animal is evidence that Washburn planned the whole thing. Add to that Washburn's precarious financial position, and you can show motive. Once a jury hears all that, I'm sure that justice will be done."

"One does hope so, but the case is still very circumstantial, Mrs. Jeffries," Witherspoon replied. "But that's up to some QC to worry about, not me. I've done my duty. I know we arrested the right person."

"Indeed you have, sir." She took a sip of her own sherry.

"But there is one thing still puzzling me."

"What's that, sir?" She held her breath, hoping that if he asked an awkward question, she'd be able to come up with an answer.

"Who was it that brought that note about Barrett's body being in the study?" He drummed his fingers on the arm of his chair. "I've thought and thought about it. For the life of me, I can't come up with a single idea of who it could have been."

"Perhaps it was one of Barrett's servants, sir. You know how some people will do anything to avoid being involved with the police," she spoke quickly. "Or perhaps it was one of the workmen?"

"Oh, well." He waved his hand dismissively. "I suppose it's one of those little mysteries that we'll never solve. But what's life without an occasional mystery?"

"Quite, sir."

"Er, Mrs. Jeffries?"

She braced herself for another awkward question.

"What are we having for dinner tonight?"

The next morning everyone gathered 'round the kitchen table to discuss the aftermath of the investigation. Luty and Hatchet, with two baskets of goodies in tow, compliments of Antoine, had arrived right after breakfast.

"Figured you could still use some decent vittles," Luty explained as Hatchet placed the baskets on the table. "I've brought some smoked ham, sliced beef, some of

Antoine's fancy croissants . . . Oh, I forget what else he tucked in there, but there's plenty here to hold you for a day or two."

"Perhaps by the time your provisions run low, Mrs. Goodge will be back," Hatchet added.

"If you run out before"—Luty popped down beside Betsy—"just give me a holler and we'll bring some more."

"That's very generous of you, Luty." Mrs. Jeffries wasn't about to look a gift horse in the mouth. Whatever was in that basket was certain to be much tastier than what they could cook.

"Madam is a very generous soul." Hatchet arched one eyebrow as he looked at his employer. "Sometimes perhaps too generous."

"Oh, git off yer high horse, Hatchet." Luty shook her finger at him. "Who was it that come draggin' Jon in when he didn't have a place to stay?"

Jon was a young lad from one of their previous cases. He was now a permanent resident of the Crookshank household. Hatchet personally supervised his lessons and vetted his tutors.

"I most certainly did not drag anybody in," Hatchet argued. "At the time, I merely suggested you take the boy into training as a footman. You're the one who insisted on educating him. However, that is a far cry from what you're doing now."

"Exactly what is it she's doing?" Betsy asked.

"What's she doing!" Hatchet snorted. "She's actually thinking of giving that murderer's sister money so she can start over somewhere else."

"You're stakin' Eliza Washburn?" Smythe asked incredulously. "But why?"

" 'Cause she got left at the altar, she don't have enough

gumption to show her face in London, and what the blazes else do I have to spend my money on?'' Luty glared at all of them. ''Now, I don't want to hear another word on the subject. That poor woman's had some rough times, and she's gonna have to watch her brother hang. Least I can do is help her to start over somewhere else.''

No one had the nerve to say a word. Even Hatchet kept silent.

''Actually, Luty,'' Mrs. Jeffries said softly, ''I think what you're doing is wonderful. If there were more people like you in the world, it would be a much better place for all of us.''

Luty's cheeks turned red. ''Thank you, Hepzibah.''

''Hello, hello,'' Ruth Cannonberry called. ''Can I come in?''

''Please do,'' Mrs. Jeffries invited.

They all greeted the new arrival. For the next half hour they talked of the murder. Ruth kept clucking her tongue and shaking her head as she learned all the details of the crime and its solution.

''Well,'' she finally said, ''it's a good thing all of us were available to help solve this awful crime. Otherwise, poor dear Minerva would probably be under arrest.''

Everyone looked at one another, not sure of what to say. Mrs. Jeffries smiled broadly. ''That's quite true, Ruth. But you do understand that we never, ever let on to the Inspector that he had help?''

''Of course I understand.'' Ruth laughed. ''When we were having dinner at Simpson's, I was as quiet as a mouse.''

Luty's eyes narrowed speculatively. ''You and the inspector seem to be gettin' on real good.''

''Indeed we are,'' Ruth agreed, blushing like a schoolgirl. ''He's such a wonderful companion. We're going train spotting next Sunday. Isn't that exciting?''

It sounded about as interestin' as watchin' grass grow, but Luty didn't want to offend her. "Train spottin'," she repeated, "that sounds real nice."

"By the way, Minerva said to thank you for all your help," Ruth continued. "She's ever so grateful for everything you did. Now, don't worry, she hasn't a clue that we were investigating the murder as well. As I said, on that subject my lips are sealed. She's getting Mr. Spears a puppy. Isn't that nice?''

They all agreed that it was. The conversation continued, with everyone asking, talking and making comments. Everyone, that is, except Wiggins.

He couldn't get the Simms brothers out of his mind. Maybe it was because they lived in the same kind of house that he used to live in before his mother died of typhoid, or maybe it was because he knew what it was to be desperate for work. In any case, he owed it to them to ask.

Wiggins cleared his throat. "Uh, Luty, do you happen to have any paintin' that needs doin'?''

"Paintin'?''

"Yeah, them painters that was workin' on the Barrett 'ouse could sure use the work."

"Let's see," Luty muttered thoughtfully. "I just had the front hall redone last year, so it don't need doin'. But Jon's gettin' mighty tired of lookin' at that pink-and-yellow wallpaper in his room, so I reckon that could use a coat of paint. You have them boys come 'round and see me this afternoon. I'll find 'em something to paint. It'll be longer than a January frost before them estate lawyers ever pay 'em what they're owed for that job they did at Barrett's place.''

"Thanks ever so much." Wiggins shoved back his

'chair and stood up. "They'll be so glad for the work. I'll just nip over and tell 'em, all right?"

"That'll be fine, Wiggins," Mrs. Jeffries said.

"Come on, boy," Wiggins called to Fred as he dashed out of the kitchen. "Let's go."

"That's most generous of you, Luty," Ruth Cannonberry said as soon as they'd gone. "Perhaps after they finish at your house, you can send them over to see me."

Soon after that the impromptu meeting broke up. Luty and Hatchet departed for home, Lady Cannonberry went off to her women's suffrage meeting, and Mrs. Jeffries went upstairs to clean the drawing room.

Betsy started clearing up the tea things. Smythe watched her for a moment, thinking of what Mrs. Jeffries had let slip early this morning. The lass had been worried about him when he'd gone out the other night, and that must mean she cared. But what if she only cared about him as a friend?

"Do you want the last of this tea?" Betsy asked, holding the pot up.

"No," he swallowed heavily. "But I'd like to ask ya somethin'."

"What?" She took the pot to the sink.

"Would ya like to go out with me this afternoon? I thought it would be nice if we went for a walk."

Mrs. Goodge arrived home at teatime the next day. She bustled into the kitchen and dropped her carpetbag on the floor.

"Thank goodness you're back!" Wiggins cried. "We've about starved to death since you've been gone."

"How is your aunt?" Mrs. Jeffries asked.

"She's fine," the cook replied. "It weren't pneumonia,

it was only a bit of bronchitis. She was well on the mend when I left.''

Smythe grinned. ''We sure are glad to see you. If it 'adn't been for Antoine, we really woulda starved to death.''

''Is that all you can think of! Your stomachs?'' Mrs. Goodge demanded as she took her usual seat. ''We've got to get crackin'. I rushed back as soon as I could. You'd best bring me up to date on the investigation, then I've got to get some bakin' done so I can feed my sources—''

''Mrs. Goodge,'' Mrs. Jeffries gently cut her off. ''I'm afraid you're a little late.''

''Late? What do you mean?''

''We've already solved the murder.''

The cook's cry of outrage could be heard all the way across the street.